PUBLIC OFFERINGS

Book Four

Children on the Altar

A novel by

Bob LiVolsi

DEDICATION

To Susan who has patiently believed in me and encouraged me for far too long for her own good. Thank you, my darling wife, for being there always and for loving me. I love you always.

To all the people in generous communities of caring around the world who continue to sacrifice their comfort and often risk their lives to bring hope to our peers in less fortunate corners of the world. And to the people of Sierra Leone whose misery at the hands of warlords and power brokers informed the very first draft of this book all those years ago in 1995.

To all those who cling to and proclaim a faith of compassion for human beings, built on service not conquest, built on hope not rules, and encompassed by love – at all times recognizing a much greater force that transcends our personal demands and yet embraces our free will and individuality.

TABLE OF CONTENTS

BOOK FOUR – Children on the Altar

PUBLIC OFFERINGS

BOOK FOUR

Children on the Altar

CHAPTER 1

Port Loko, Sierra Leone
December 20, 9:52 a.m. Greenwich Mean Time

The ashes and mud smeared on his face hid ten year old Jacob Karanja amidst the brush that lined the outside of the modern glass and stone building in Port Loko. He lay prone, cradling a rifle nearly as long as he was tall. Sieramco, a subsidiary of a Swiss company, housed its executive offices here. The company had closed the offices when the civil war had made it untenable for its white Swiss managers to stay in country. The closing had impoverished Jacob's Lokoma tribe. For decades, the tribe mined bauxite for a subsistence living while Sieramco's executives and shareholders grew wealthy on the sale of bauxite for aluminum production in the West. Without Sieramco's administrative and transportation infrastructure, the economies of scale made further bauxite mining a money-losing business for the Lokoma.

Jacob understood none of this. Fela, the Abo chief, understood it well. So did Adrian Guerra who viewed reviving the local economy as an important part of his and the World Bank's mission. Fela and the Abo offered a means to consolidate the bauxite lands, creating enough concentrated revenue to either attract Sieramco back to the country or to allow a new company to start up with sufficient scale to achieve sustained success. And Chief Fela planned to do so at the expense of the Lokoma.

That much Jacob understood.

Visiting Abo village, pretending to be just a little boy there to play, Jacob had learned Chief Fela would be in Port Loko today. He did not need to understand the business issues or rationale. He only knew that Fela had somehow been behind the invasion of Lokoma village, behind the murder of his grandparents and the dislocation of his family. No system of justice could be relied on to fix the matter. Jacob thought it likely that the government somehow had a hand in supporting the chief.

Fela exited the former headquarters building with Adrian Guerra. While Guerra wore a white Hawaiian shirt, Fela wore robes to the ground, a length of cloth wrapped around his head into a cone. He had made the pilgrimage to Mecca, making him a haji in the Islamic community. Jacob had asked his father about that once, wondering why men would wear such clothes in the humidity and heat.

"It's a statement," Hamara had told him. "For most, it's solemn, well-meant. For some, like our friend Fela, it's more like a dog marking his territory."

Guerra's presence with Fela only confirmed Jacob's suspicions that the government and the Abo worked hand-in-hand. Guerra always represented himself as someone close to the Leonean leadership and his body language made it clear he was catering to Fela.

Working to choke down his anger in order to remain steady, Jacob peered through the rifle sight. Fela, moved unsteadily into the crosshairs as he approached his chauffeured Mercedes in the parking lot. Holding his breath, Jacob squeezed the trigger. As he did, a military jeep drove across his line of sight. The bullet hit the metal around the windshield, ricocheting loudly. Fela, Guerra and the other men dropped to the pavement. Five shouting soldiers piled out of the jeep and raced toward Jacob, rifles and pistols positioned to fire.

Jacob remained flat on the ground for several seconds, stunned. Then, fear and experience rushed in. He calmly aimed his rifle, taking down two soldiers with deadly accuracy. The three others took cover. Jacob used the opportunity to slip down an embankment and race down a pre-planned escape route. He put the rifle into a slot in a tree trunk that he had identified earlier. Pulling a towel out of the same slot, he wiped the camo off his face as he ran. Climbing an embankment, he raced into a crowded open-air market, just another unruly child annoying the merchants.

Loud shouting erupted behind him. People started scattering to the sides. Pounding footsteps on the pavement. A line of people wound into a large white tent. Jacob scooted into the middle of the line, disappearing behind a large woman in a bright kaftan. The soldiers stopped outside the tent, yelling at each other in the Abo's Krio dialect. Jacob understood most of it. One of them described the shooter as a boy. Another disputed this, commenting on the assassin's accuracy in taking down two of their comrades. No child could shoot that well.

"Move along, boy," the large woman said as she pushed him by the scruff of the neck.

He tried to shrug her off, but she clamped her hand on his shoulder.

"You wanted to break into queue. You pay the price." The woman smiled, a glimmer of mischief in her eyes. He tried to shrug off her grip one more time.

"If they be lookin' for you, boy, you best stay wid me."

One of the soldiers poked his rifle into the tent and peered around. Jacob pushed close to the woman now and she held him to her enormous bosom as though he were her own.

The soldier looked straight at Jacob, but Jacob didn't see him with his head buried in the folds of the woman's dress. Not seeing a lone boy, the soldier left.

"Thank you," Jacob said, starting to pull away again.

"Stay here, boy. Give the soldiers more time to go. Anyway, you look well. Keep it that way."

She shoved him toward a woman in a white smock. She rubbed alcohol on his arm with a cotton ball and nudged him gently toward a man with a large syringe. Fear surged through Jacob. He hated needles. I have to be a man, he thought.

As the needle penetrated his skin, tears dribbled out of his squinting eyes.

"Now you won't be gettin' no more malaria," the big woman said as she wiped the tears from his face with her big sleeve.

CHAPTER 2

Peggy's Cove, Nova Scotia
December 20, 7:27 a.m. Atlantic Time

Little Marie lay under her covers playing. The cry of gulls outside her window, braving the frigid North Atlantic winds of Peggy's Cove, awakened her just after dawn. Her Barbie doll leaned over the keyboard of the smartphone and pressed on the keys, typing an imaginary message. The phone's screen remained as blank as it had been for over six weeks now.

"Save us," said Marie. "Smoke is filling our cabin and people will die and lose their eyes."

"Don't worry," Marie said in a deeper voice. "We will send someone to save you."

"Oh, no," Marie said in her normal voice, the one she assigned to Barbie. "No. It's too late."

Marie plunged Barbie headfirst into the mattress. "I'll save you, Barbie. I'm Marie. I'll go on the beach and save you."

Then for no clear reason, Marie curled up and started crying.

A gentle hand touched her shoulder. "Marie? Are you all right, sweetie?" It was her mother. She pulled back the covers. As she felt the movement of the blanket, Marie scooped up the phone and pushed it underneath her stomach so her mother would not see it.

Annette Louve saw the tears and the fear on her eight year old's face. Jack still slept so he was not the problem this morning. Anyway, he had been sober for a month thanks to Father LaBonte's efforts, and, of course, the shock of the airplane tragedy.

"Marie, why are you crying?"

"Go away, Mama. I need to be alone." Nothing about this behavior added up to Annette.

"Look at me, please, dear. Now."

Marie turned her head to face her mother. As she did, her chest rolled revealing the edge of the phone.

"What's that?"

Marie curled up again, but her mother's hand was beneath her extracting the device. "Where did you get this?"

Marie sat up on the edge of the bed, prepared to run. Annette read her intentions and blocked the doorway with her body.

"Well?" Annette said, waving the phone at Marie.

"Don't break it, Mama. It's important."

"And why is that?"

Her lips curled into a cry as she explained, "It's from the plane crash."

"The plane crash?"

"Yes," she said tearfully.

"I don't understand," Annette said as she turned the device over and over in her hand.

"I found it on the beach when I wasn't supposed to be there. I thought Daddy would hit me."

Annette crouched in front of her daughter and hugged her. "Oh, honey. Daddy was having a very hard time back then. He would never touch you now. He loves you very much. We both do."

Marie whimpered, her head tucked into her mother's shoulder. Annette pulled back abruptly.

"Now, how do you know this is from the plane crash?"

Marie chewed her lip as she pondered her mother. "It told me," she blurted out.

"How did it tell you?"

"I could read it," Marie spoke very sincerely. "Until its battery died. "

With a face full of concern, Annette put herself at Marie's eye level. "What did it say to you?"

"It said somebody crashed them on purpose."

Annette's heart raced. This could not be real. Marie was imagining.

"Did it say who that somebody was?" she asked, feeling flush.

"It said that the answer was inside it."

Annette turned the phone over in her hand again. She thought they had a charger for it. "Jack," she called quietly and then very loudly, "Jack!"

Five hours later, the family sat in the rectory of the windblown church at the top of the cove.

"Why did you bring this to me?" Father LaBonte asked.

"The note on the phone is very specific," Jack said, sitting forward on the couch between his wife and daughter. "It's my fault that it didn't appear sooner. Marie was afraid of me."

LaBonte place a hand on Jack's forearm. "So what does this note say?"

"It asks that we take it to a parish priest, to someone not beholding to the United States government, that the US government could not be trusted."

"What about our government, the Canadian government?" the priest asked.

"Too friendly with the Americans I figure."

"What else does it say?"

"I don't know, but the phone has a storage card in it with a list of document files on it. Most of them are password protected, though, but a reminder popped up after we re-charged it. It said that the phone's owner was supposed to be at a meeting at some lab this past October. One short note without a password names the lab. Says it is guarded by an extreme IRA faction…"

"IRA? Irish Republican Army?"

"The same, Father. I think this guy thought the IRA sabotaged the plane."

The priest navigated the phone and found it was named Evan's Phone. He searched contacts for Evan and found only one. the owner's name and address appeared briefly on the opening screen. He turned it off.

"We can start by confirming that this is really from the flight, I suppose," the priest said.

"How can we do that without involving the authorities?" Jack asked.

"We'll just have to get an old paper and see if…" The priest paused while he turned the box back on and read the name and company on the opening screen again. "We'll just have to see if Dr. Evan Conger of the World Health Organization died on that flight."

CHAPTER 3

Fort Collins: Clement home
December 20, 11:12 a.m. Mountain Time

Dave did not want to wake up the next morning. His head still pounded, but medication and sleep diminished the intensity to a bearable level. Opening his eyes did not seem like a good idea.

Liv carried a tray into the room at 11:12. She did not know whether to bring breakfast or lunch. She opted for oatmeal with sliced bananas. Dave ate oatmeal for his health; bananas had potassium, good for his heart. Coffee and a newspaper still in its plastic also sat on the tray.

Before Mel headed off for a closing, mother and daughter, eating a quick breakfast of hot tea and English muffins, worried that the hit on the back of the head had done more serious damage than the emergency room physician thought.

Jennifer remained sequestered in the guest room where Mel had instructed her to stay after the break-in. The intruder had seen her. If not a run-of-the-mill burglar, the man posed a clear threat to the well-being of the entire household. Mel wanted to believe the man to be just a burglar. Jennifer insisted that she thought he was. Mel's sixth sense picked up a level of anxiety in Jennifer that suggested she knew more than she admitted.

"Good morning, sweetheart," Dave said, his eyes still closed.

"It's almost afternoon, Daddy," Liv said, "Were you planning on sleeping all day?"

"I would love to."

"Does it still hurt?"

"It's not too bad right now. I think if I stand up it will start all over again."

"You're supposed to stay in bed all weekend so that shouldn't be a problem."

Liv picked up a pillow and Dave sat up in bed as she stuffed it behind him. She put the tray down over his legs. Fearing that the sloshing, overly full cup of coffee would spill its steamy contents in his lap, Dave risked burning his tongue, taking a quick sip.

Her hands free, Liv felt for the cell phone in her jeans pocket. Earlier that morning, at Mel's instructions, she had programmed "9" as the speed dial for 9-1-1.

Dave saw her patting her pockets. "Is the alarm on?" he asked.

"Yes, sir. Mom gave me a full security briefing before she left."

Liv's wording caused Dave to smile.

"Security briefing? What are we? The CIA?"

Liv blushed. "It seems to describe it," she said.

"I don't think there's anything to worry about. Some dumb burglar that didn't realize we had a house guest."

"What if it's the people that are after Jennifer?"

"If they exist, they're professionals. They would have finished the job."

Liv's shoulders relaxed. Her dad made sense. The bad guys would not have just visited and left.

"Do you want to watch TV?" she asked, picking up the remote from the nightstand.

"I'd rather not. The noise might be too much. We can read the paper."

He pulled the newspaper out of its plastic and handed Liv the front section.

CHAPTER 4

Liv's Diary
December 20, 10:47 p.m. Mountain Time

Tonight, I feel as good as I can remember. It may be too much to hope, but the doctor might have found a medicine that works for me.

Life has been very busy. Of course, life may be short, too, if the medicine stops working like all the others did. Mom and Dad try to keep my hopes up, but I know from reading online and from my response to the meds that I'm probably going to die from this sooner or later. Not eventually like everybody else. But soon for some reason.

I've spent a lot of time feeling sorry for myself. The other night was the end of that, though. A week ago, Chelsea embarrassed me beyond hope in front of Michael. She made me an untouchable. He hasn't said so and he's been nice, but... I don't know. I cried so much that my eyes stayed swollen for almost the entire week. Everyone at school probably knows by now. If I were them, I'd be scared of me.

But seeing Dad lying in the snow bleeding opened up a whole new level of pain. I thought he was dead. I've never been so scared. It was so sad, so horrible. I had no idea how much I love him. There has been so much resentment from me about his work or how he acts.

We were covered in snow, but I held his head in my arms. We rocked. He didn't know it. He seemed to barely breathe. His blood dripped on my sweats. I didn't care. I only knew how much I loved my Daddy, how hard he had worked for us. I don't think I ever realized he could get hurt until then. He's always the strong one, the one nothing bothers.

Mom told us that I screamed loud enough to wake the dead when I found him. Dad said that must have been why he woke up. I saved him, he said. Even laying there in the emergency room, covered in blood, his eyes barely able to open, he made me laugh. That's the Daddy I remember and love. That's why I hate it so much when he's gone.

So I'm not feeling sorry for myself anymore. When I pray from now on, I'm going to thank God for my dad and my mom. I already started today. I thanked him for the time I've had here and how good that time has been. Sure, I prayed for the AIDs to go away. Still, I think that may not be what God has in mind for me. It's the first time in a long time that I just thanked Him. I paused for a long time on the words 'thy will be done' in the Our Father. I said them again and again. I think I mean them now... finally. It takes a lot of pressure off. I wonder if God feels the same way.

Here's my prayer tonight. God, thank you again for saving my dad. I feel strong tonight. I don't know if I'll still feel so good tomorrow or the day after or the day after that. Whatever happens, please let me know how to handle it and what you want me to do. Please, God.

Clement Home
December 20, 11:24 p.m. Mountain Time

Mel simultaneously tapped on the door and cracked it open. She caught Liv quickly sliding something under her bed. "Sweetie, time to get to sleep. You need your rest."

Liv popped up and gave her a mother a long, tight hug. "Are you okay?" she asked.

"Am I okay?" Mel responded, surprised. "You're the one we need to worry about, Miss Energizer Bunny."

Liv pressed her head into her mother's shoulder, a small smile creasing her lips. "Don't worry, Mom. I'm doing so much better."

Mel placed a hand gently on Liv's head and slowly stroked her hair. Dave's injury had frightened her, too. He seemed so unconquerable, so determined and bull-headed. Seeing him lying helpless in the snow had made her feel vulnerable, exposed. It terrified her. Worse, it shamed her to think that she thought first of herself at that moment.

It had caused her to re-visit her priorities. On what foundation had she built her life? What kind of relationship did she and Dave have? She needed to take care of him. Spending the next morning and half the afternoon at the office seemed absolutely the wrong priority. But she needed to earn a living. And Liv did a great job of playing nurse.

Liv's hair felt like it needed washed, but Mel decided not to bother her with that tonight. She would wake her early in the morning instead. Liv did not seem to find much peace lately. For now, she should be able to savor it.

So should I, thought Mel. A wave of fear shivered through her, the constant foreboding that had seemed only to intensify since the diagnosis.

She pulled Liv closer.

CHAPTER 5

Loveland, Colorado: Josie's Café
December 21, 9:20 a.m. Mountain Time

Dave's wooziness assured him that he should have stayed in bed this morning. The call surprised him. He thought the priest still kept himself busy in the mountain villages south of Freetown. This morning, however, Fr. Jim walked through the door of Josie's. A little ruddier because of the Colorado cold, he still poured sincerity from his eyes.

"This is a real surprise, Father. It's great to see you again. I'd heard that either bandits or rebels had killed you."

"And here I am in the flesh, Dave. Your PDNA is what brought me here."

"How?"

"I know you have a house guest."

Dave's hands tightened on the edge of the table.

Fr. Jim leaned toward him and spoke quietly. "Relax, if you work with me, it won't bring you any more harm."

"What harm?"

"I'm the guy who broke into your house."

Dave tilted his head and studied the priest. He felt his heartbeat accelerate. "You're what? You're the guy that damn near killed me?"

Jim held Dave's gaze. "No, I didn't hit you."

Dave thought of Jennifer's comments about a rumored Vatican plot. "One of your fellow priests then. What are you guys? Jesuits, right?"

"No, I'm just a simple missionary that stuck his fingers in too many electric outlets when he was a kid. Can't seem to break the habit."

"So who slugged me? And why the hell were you in the house?"

"Dave, listen. Revenge is the last thing you have time for. Things are not what they seem."

CHAPTER 6

Liv's Diary
December 21, 11:05 p.m.

What a night. Not a minute of playing time for me. Plus we lost. We only won one set. Coach said I'd missed too much practice time to put me in, unless we built up a good lead. I have no doubt he blames me for losing the match against Poudre when I passed out. On the way home in the car tonight, I asked Mom and Dad if I should have told the coach the truth. Thought maybe I made a mistake. They had the right idea. If the coach knew about the HIV, he probably would have wanted me off the team.

I don't hate him. I just...

It was our last match for the season, but... for me... it probably was my last chance ever. I'm feeling really weak again. For the last week, I'd been feeling stronger and stronger. Then today, I woke up feeling a little nauseous and dizzy. By the middle of the day, I had a killer headache. By game time, I had four acetaminophen in me and two ibuprofen so the headache was under control, but I still wasn't right. So the Fuzeon shots worked for a while, but I think the HIV's already building resistance. I told Mom when we got home. I'm such a baby. Cried hard for ten minutes. Mom didn't. She was good. Said I was probably wrong. This is just a dip, that it was way too soon to tell. She thinks it may even be my body adjusting to the drugs. I want to believe it, but it's hard to stay positive all the time. Both other times I had drug resistance, I felt just like this at the beginning.

But I'm still strong enough that I could have played tonight. It's weird how important that seems when I'm literally facing death.

Then there's Michael Winston. He didn't show up for the match at all. Chelsea's little drunken thing must have gotten to him after all. So, first Chelsea gives me HIV and then she drives my boyfriend away.

Confession: We played stupid kid games three years ago. Middle school. Everybody does stupid stuff in middle school. It is so embarrassing now. But Chelsea liked it. A lot more than I did, I guess. But if she gave me HIV, then she should have it, too. She could be a carrier. Has to be her. That is the ONLY way I could have picked this up. She completely denies it, of course. Maybe she just doesn't know. She still refuses to be tested. I'm trying not to judge her. Hard not to. The party has definitely adjusted my perspective.. She's hella cray cray.

So, there it is, dear diary. No boyfriend. A best friend that totally betrayed me. Oh, yeah. I'm dying, too. How cool is that?

I'll tell you how cool. So cool that I'm not going to let it happen. I'm going to find a way to fix my life myself. I don't know how, but I will beat this stupid thing. I pray about it EVERY day. God will help me. I know it. If he doesn't... Well, if he doesn't, he isn't so loving, is he? I'm having a much harder time with "thy will be done" tonight than I did last night.

At least, I think Daddy's head is okay now. Not sure, though. He went out this morning for a meeting after Mom and I both told him it was too soon. He came home acting weird. But not like he gets about work. Much more intense – as if that were possible. Might be just his head still recovering, but I don't think so. Something's up. Something big. Or bad.

CHAPTER 7

Clement home
December 22, 5:10 a.m. Mountain Time

Sitting in the darkness in the Clement's family room, Jennifer closed the app and put her phone down. She had been there since 3:30 when she woke with a start. She thought she heard something scraping at the basement window over the guest room. It may have been part of her dream, but she did not want to risk it. So she moved upstairs where she felt safer.

She listened again for the noise. She heard the drip of the kitchen faucet, the hum of the dishwasher in its dry cycle, the quieter hum of the ballast of the fluorescent light over the sink.

She got up from the couch in the family room and walked toward the kitchen. She carried the TV remote with her and entertained turning the TV on. No, she thought, I need to hear everything.

The hit man could come back at any time. Mike had not contacted her since his visit the night of the break-in. Why had the hit man not come back? He had to know she was there now.

Click!

Jennifer jumped. She listened intently. The fans of the heating system blew, explaining the clicking sound as they switched on.

She dialed 911 on her phone, but did not tap the call button. Instead, she let her finger hover over it, just in case. She walked over to the sliding glass doors and pulled the drapes tighter, making certain to leave not even a slight crack for someone to look in. She headed toward the front door where she again confirmed the alarm was on and working.

Back in the kitchen, she put her phone down and pulled two butcher knives from the drawer. Returning to the family room, she sat back down in the couch, but did not pick up her phone again. She did not want to risk being distracted. She could not afford to be surprised.

CHAPTER 8

Cameron Pass
December 22, 5:25 a.m. Mountain Time

Claire sipped her hot cocoa. Up too early with too little sleep. Again. She still had not slept more than three or four hours in a night for over a month. She pressed a button on the intercom.

"Yes, ma'am?" responded a voice over the speaker.

"Where is she, Farley?"

Mike snorted audibly on the other end.

"Don't get frustrated with me, Mike. She's still not here. You promised me she'd come after you finished your little charade."

"Tomorrow," Mike said, his voice coming through the speaker. "At the latest. I know her too well."

"Maybe you should have just grabbed her as soon as you found her."

"No, Ms. McQuaid. Your pieces are fallin' into place like ya wanted. She's probably been giving the Clements an earful about a Vatican conspiracy. The real fear in her eyes is sure to make it believable. And now we know my baby brother is capable of killin'."

Claire sucked down more cocoa. That had been all her idea. She wanted to know how much of the killer still lived in the priest. She wanted to know that he was more than a puppet all those years ago. She needed to know that she still stalked a killer. But she did not agree with Mike about the outcome; she still did not have certainty. She only knew that when he could have pulled the trigger, Fr. Jim hesitated. She knew all along he did not have it in him. Otherwise she would not have risked Jennifer's life. But it would have been so much easier if he had tried, if he had even held the gun to her head. Then she would know with certainty that she pursued the right course.

Her head started to pound. "You cut it too close in that basement. It should have never gone that far. I need Jennifer up here. How can you be certain she doesn't think I sent the hit man?"

"Because I told her you didn't. She thinks Eldridge has gone rogue on you, that he's workin' with the Vatican. Now she can't wait to get here and help save you from his plotting."

Claire felt irritated. She did not like Mike making her chess moves for her. "But if she really believes Eldridge wants her dead, she'll never walk in the front gate. If it were me, I wouldn't know friend from foe."

"She's right, isn't she?" he asked. "If you thought she'd blow the whistle, she'd be finished."

Claire pondered the speaker box and shook her head. "Mike, sometimes you're a complete idiot. She's an intelligent woman and a scientist that we need, not an Irish kid filled with anger at the British establishment. Takes a little more subtlety than death threats to keep her on the team, you dumb thug."

It reassured her that she only had to put up with him a little longer.

"You wanted Sean to think we trusted him. He thinks we trust him. And my brother will continue to convince the Vatican that all that science you had Eldridge plant on Sheila's computer remains credible."

"That's true, Mike. You did what had to be done."

"I still wish you would tell me what the end game is on that one."

"Compartmentalization," she said. "You understand that." She changed the subject. "What about Clement?"

"Our Jennifer's made him dangerous," Mike answered. "He's started second-guessing everything because she went so damned paranoid. We'll have to rein him in. He needs to believe you're one of the good guys again."

Claire pressed her face against the cold window glass, staring out into the dark. Spotlights dotted the snowscape on the moonless night.

"I'm not worried about him working with us," she said. "I have leverage. He'll think I'm the second coming before this is over. I'm asking about his head. Where you hit him. He's my key resource at Prodeus and you hammered him."

"He would've recognized Sean from Sierra Leone. Anyway, he's got nothin' more than a nasty headache as it turns out."

"You put two of our most important resources at far too much risk with your handling of this."

"Desperate measures," he said. "Don't forget that you're the one that thought firing Jennifer would drive her back to the lab."

"We had no choice after she found out about Sheila. That was sloppy work on your part."

"We didn't know about the tattoo."

"You should have, Mike. And you still don't know whose phone number it was. Another loose end."

"She might have had it for years. It was in a place where only an intimate would find it."

"Just get Jennifer back in the fold. Quickly. We've planned this thing too well to let the little things trip us up."

"Aye, aye, your ladyship."

Just a little longer, she thought.

CHAPTER 9

Mangui, Middle African Democracy
December 22, 1:45 p.m. West Africa Time Zone (WAT)

Joseph Mossoumou's colonnaded palace stood deep within an elaborately landscaped compound of enormous banyan trees and dense thickets of flowering plants, their enormous and fragrant blossoms exploding from their buds in bright hues of red, pink, purple, blue and yellow. Camo-clad soldiers, armed with up-to-date weaponry, stood guard at numerous points, their uniforms impeccable and black boots gleaming, unlike their peers outside the Presidential guard.

Adrian Guerra arrived late the prior evening. He appeared this morning, as directed, at a private breakfast with the president in a surprisingly humble dining room. While substantial in square footage, it had only a round, democratic table with no head. Made of dark mahogany, the table had thick, gnarled legs, well-suited to the president. The chairs had wooden backs embedded with intricate carvings of tribal ceremonies; no cushions. The walls had only military maps of the region, apparently the most common topic for discussion over meals. Dark green concrete floors provided additional echo for Mossoumou's already sonorous voice. The President allowed no carpets to insure that he would always hear the footfalls of anyone – friend or foe - that approached.

Greeting Adrian with a bear hug, Mossoumou was only slightly taller than Adrian, but his taut girth enveloped the slimmer man. Few pleasantries passed before the president focused on business.

"I'm not happy, Adrian. Fela needs to stay well a while longer. You can't allow him to expose himself like that."

Adrian viewed the assassination attempt as a freak event without any indication of an organized effort. He chose not to explain this to the president. The man did not tolerate excuses well.

"We're working to improve his security arrangements."

"While you're working at it, he could be killed. Working at it is not acceptable. Unless you think that perhaps you were the target and not our friend."

"I'm not that important."

Mossoumou laughed. Not a comforting laugh, but a loud, deep intimidating laugh. "My American friend, if people knew what you were up to, you would be on almost everyone's hit list."

Guerra tore off a piece of croissant, easing it into his mouth with the manners expected of a man who had attended cotillion for four years from the age of ten. He chewed and swallowed before speaking.

"We'll hang together, Mr. President."

"No, Adrian. If there's hanging, you'll hang alone."

Again Mossoumou laughed. Guerra tried to laugh, too, but produced only an awkward titter. He fingered his croissant, but could not bring himself to put a piece in his dry mouth. He stole a sip of orange juice instead.

"My generals reviewed the timetable with me last evening. They remain concerned that the US will intervene."

The orange juice tasted sweet and pulpy. Adrian hoped the Vitamin C would help his stress levels.

"We will welcome a little pro-active assistance here," Adrian responded. "This operation has the complete accord of those that matter."

"Does that include your President?"

"Presidents come and go. I said those that matter. The President will react as needed."

Mossoumou's thick, powerful fingers drummed the table. He snorted through his wide nostrils. "So, Adrian, how does it feel to be on the bubble of history?"

"I should ask you first. You're the lead actor on that stage."

Mossoumou smiled. Indeed, the lead role had been bestowed on him. Adrian had heard him talk about it before: The convergence of history and destiny had not been as strong since the time of the Pharaohs. Mossoumou's destiny would dwarf theirs.

"Through our work, we will redeem the very cradle of civilization, returning middle Africa to its pre-destined place as pinnacle of mankind."

"Hopefully, it won't be too bloody," Adrian commented, immediately second-guessing his carelessness.

"Does it matter when it's redemptive blood? What greater honor than to bleed for redemption?"

Mossoumou's bluster seemed to be reaching new heights. Or was it bluster? Adrian wondered if they had created too much of a monster. He wondered if he should give a heads up to the folks back home.

Mossoumou's wide brown eyes bored into him, demanding an answer. Adrian cleared his throat.

"No greater honor, Mr. President. None whatsoever."

CHAPTER 10

Foothills Mall: Fort Collins
December 22, 11:15 a.m.

Mel glanced at the time on the tall clock in the middle of the mall. 11:15. She looked to her left. Dave. He actually broke away from the office to meet her for Christmas shopping. She could not remember another time he had done this. When he walked straight, his little paunch disappeared. Or, she thought, maybe it's the leather jacket? No, it really disappears. It's still nice to just look at him.

She reached her hand out and met his. They walked by the fountain in the center court like teenagers, slowly swinging their entwined hands. She could sense the tension in his grip, hot and shifting slightly every few steps. His pulse thumped against her palm, his racing thoughts and anxieties affirming their omnipresence.

But he was here. Desperately trying to be in her moment.

He felt her attention. "You all right?" he asked.

"I'm worried about you."

"Nothing to worry about."

"You have a lot on your mind. I understand."

He walked along quietly for a moment. She watched him, said nothing. They walked by Auntie Anne's Pretzels without stopping, very out of character for a guy who in the past had made special trips just to buy a single soft pretzel.

"Want a pretzel?" she asked.

"If you do."

"No, thanks."

"It's just that it's all tied together now." He let go of her hand to gesture. "My work, this insanity with Jennifer, the PDNA launch. Most of all, Liv's health. Her life itself."

They drifted past the Macy's entrance.

"I feel punch-drunk. It's like I can't really control anything."

This amounted to a completely new Dave.

"There are some things you still can control," she said.

He held his hands in loose fists. "Not the right things. I'm in biotech, for God's sake. My partners do drug discovery. I can't even get them to admit they can help my daughter."

"Maybe they can't."

"Then why are we baby-sitting Jennifer?"

"Hope, Dave. Desperate, clinging hope."

He stopped. Two steps ahead of him before she realized it, Mel turned to face him. Dropping his hands to his side, he stepped toward her. He embraced her. "Let's cling to each other," he said.

Mel held on to him for a moment, grateful when her cell phone trilled. She had never known him to be so openly needy. Stepping away, she answered the phone. Dave looked into the sporting goods store while she talked. She saw him look her way when she said "Paul" to the caller.

"How low?" she asked, "So what do we do now?"

He drew closer to her, leaning in amidst the loud hum of Christmas shoppers in the mall.

"Won't that make her really sick?.... Do you think it will work?.... Then why bother?...What do I tell her?... We'll be there."

She pressed the end button.

"Doc Resnick?" Dave confirmed.

"Her CD4 count's still below 300 and the ratio's not improving. The Fuzeon may not be working at all."

"Now what?"

"God knows. Resnick sure doesn't." Mel covered her eyes, pressing back frustration and fear. She looked up at him, fire in her eyes. "It's on you," she said. "You need to get Claire to open up."

"Right," he said. "You're right. It's time for bigger risks."

"I'll finish the shopping," she said.

Dave walked away. Mel let him.

CHAPTER 11

Boulder, Colorado: The Aldrich Institute
December 22, 1:20 p.m.

Ten minutes after Claire's chopper landed, Dave stood in her office.

"This is a surprise," Claire said, looking up from paperwork. "I can only give you a few minutes. Lots of last minute prep for the trip tomorrow and I have to be back in Cameron Pass before dark."

"That won't be a problem."

"So, what is it?" She scanned her desk and reached for a file folder in the corner. She grabbed a pen and made a quick note.

Dave walked to her side of the desk and stood over her. "Claire, we're about to launch a program that will ultimately save millions lives. But right now, there's only one life on my mind."

She did not look up. Rolling the pen between her fingers, she spoke, "I know what this is about, Dave."

"No, you don't. You don't know that the only kid in the world that matters to me right now could be dying. You don't know that no drug seems to get any traction with her."

Still looking down at the papers, she asked, "Which one's have failed?"

"Fuzeon is the latest. Ten days in and her CD4 count is not moving."

"It's too early for a result. You need to be more patient."

"I know the science, Claire. There should've been headway."

She pushed her seat back, nudging Dave aside. "What do you think I can do to help?"

She looked at him now. Dave leaned back against the edge of her desk.

"I'm not asking you to spill any secrets. But you know the latest on all the discoveries around AIDS. Pretend she's your kid. Tell me what you would do."

She looked at him as though he were a child that needed placated. Dave choked down anger.

"All right," he said. "You can't really understand this. You have no children. What would your father have done if Liv were you?"

The question struck her like a dagger. She remembered her Dad every day, thought of him frequently. His voice, recorded by Claire years ago, narrated the video montage of terror. His memory kept her going in the worst of times. He watched a child suffer. She felt his anguish, twisted inside with his pain. He would look at her, ask her things, hoping for reassurance, wanting only her happiness. She remembered him in his wheelchair. The cumulative stress on his back had finally relegated him to spending most of his life in the chair. She took care of him between work and her college course load. She remembered telling him how her friends planned to go to the beach. She told him that they invited her.

"Were you able to say no without hurting anyone's feelings?" he asked.

She could see the pain on his face, ten years older looking than he really was, his hair a stark white.

"Of course, Da. I've become quite good at that."

He nodded, his lips pressed together. He blamed himself. No matter what she said to reassure him.

"Don't, Da. Leave yourself alone. None of this is your fault."

"I should have died," he said. "At least the insurance would give you some comfort. You wouldn't have an old man to watch after."

"If I didn't want to be with you, I'd hire someone. We can afford that. But I don't choose to."

"You're living a lie because of me."

"Not you. Not you. You know that."

"I can't stand to see your embarrassment. It's my fault you don't have a man in your life."

She lied. "Wrong again. It's about choice, my choice."

He tried to push up from his chair to hug her. She stepped forward instead, leaning over and squeezing him close. After a moment, she let go.

"You make the best of what you have, Claire. Always. You can do it because it's your gift. Don't let this useless old man drag you down."

"Dear Lord. Why do you think you're useless?"

"I've lost nearly everything. All we have left is this house..."

"And it's a grand house with lots of land."

"... this house," he continued. "And my life insurance."

She should have known then. She feared it, but refused to believe it. She should never have gone to work that night.

Claire's thoughts returned to the present. She looked at Dave, recognized the tortured look on his face. "I have an idea," she said. She picked up the phone and dialed an extension.

"There's good unpublished research on better ways to supplement Fuzeon," she said while she waited.

"Bill," she said into the phone, "I want to do a pre-clinical for a friend. Bring me CADA, CXCR4 antagonist AMD3100, and the GNA/HHA combo… Right. Fuzeon's not cutting it with her current cocktail… Me. Either… Thanks." She hung up.

"This is what you've been working on?"

"No, others have. We analyze it as part of our own discovery process."

"Does it work?"

"Combined with Fuzeon, it seems to extend the period of drug efficacy. I think when your doctor gets all the data, he'll find the slow response of the CD4+ count to be insignificant. What's probably wearing her down is the viral load starting to move back up. This is a broad spectrum solution that should get that under control for a while."

"How certain is it?"

"It will certainly buy some time."

"How long?"

"I don't have that answer."

That depends almost entirely on you, Dave, she thought. It's all up to you.

CHAPTER 12

Clement Home
December 23, 1:12 a.m.

Jennifer turned the bedside lamp off and closed her eyes. The presence of the Clements in the house helped her relax. Waiting in the dark for the hit man to re-visit had been a very tense ordeal. Her forearms and hands felt sore from gripping the butcher knives so intently, the rest of her body simply drained.

She rolled over on her side and snuggled into her pillow. She heard a window rattle. Probably the wind.

Not that the Clements could protect her. Dave had proven pretty useless the other day. What if it wasn't the wind? She wished she had kept one of the butcher knives with her. She felt very exposed, pulled the covers tighter.

Mike Farley had not been in touch since that night. He left in a hurry. Left her with a racing pulse and orders for her next step. Told her she had to be at the lab before Christmas Eve. That was her drop dead date – maybe literally. And she needed to bring Liv Clement. Nothing about Jennifer wanted to walk in through the front door of the lab. Eldridge or whoever really wanted her dead could be waiting for her, watching her arrive on the security monitors. She might not even make it across the parking lot.

She thought of Liv upstairs in her bedroom. The kid did not know it, but Jennifer had a plan that included an early wakeup call planned for Liv at 4:30. Liv's fear about her HIV was far enough along that Jennifer thought she would go along with the plan.

The window rattled again. Jennifer sat up in bed, hanging her legs off the side. She rubbed her hands down her thighs, stretching nervously. Why the hell had Mike not been back in touch? Maybe Eldridge is not the only one behind the plot against Claire. If Sheila had been expendable, she certainly was.

Within 24 hours, she would know. She pressed the home button on her phone to see the time. She could still get a few hours' sleep before heading out. She thought Liv would buy it. She kept walking through the dialog in her mind. And every time she nodded off, she soon woke up obsessing.

Lying there, staring at the ceiling, she thought she heard voices upstairs in the family room. She realized it was the television. Sounded like *Finding Nemo*. Liv. If it was her, the next steps might be a little easier than surprising her at 4:30.

She reached for her robe.

In the family room, Liv awoke with the television still on. The time on the cable box said 1:50. Still a lot of night ahead.

She stuffed her hand under the pillow and found her diary, relieved that it remained safely out of the hands of others. Mel had let her sleep down here in front of the TV to get her mind off the day's bad news.

The horrors of her life ran on a loop in her mind. No amount of *Frozen* and *Maleficent*, the two movies she had found on the two Disney channels, could distract her enough to forget the latest CD4+ count. Not even quietly singing the lyrics of *Let It Go*, normally uplifting for her, helped tonight. She sensed where things were headed even before the latest test results, but she hoped to be wrong. In the last week, her energy began fading earlier and earlier in the day. Now, by dinner time, she had nothing left – not normal for a fifteen year old.

"So where are you, God?" she said out loud, staring up at the family room ceiling, lit only with the luminous blue from the TV screen.

She looked toward the coffee table at the bag of experimental medications her Dad had brought home from the Aldrich. He had told her she could expect these to at least buy some more time. "Significantly more," he had said.

She brushed back a tear as she stared toward the ceiling in the dark room. "Are you just teasing me, God? A little more time? Again? When will something last? Are you even there? Or is this whole God thing some kind of supernatural joke? Instead of getting better, things seem to get worse by the day. What's with that? I trusted you."

"Sometimes you have to trust yourself," said a voice in the darkness.

Liv nearly jumped off the couch. Turning her head, she saw Jennifer and quickly regained her composure.

"Why aren't you in bed?" Jennifer asked.

"My parents felt sorry for me so they let me sleep in front of the TV."

"You're going to be really tired in the morning. How will you stay awake in class?"

"It's the last day before Christmas vacation. I'll probably sleep in class. Teachers won't care."

Jennifer nodded and then walked to the kitchen. "Want a cup of tea?" she asked as she opened a cabinet.

"Decaf."

Jennifer took two mugs down and filled them with water from the hot tap. In the pantry, she found English breakfast decaf.

"Heard anything from Michael?" she asked as she grabbed a handful of sweeteners and tucked the milk under her arm.

"I am so over him. Jerk didn't show up at our last game."

Liv rolled off the couch and joined Jennifer at the kitchen table. Jennifer glanced at the sliding glass door as she sipped her tea. The pushpin that kept the doors from opening appeared to be in place. A dowel rod lay on the track as a backup if the pushpin failed.

"Maybe he had some kind of conflict."

"That would be nice."

Jennifer stood and went to the sliding glass door. She pressed on the pushpin, reassuring herself that it could not easily be knocked out. She returned to the table.

"Doc Resnick and the specialist both think that my HIV is already fighting off this new drug. They act like they haven't seen this before."

Jennifer did not respond right away. "I'm not surprised," she finally said.

"Why not?"

"I think you have some sort of weird mutation. It requires a very targeted medication."

"Dr. McQuaid gave something to Dad for me. Said it will help for a while. It's a good thing. I'm just having a little bit of a pity party tonight."

"Can I see them?"

Liv walked back to the family room and got the bag from the coffee table. She handed it to Jennifer.

"When did he get these?" Jennifer asked as she opened the bag and studied the labels on the drug bottles.

"Yesterday."

"He's right. These might buy a little time, but they're not a fix."

Jennifer warmed her hands on her mug. She pondered the teenager, seeing her clearly as a human being. She felt her angst, for the first time only one step removed from this curse, connected through a friendship she never anticipated and did not want.

"So, Liv, do you want to help yourself? Or are you going to keep waiting for some miracle to just fall into your lap?"

"If I knew how, I would go after it."

Jennifer placed a hand on Liv's shoulder. "What if you and I could do something about it? What if we could go to that lab and get the cure to stop all this?"

"I probably should give the Fuzeon a few more days with the new stuff."

Jennifer slowly rubbed the mug in her hands. She looked again at the pushpin and then back at Liv.

"Listen, Liv. My career involved understanding HIV and everything that can happen with it. I know it's not what you want to hear, but the new stuff will lose its effectiveness just like all the others."

"I know that, but it will take a while."

"What if it's quick?"

Liv felt herself getting emotional. "I sort of expect that, but I was just hoping…"

"We have to get you to the Aldrich lab."

"I've heard Mom and Dad talk. Dr. McQuaid said there is no cure."

"She's hiding the truth. I know that because I was there."

"She lied?"

"Yes. Do you want to go?"

"They won't let us in."

Jennifer looked again at the pushpin in the sliding glass door. Mike Farley's face flashed in her mind. Then Sheila's. Then Eldridge Perry, the sonuvabitch. She could wait for Farley or her killer to determine her fate. And Liv could wait for the HIV to overwhelm another pharmaceutical stopgap. Or not.

"Not acceptable," she mumbled to herself as she rubbed her forehead.

"What's not acceptable?"

"Think you can get your climbing gear together without waking your parents?" she asked.

Liv put her cup down and sucked in a deep breath. "You're serious?" she asked.

Jennifer nodded affirmation.

"Not a problem," Liv said. "They won't hear me over my Dad's snoring."

"Make sure of it."

Liv got up from the table and then turned back to Jennifer. "Only if I can drive."

"Deal. Now get going."

Jennifer watched as Liv tread quietly up the stairs. We both could die tomorrow, she thought. She glanced at the clock on the cable box. Today, she corrected. A spike of fear raced through her midsection.

"So why put off the inevitable?" she mumbled.

CHAPTER 13

Poudre Canyon, Route 14
December 23, 5:05 a.m.

In the pre-dawn darkness, almost an hour before Dave's alarm woke him for the day, Liv and Jennifer drove up Colorado route 14 between the granite cliffs of the Poudre Canyon. The snow had not yet arrived and the tires spun over bone dry roads. Overhead, billions of stars and their cloudy galaxies filled the clear night sky. With the temperature in the mid-teens, Liv ran the defroster constantly to melt the fog off the SUV's enormous windshield. The forecast projected that daylight would bring a chance of snow and highs in the low thirties. That would probably mean low twenties at 10,000 feet. Rough but do-able conditions if the sun stayed out.

Get On Up by Malia Grace played on the MP3 player plugged into the car's aux jack. Its lyrics fortified Liv's resolve.

> Get on up. Stand your ground.
> Don't let anyone or anything keep you down.

The song pulsated from the speakers, firing up Liv's adrenaline as she struck out into Colorado's wilderness. Still, the knot of fear curdled in her stomach, rolling up into her throat, drying it out.

> People say things happen for a reason,
> that we learn from our hardest times.
> I can tell you I been knocked down on my knees
> and I don't feel any more wise.
> Sometimes it ain't about the lesson.
> It's about not layin' down to die.

Liv swayed in her seat, her gloved fingers drumming the music's beat on the steering wheel. Jennifer, a wary eye on the highway, unconsciously bobbed her head. Soon, both sang in full voice.

> Get on Up. Stand your ground
> Don't let anyone or anything keep you down.
> Stamp your feet. You're here to stay.
> Just throw all your dust and heartache out your way.
> Get on up…

As the song ended, they laughed and did a quick fist bump. "It's about not layin' down to die," Liv said, quoting the song. Jennifer placed a reassuring hand on her shoulder.

As they continued up the canyon, Liv reached again and again for the coffee to wet her mouth, oblivious to the dehydrating effect it would ultimately have on her. Though the SUV's heater had long since warmed the cabin into the high 60's, Liv still frequently re-adjusted the vents in her direction in a futile effort to warm a chill that came from deep within.

"Can you believe we're doing this?" she asked..

Well aware that Liv still had only a learner's permit, an edgy Jennifer kept her eyes glued to the winding mountain road, her foot occasionally pressing an imaginary brake pedal on the floor in front of her.

"It's all good," Jennifer answered, reaching over and turning the volume down. "Just go easy. We have lots of time." She looked at the speedometer. Liv kept it right at the speed limit. "The speed limit's an upper limit," Jennifer said. "You don't need to go that fast."

She had proposed she drive when they left the house, but Liv reminded her of the promise made in the middle of the night. When Jennifer tried to renege, Liv offered some lame argument about Jennifer not being insured on the family vehicles. Rather than risk Liv backing out, Jennifer gave in and kept her fingers crossed. Insurance, she knew, would be the least of their issues.

Out the right side of the car, dropping straight down about 50 feet, Jennifer glimpsed the Poudre River cascading down from the Continental Divide. It brought water that would ultimately make its way thousands of miles to the Gulf of Mexico if it was not siphoned off for irrigation or other human uses first. Under the moonlight, the white rapids racing over the rocks of the Poudre looked fluorescent and all-powerful. She remembered meeting Sheila to sunbathe somewhere along this road only a few months earlier. Sheila had hinted at problems then, trusting Jennifer implicitly. That day, Jennifer knew Sheila had become confused about the mission. That day…

She let Liv's raucous rendition of Malia's *Mama Didn't Raise No Fool* intrude on her thoughts. It helped suppress the twinge she felt in her heart.

Liv braked the vehicle and tightened her grip on the steering wheel in preparation for a 90 degree angle to the right in the road ahead. Jennifer stiffened. As the Ford entered the turn, a sheer rock wall rose within a yard of Jennifer's side. Small rock outcroppings brushed even closer to the metal and, with the moonlight casting long shadows, Jennifer feared they would crash through her passenger window.

Liv saw the rocks, too. Her forearms ached from the force of her grip on the wheel. The Expedition's tires squealed into the switchback. She pumped the brake. Jennifer pumped the floorboard. Terror rushed through both women as they felt the two right wheels leave the ground. Liv jerked the wheel left and the three ton SUV crashed back down to the ground.

Finally, Liv pulled out of the turn into a short straight-away. She blew out the breath she had been holding. "I'm not used to that."

Jennifer exhaled slowly. "Dammit," she said quietly. "Pull over."

"I'm not letting you drive."

"Then slow the hell down."

"Promise."

Jennifer looked at the speedometer. "Try 30 in here."

Liv flashed a glance at Jennifer. "You sound like my mother."

"Then, good for your mother. We're out here to save your life. Not kill us both."

"Sorry." Liv drove quietly for a moment. Then, she began singing again, a grin emerging on her face. "My mama didn't raise no fool…"

Ninety minutes after leaving the all-night gas station in Fort Collins where they had filled up on coffee and gas, the women pulled onto a side road just beyond Joe Wright Reservoir as Route 14 entered Cameron Pass. Liv threw the Ford into four wheel drive. Between stands of tall pines, the SUV rolled slowly over crunching snowpack on the pitted dirt road. With the snow only a few inches deep, dry spots were visible in the dark. Down the mountains in the direction from which they came, the sky showed the first signs of daylight as black turned to gray.

After ten minutes of bouncing and swaying on the rugged road, Liv pulled the vehicle into a small trailhead park illuminated by the headlights. The women exited the car, stopping first at the porta-toilets lined up beyond the picnic benches. They met back at one of the tables.

Jennifer aimed a flashlight at a topo map. "I think we can get a good look at where we're going from a vantage point just up the trail."

They walked about fifty yards over frozen ground and very little snow toward the top of a hill overlooking a moraine, an ancient valley cut in the terrain by a glacier. As they walked, preceded by clouds of frigid breath, darkness evolved to gray, little by little revealing more of the landscape.

The moraine ran like a narrow valley between where they stood and high land on the other side. It was a like a bowl; they were on one lip in need of going to the opposite side. Positioned well to catch the winter sun, the moraine had almost no snow on it.

"We won't need our skis," Jennifer said.

"I guess that's good," replied Liv. "Less to carry. Is that where we're going?"

Jennifer's eyes followed Liv's pointing arm to what looked like a sheer, smooth face rising from a more gradual slope of rocks to a height well above the floor of the moraine. In the distance, far beyond the rock face, stood the majestic white cap of Clark's Peak at just over 12,000 feet, the first glint of pink and orange from the dawning sun casting long shadows from the sub-peaks surrounding the highest peak in the Rawah Wilderness. They would not be going that far on this journey and once they got close enough to the other side of the moraine, the cliff would obstruct their view.

"That's where we'll need our climbing skills," Liv said, arms folded against the cold wind blowing across the moraine. "How high do you think that rock face is?"

Jennifer rubbed her glove hands over her frozen cheeks. "Hundred and fifty feet?" she guessed, "Maybe a little less."

"What's the topo say?"

Jennifer stooped, re-opening the map on a flat rock. "I can't tell," she said. "The total rise looks like it's about 380 feet, but most of that's walkable."

Liv looked across through her binoculars. "Our rope's eighty feet long. So with a hundred and fifty feet of climbing, we're looking at two pitches."

Jennifer took the binoculars. "We can do it," she said as she moved the binoculars over the rock face, "It's that or turn back?"

"I'm not turning back. Not now."

Jennifer scanned the top of the cliff for evidence of the lab site. At first she saw nothing, then, as the orange sun fired its early rays across the moraine, something glistened at the top of the far cliff. She focused the binoculars on the spot. There she saw a blue jogging suit with fluorescent orange stripes for safety. Someone from the lab out for their morning run. Something glistened again, this time clearly from the wrist of the runner who occasionally disappeared behind groups of trees. Jennifer looked for a fence but could see none. Nothing had changed. Claire's security team still considered this side unapproachable; a fence and guardhouses were not needed.

"No guards," Jennifer said. "That's the good news. Bad news is that someone clearly thinks that rock face is a tougher climb than we imagined."

In spite of the long night, Liv felt energized, a combination of the caffeine and perhaps the new drug cocktail kicking in. Plus she always felt better in the morning.

"We're up to it," she said. "Let's get our stuff. We should try to get across the valley before many more people wake up."

It was 6:25.

They stood almost 5,000 feet above and 55 miles distant from the mouth of the canyon at the northernmost outpost of Fort Collins. Beneath a deep blue sky, reflected sunlight crept down the crags, carving shadows in the gray and brown cliffs. From their vantage, Liv and Jennifer could see roiling snow clouds north of them just across the Wyoming border. They seemed to mushroom from the Medicine Bow Range, churning clockwise around it, heading southbound down Colorado's Front Range into Fort Collins, leaving the high pass unscathed.

"Good thing we're up here," Liv said. "Looks like home's in for it."

"And we're not?" Jennifer said, pondering the climb ahead.

Clement Home
December 23, 6:02 a.m.

As Dave made coffee at six that morning, he noticed the family room couch was empty. Liv had not spent the night there after all. Probably too afraid, he thought.

He entertained going upstairs to kiss her good-bye. He decided that waking her when she could sleep later would not go over well. He needed to get to work anyway. Weather Channel showed a bad snowstorm inbound. If he wanted to get any work done, he needed to be in early. Looking at his watch, he thought again of checking on Liv, but realized Mel would be up in 15 minutes. She would look in on her.

He peered through the front door peephole and saw the splash of distorted black parked on the curb in the pre-dawn gray. No one had taken the time to clear his side of the driveway since the snow showers yesterday morning. So he left the Volvo on the street when he arrived home from work at eight-thirty the night before. He planned to get out the snow shovel and pull the car inside before he went to bed. Instead, he and Mel talked about Liv's situation until almost one before finally falling asleep. Dave wanted to tell her about his meeting with Fr. Jim, but he stopped himself repeatedly. In the first place, neither he nor the priest knew the whole story. Secondly, having knowledge of the matter could be a very dangerous thing for Mel.

He punched the alarm code and closed the front door behind him, careful as he walked over the icy sidewalk to the car. The cold cut right through his clothes, chilling his skin. He thought about going back inside for an overcoat, but decided he would be fine once the car's heater kicked in.

In the car, he reached for his sunglasses, but they were not in the cup holder where he usually left them. He had another pair in the Expedition. He looked at his watch. He decided not to take the few minutes to open the garage and find the other pair.

As he pulled away, he had a strong sense of foreboding, that somehow he made a mistake not going back to the SUV. Silly, he thought.

Cameron Pass
December 23, 7:05 a.m.

By 7:05, the women had successfully hiked across the moraine leaving the big SUV far behind them in the small parking area. They took turns carrying the rope over their shoulders as they climbed over small rocks and rubble accumulated over millennia of erosion. Liv remarked that the distance seemed a lot shorter looking across the moraine. Jennifer suggested the elevation of the mountains surrounding them created the illusion.

By 7:40, they had scrambled up the side of the mountain to the point where they needed to begin their technical climb up what they hoped would be less than a hundred and fifty feet of unaccommodating granite. Thus far, they had managed to stay upright and walk most of the way, but now they would need to go to ropes.

In one way, the rock face did not look nearly as ominous close-up. From a distance, it appeared straight up. From their current perspective, they could see that the slope was much more gradual than they feared -- except for what appeared to be the last 20 feet or so. That stretch actually had a slightly protruding shelf and would require a great deal of upper body strength and determination to overcome.

"What do you think?" Liv asked.

"You're the climber."

"You're the Outward Bound survivor. We both have to be climbers to get over that shelf."

Jennifer rubbed her gloved hands over her red cheeks to warm them. She watched the frozen breath float from her mouth as she exhaled.

"Liv, we've come this far. We'll figure out a way to make this work. All those pull-ups should come in handy."

Looking up and down the length of the cliff, they sought a better spot for climbing, one that might have both an easier and shorter climb. As they scanned the wall to the north and south of them, the other options all looked even more difficult. This was it. They spread out their gear to organize it.

First, they put on their harnesses and belay devices. They carefully attached carabiners, chocks, and nuts to rings around the harnesses. Each slid a hammer through a slot in the harness, bouncing it to make sure it was secure. They had no helmets, one thing Jennifer regretted. The rock looked loose and they were bound to catch flak. Unlike most of the equipment, Liv had never bought a helmet, always choosing to rent one at the gym because of the price. Nor did they have climbing shoes. For the same reason. They had discussed the issue when they loaded the SUV and convinced themselves that their racing flats would be nearly as good. Short of delaying their departure to go shopping, they had no choice. They agreed they might lose their courage if they waited.

After they secured the rope through Jennifer's belay device, Liv concentrated on the task ahead. She would climb lead. Everything else had to be pushed from her mind. HIV, Chelsea, Michael Winston: none of them belonged with her on this climb. She owed herself and Jennifer 100% concentration. If she did not give it, then they could both be badly hurt or even die.

Surveying the wall, she identified a thin crack fifteen feet overhead that ran at a sixty degree angle toward a narrow chimney about fifty feet up. The chimney went for another twenty-five to thirty feet before it played out. After that, a wide horizontal crack could be used to traverse the face until they arrived at an angled pillar that could allow for some easy climbing for forty feet or so. That would bring them to what appeared to be the least challenging spot from which to approach the intimidating outcropping. Somehow they would have to muster the upper body strength to climb up a section that pitched outward at about ten degrees, not impossible but very difficult.

"Look," she said, her gloved hand pointing. "It looks like a small chimney in that outcropping. That could give us the little bit of a break we need to make it over the top."

Jennifer followed Liv's finger. "It looks perfectly horizontal," she replied when she spotted it. "It goes to the edge of the big section of rock sticking out. I can't see if it keeps on going or not."

"It's cool. At least it gets us right to the lip of the upper ledge. If we can pull up over, it's an easy ten foot ramp to the top."

The women stood there looking at the chimney, a cut in the rock with walls wherein they could lean on both sides of the walls at once. They could wedge themselves in between the walls as they shimmied up, thus getting extra support at a point in the climb when they would already be very tired, a time when they would be facing the most physically challenging part of the climb.

The sound of the wind whipped past their ears. Jennifer started getting dizzy from staring up at the cliff. She looked down and rubbed her head. Turning, she looked back across the moraine. The sun shone above it now in a cloudless, deep blue sky. The heat from the sun felt good on her face, but the twenty mph wind chilled it just as quickly. She looked to Liv who stood almost catatonically as she faced straight ahead at the immovable granite.

"Should we tie on?" Jennifer asked.

Liv did not answer immediately. Both women could feel their stomachs twisting. This was not the gym. This was the real thing.

Liv shifted her eyes to the stretch of rock just above her. If she just took this one section at a time, she could do it. That's what they taught at the gym. She looked down and undid the rope from her pack.

"Tie on," she said, handing Jennifer an end of the rope.

The whipping sound of the wind pervaded the mountains. Preparing the rope, cinch knots, belay devices and anchors, they could hear each other's breathing, the occasional clanking of the metal parts, and the noise of the wind. Nothing more.

They changed gloves to pairs with finger holes for gripping. Each tied their ends of the rope to their harnesses. Jennifer put hers through a belay device attached to the harness. The belay device, a simple metal piece, allowed her to both pay out rope to Liv as she climbed, and to quickly brake the rope, pulling it tight to stop a fall by Liv. Finally, Jennifer anchored her back-rope, a short length separate from the long climbing rope, by tying one end to her belay harness and the other end to a small pine tree protruding from the rocks. That way if Liv fell from above, Jennifer would be tied in and unable to fall. This created a fail-safe system with Liv most at risk as the lead. Jennifer secured her through the belay device and its rope-braking mechanism. The back-rope secured Jennifer to a fixed object in the ground.

Looking over her shoulder to Jennifer, Liv spoke. "On belay?" she asked, the climbing call for getting started they had learned at the gym.

Jennifer tugged the back-rope behind her one more time to make sure her anchor was in place. She checked to be sure the belay device holding and guiding the rope was still properly hooked to the harness around her waist and thighs. She shuffled her feet, clearing the loose pebbles away. In the silence of the wilderness, her feet shuffling gruffly against the dirt and the crackle of the pebbles sounded like thunder to her, ready to draw attention from the lab above.

"On belay," she finally responded.

Liv acknowledged by the book, "Climbing."

"Climb on," Jennifer called to let Liv know she was ready.

The teenager started skyward, first placing her hands on a couple of pre-planned holds just above her head. She then placed her feet on two small ledges, also pre-planned. She looked back wide-eyed at Jennifer who gave her the thumbs up sign. Liv smiled slightly and then gulped a huge amount of air. She placed her head against the rock and mumbled a quiet request for God's help and their safety. From a gear loop on her harness, she unclipped the first anchor, a metal wedge known as a rock that had a wire sling hooked to it. She twisted the metal rock into a small vertical crack just above her to the right. Pulling on it a few times, she made certain it was secure.

Next, she grabbed a "runner" made of nylon webbing and hooked it through a carabiner she attached to the end of the wire sling. She then placed another carabiner on the loose end of the nylon runner and clipped it to her rope. The extra length provided by the runner made it less likely that the metal rock would be dislodged as she climbed. Liv did not completely understand the physics. She just trusted it was the right thing to do.

Moving her right foot up to grip a small dent in the rock by her thigh, Liv began her caterpillar like movement. First she reached out with her arms. Next, she moved her legs up as near to her hands as possible without losing her balance, causing her butt to stick way out. She then stretched out again with her hands, imitating the crawling motion of the fuzzy insect.

"Good luck," mumbled Jennifer as she watched her young friend move away. She thought to free a hand to bless herself, even though she had been raised Presbyterian, but the instructors at the gym has taught her that the belayer must always keep both hands on the rope. This did not seem the time to test their wisdom. Instead, she gradually let out rope with her brake hand as Liv went higher.

CHAPTER 14

Loveland, Colorado: Prodeus Offices
December 23, 8:32 a.m.

Swirls of gust-driven snow spun outside Dave's office window, the Front Range invisible in the bleakness. With just two days to go, a white Christmas now would be a near certainty. The storm had first announced itself with frigid straight line winds as Dave crossed the plant parking lot an hour earlier.

Even without the forecast, he would have expected this to be a bad one. The winds came from the north, Wyoming. Nothing good in the way of weather ever came out of Wyoming. The bow-like turn in the mountains at the border, just 25 miles north, somehow sheltered Fort Collins from the harsh winds and storms that peppered its northern neighbor. But every now and then a storm swept around that corner, veering due south, dumping its wrath on the foothills of Colorado's northern Front Range.

Now, reflected in blue luminescence from the computer monitor, Dave sat at his desk, huddled in the dark with a warm cup of coffee, its steam drifting past the e-mail filling the monitor. He did not turn the overhead light on, preferring the coziness of the room darkened by the storm clouds.

The last week had been very difficult. More difficult than dealing with the blow to his head and de-ciphering the priest's intrigue, watching Liv adapt to her diminished role in life broke his heart. He knew how much she wanted to be back to normal. He and Mel worked to look on the bright side, but both feared that no meds would work for Liv, that her death could be just a matter of months away.

He tried to put aside his worries at home and plow through his e-mail. Fortunately, the dreary weather proved conducive to curling up behind a desk and reading.

He glanced through his Outlook calendar. In less than twenty-four hours, the malaria vaccine press conference took place in Sierra Leone. Claire and Ed had both encouraged him to go, but he viewed the Christmas holiday as sacred family time and chose to stay home. He had already put Mel and Liv in second position far too often. Plus he knew Claire and Pamela Thatcher would give appropriate credit to the PDNA. That meant revenue and credibility. Dave did not need to be present for that.

An e-mail from Eldridge Perry at the Aldrich updated the progress on the vaccine. A lengthy attachment provided details. Dave opened it. Making liberal use of the down arrow, his eyes scanned the screen for meaningful data. The report clearly had been put together by several different people reporting on multiple aspects. He looked for inconsistencies and contradictions to ferret out the hard facts from the puffery.

"You want some light?" Brian Middleton said quietly at the door, not wanting to disturb his boss's concentration too abruptly.

Dave did not respond. A table specific to the effectiveness of the PDNA deployment had his full attention. This table, put together over the weekend by the Aldrich team director in country, told of 16,734 people already tested and almost forty percent of them inoculated. More importantly, roughly twenty-three percent had not and would not be inoculated because genotyping on the PDNA showed either that the vaccine would not be effective for them or that their genotype already provided resistance to malaria.

Middleton knocked on the doorjamb. This time Dave lifted his eyes.

"I will have some light. Thanks, Brian."

Middleton smiled as he flipped the switch. His red, puffy eyes betrayed a lack of sleep.

"Have you seen this?" Dave asked as he shaded his eyes with his right hand while they adjusted.

"I looked at it last night at home. The PDNAs are doing the job." Middleton sat down.

"4,000, Brian. Almost 4,000 inoculations salvaged that would have been wasted. That's a huge increase in efficiency and cost savings. That means a lot more people will be helped."

"What's the percentage of the total tested that was ruled out?"

"Twenty-three."

"I thought the projections were for over thirty percent."

"So it's a little disappointing," Dave conceded. "But it's still a very significant number."

"And it's going to be good for our stock," Middleton added.

"Don't. I'm having a moment of pure altruism here."

Sitting on the edge of his chair, Brian folded his hands and tapped his knuckles on his lips. His head tilted downward, he peered up through his dark eyebrows. "Enjoy it, boss. You're not going to feel so pure when you hear what I have to say."

Dave pushed his monitor aside. That sounded threatening.

"We spent all night on it," Brian said. "We've been sandbaggin' you. My guys never stopped working on the reverse engineering. You'll be glad we didn't."

Dave inhaled and sat back, arms folded.

"Here," Brian said, handing Dave a CD in a clear plastic case.

Dave took it, turned the case over and saw nothing was written on the CD. "I don't get it."

"You're holding the smoking gun. You did the right thing to fire Jennifer."

Dave put the CD down on the desk. "Now, I really don't understand."

"We found it in Jennifer's PC, in the CD drive. She got careless. It has a compiler and de-compiler on it. It also has an encoding scheme. She probably used it primarily for encryption and decryption. It's family jewels to the Aldrich."

"Are you sure it's current. Maybe it's just a scrap CD she brought over from the Aldrich with her."

"No, it's the real thing. We've already used it to decrypt and de-compile a lot of their files. Plus her e-mails. We plowed through anything that ever passed through her inbox and her hard drive. It led us to the key to accessing the source code. We haven't completely figured it out yet, but there's something wrong with the code. It looks like it's designed to give false readings in the field."

"Something they blew in the de-bug?"

"They did it on purpose."

Dave dropped his head back against the chair in exasperation. "Why? The Aldrich needs this thing to work as much as we do. They're not going to sabotage their own program."

"Maybe they have a rogue coder, Dave. I don't know. We should meet with them and confront them."

Dave swiveled his chair and watched the snow. Why had Jennifer not told him about the CD? What was she doing with it in the first place?

"There's something else, too, Dave. An e-mail to Jennifer from Sheila Stratemeier right before she left them. She's telling Jennifer that the project's gone off the rails, that there's something very wrong at the Aldrich lab. Sheila said she was going to blow the whistle."

Dave swiveled his chair back around to face Brian. He processed the information and then processed it again.

"Did she say what it was about?"

"Maybe. There's over a half million lines of code involved. It's pretty labyrinthine. We have some ideas, but we're not able to confirm them yet. We think the firmware causes the PDNA to read a gene marker as true for a good response to the malaria vaccine whenever HIV is detected in the first pass through the analyzer. This happens whether or not the HIV positive person genotypes well for the vaccine."

Dave paused to think. "So that means all HIV positive people get the vaccine."

"Right."

"And a significant portion of that group will get no benefit from it?"

"Right."

"That means they deliberately designed it to waste vaccine. Why? So they could sell more of it? But they know they'll be well over a year before they can manufacture enough of it. This makes no sense."

Middleton sat back and threw his hands up. "I don't know. My team's just trying to connect the dots."

"They're not connecting for me."

"Maybe that's why we're only seeing twenty-three percent as no-go's for the vaccine. If they weren't giving us false readings of true on all HIV positive people, we'd probably be much closer to thirty percent not inoculated."

Dave's fists clenched and unclenched in his lap. His teeth ground into each other with an intensity that started a dull ache in his temples.

"It doesn't add up," he said. "Maybe it's a plan to somehow sabotage us and own our technology. Or maybe there's a reasonable explanation. Whatever it is, we need to fix it."

"What do you want me to do? I think we need to meet with the Aldrich."

"Have any of your folks let the Aldrich in on this activity?"

"Heck, no. We've kept it very secret. We didn't want to risk anyone finding out until we cracked it. We figured you'd shut us down otherwise."

"So why tell me now?"

"Because we think the program's been compromised. And because there are people in Sierra Leone who might suffer because of it."

"In what way?"

"By not getting the vaccine, I guess. People who don't need it will get it and some people who do need it won't get it because of limited supplies."

Or worse, thought Dave. The entire activity had been built on partnership and a level of trust. Dave felt none of that now. Claire McQuaid and possibly Jennifer had used them, even conned them. For what? Why the secret agenda?

"How many engineers do you have on this, Brian?"

"Two. We can trust them."

"Who?"

"Billy Zopf and Scott Lawrence."

"Good. Add more. We need to get our arms completely around that code. Pick only people you are completely certain will keep their mouths shut."

"Don't we need to tell Ed?"

"What if it's a wild goose chase? Hepp would not be very happy if he thought we were on a witch hunt with his friend Claire as the target."

"You're right. We should have more data first."

Ed would go right to Claire, thought Dave. If she was up to something, he did not want to give her forewarning that they were on to her.

"Also, forward to me all of Jennifer's e-mails to and from Claire and Sheila Stratemeier."

"They're not all decrypted."

"You mean everything they sent each other was encrypted?"

"Just the attachments."

"How often did they send attachments?"

"Almost every time."

So Jennifer had betrayed them from the outset. More than that, she had been an outright plant, a spy.

Dave stood and walked Brian out the door. "Keep me apprised round the clock," he instructed.

As soon as Middleton left, Dave shut the door and picked up the phone. "Mel, take Liv and get out of the house. Without Jennifer... Something's very wrong... Jennifer seems to be involved in some plot with Claire to undermine our software... No, I don't know anything for sure. I just want you and Liv away from her and away from the house until we figure this out..."

The color drained from Dave's face. "She didn't say anything to me. I thought she slept upstairs. Have you gone downstairs to see if Jennifer's there? ... I'll hold on."

Dave held the phone to his ear as he walked to the window. With the index finger of his right hand, he drew in the condensation. He etched a large circle to represent the people of Sierra Leone, a smaller concentric circle inside to represent those with HIV and an overlapping circle for those who would not benefit from the malaria vaccine.

"Why?" he said as he stabbed his index finger into the overlapping area. "What are you up to, Claire?"

He adjusted the phone closer to his ear as Mel's voice came back on. Jennifer was gone, too.

"Then where is she, Mel? She's supposed to be hiding out... I'm sorry. I don't mean to jump all over you. Maybe they're at the climbing gym... Call me as soon as you know something... Just let me know if you do... Love you, too."

Dave grabbed his keys off the desk. He hurried downstairs to the parking lot. As he turned the engine over, the radio came on, tuned to the all-news station. The newscaster warned everyone to stay inside. A front originally expected to stay north in Wyoming had shifted south, he said. Dangerous blizzard conditions had descended on the Front Range.

Finding Fr. Jim Reilly's mobile number, Dave dialed it. He looked at his watch. The priest said he would be at the mountain lab at 9:00. It was 8:15 now. He was probably halfway there.

"Father, we need to continue the conversation we started at Josie's. My team may have found a smoking gun... Where are you now?"

On the other end of the line, Jim evaluated his options. He started out earlier to drive up to the Aldrich Lab in Cameron Pass, but an endless line of red brake lights floated in the haze of snow in front of him; headlights and parking lights marked the trail behind him. The radio said an avalanche at the foot of the Poudre Canyon had shut down route 14. They expected to have it cleared in the next hour. So he could wait an hour in traffic and keep his fingers crossed or he could make a u-turn and humor Dave Clement.

The lure of an empty highway and unencumbered movement proved too tempting. He turned around.

Rawah Wilderness
December 23, 8:38 a.m.

Claire charged down the corridor and found Mike Farley in the communications center. "What the hell, Mike. We need the two of them on the plane this afternoon. Why hasn't Jennifer returned? And since she hasn't, why haven't you gone to get her and the Clement girl yourself?"

Mike nodded at one of the displays that showed the storm front north and east of the lab. "Weather. This storm was expected to stay north, but it's dipping down into Colorado. We can't get in with a helicopter right now. Not safely."

"One way or the other, Jennifer and the girl are going to Sierra Leone today."

"We can risk the chopper, but it's wiser to wait a few hours and look for a weather window. We think there will be a few breaks before the storm intensifies again this afternoon."

Claire folded her arms and contemplated Farley. "You waited too long, Mike."

"We timed it the way we had to," he said. "The Clements weren't going to let Liv just go off to Sierra Leone at Christmas. Jennifer had to make the parents think the kid came to us on her own. Then you get to be the hero with the whole Christmas vacation in the Canary Islands and the hope of a cure."

Claire reached up and placed a hand on each of Mike's shoulders. "Well, security expert, we may be back to the drawing board. Have you tried to reach Jennifer? Did she know you were planning to come and get them."

"No. She promised me she would be here by today."

"After you made her a wreck about a hit team set up by Eldridge? You knew damned well she wouldn't walk in the front door without an armed guard."

Mike nodded. "You're right. But there are so many moving parts in this whole scheme, something was bound to go wrong. Lucky for us, I'm good at improvising."

Claire pressed her lips together and took a deep breath through her nose. "It's not a scheme. It's a chess game. With the highest stakes. If you can't think five moves ahead, then I picked the wrong security chief. And this program will fail. That's not acceptable."

"So what do you want me to do now?"

"Figure out how to get them up here in time to make the flight to Sierra Leone on Pamela's plane. Assuming we can get to Grand Junction from here."

"That one will be easy. Good flying weather going west from here."

"If you can't get them here, then your carelessness may mean we need to plan to go forward without Dave Clement. That would be a shame for his widow and his dying kid. And a major pain in the ass for me."

CHAPTER 15

College Avenue, Fort Collins
December 23, 9:10 a.m.

Thirty-five minutes later, Dave found himself just over halfway to Vern's Place, a drive that should have been thirty-five minutes in total. Vern's was halfway between Dave's home and the entrance to the Poudre Canyon. Dave and Jim agreed it would be the best option with the road conditions.

Driving slowly, Dave locked his fingers in a death grip on the steering wheel. Holding the road proved difficult since sand trucks had not yet coated the highway. His windshield wipers clicked back and forth at their highest speed and the defroster stayed on. As cold as it was, he kept his window cracked because the heat from the defroster became suffocating.

College Avenue turned into 287 North, the most direct route to Vern's. Normally, the interstate would be faster, but the radio said I-25 had been closed just north of Fort Collins. With the rate of snow accumulation, Dave expected the most northerly Fort Collins exits would be next, likely forcing him off the highway into a traffic jam with a lot of other diverted motorists. He knew 287 well and could always find his way to other back roads if it became too problematic.

"Dave?" Mel voice came across the car's speakers..

"Anything?" Dave responded loud enough to be heard above the hum and clatter of the windshield wipers.

"Nothing. Why are you on your mobile?"

"I'm on my way to Vern's Place for a meeting. I thought meeting at Vern's would get me closer to home in case the snow didn't let up."

"What meeting could possibly be so important with Liv missing?"

Jim had sworn him to secrecy about their contact. Dave felt a compulsion to do what the priest asked - because he was a priest and because Dave was cradle Catholic, psychologically committed to the lore of the Church.

"The guy swore me to secrecy."

Mel said nothing for a moment on the other end. "Cancel the meeting, Dave," she finally said.

"It's a meeting about Liv. About the possibility of a cure."

Silence again. Then slowly. "She's missing," Mel said. "With Jennifer. Who may be a killer. Has it occurred to you that she has to be around to benefit from the cure?"

"It's complicated. I'll explain when I see you."

"That's not good enough. Come home. Now."

Dave sighed. "All right. Look. It's Father Jim."

"Father Jim? He's dead."

"No. I've seen him. He's very much alive and thinks he knows how to help Liv."

"My God."

"I'll explain more when I see you. What did the school say?" he asked.

"They don't take attendance until ten."

"Can't they check her earlier classes?"

"I begged them. They gave me an excuse about the rules and how they would have to do it for every student. Bureaucracy. Unbelievable. I'm stranded here without a car. Otherwise, I'd be at the school and in their face."

"How about a cab?"

"I already called. They have a two hour wait because of the weather."

Dave pressed the accelerator too hard. The car lost traction, sliding sideways across the ice. He lifted his foot off the gas and stayed away from the brake, holding the steering wheel with both hands until the Volvo straightened out.

"Are you there, Dave?"

"I'm here. The car skidded."

"Be careful. We don't need to deal with anything else."

"Should we call the police?"

"I did. They won't do anything until she's missing 24 hours."

"For a minor?"

The windshield suddenly fogged over. Dave turned up the fan on the defroster. A small clearing started along the top of the dash and he leaned down to peer through it.

"Especially without an attendance report."

"Did you tell them about Jennifer?" he asked, speaking louder to overcome the loud whir of the defroster.

"Of course not. A conspiracy theory won't exactly help our credibility."

"Look, what if I swing by and you drop me at my meeting? The high school's near there. You can go straight from Vern's. Maybe Liv's at school. She could have wanted to sneak out with the car and brought Jennifer because she needed a licensed driver."

"That's a reach. How soon will you be here?"

CHAPTER 16

Rawah Wilderness, Medicine Bow Range
December 23, 9:40 a.m. Mountain Time

The fingertips of her right hand struggled to grip the tiny hold straight overhead. There, she thought, I've got it. Now instead of pulling up with her fingers, Liv pushed with her legs, conserving precious arm and finger power. By keeping her legs and hips relaxed, she minimized the risk of cramping, a treacherous possibility if it proved ill-timed. So far she had done this quite well. And her strength seemed intact.

She searched for the next hold. Her left hand, jammed in a small waist-high crack, needed a new home. The chimney she wanted to climb ended a good ten feet up from the end of the thin crack she had been following, not the arm's length presumed by her inexperienced perspective when she planned the climb from below. So now she perched precariously between the crack and the chimney.

Some 40 feet below, Jennifer remained anchored at the original belay point, 30 feet to Liv's left because of the traverse of the inexperienced climber. This caused the rope to slacken. Liv felt the slack. If she fell, her last runner would allow her to swing some seven feet below, a long drop that could possibly crack her head or break a shoulder, but the extra slack in the rope could increase the net fall by another five or six feet, dramatically aggravating the risk of injury. Liv had no desire to fall at all, but there was no sense in making things any worse if she did.

"Tension," she called facing the wall, but Jennifer did not respond. When the wind occasionally gusted up to howling speed, they could not hear each other, even when shouting. Liv tugged on the rope to get Jennifer's attention. It remained too loose. She called again over her shoulder with similar lack of success. Carefully, she turned to look down to Jennifer and direct her voice.

"Tension," she called.

Liv felt the rope tighten, but something else was wrong. When she made the last call, she had looked down. She was high and the wall nearly straight up. She saw down to Jennifer and beyond, including the next 200 feet over the rocky terrain to the moraine below. She was up very high. Terror charged through her. Her fingers tensed on their holds, her hips now pressed tightly against the wall.

Oh my God, she thought, get me down from here. What am I doing? This is not the same as the gym. C'mon, fingers, hold on.

Her breath came in quick shallow gasps. In spite of the cold, she sweated beneath her parka, her fingers growing moist and slick on their holds. A voice called to her in the distance, but she could only think of the wall, the wall and the fall.

"Deep breaths! Deep breaths! Liv! Deep breaths!"

Jennifer's voice. Deep breaths. Focus. She struggled to slow her breathing down long enough to inhale, but she could feel the fingers of her left hand slipping off the hold at her waist. Instinctively, she tightened the fingers of her right hand to compensate. So concentrated was she on her fingers, that it surprised her when her right foot slipped off its hold.

"Oh, God!" she cried as she slipped back.

"No!" yelled Jennifer from below.

Liv flailed with her hands and feet to find a new hold. Jennifer thrust the rope to one side, braking it hard on the belay device to take out any remaining play, shortening Liv's potential fall.

Her frenetic scrambling unsuccessful, Liv slipped backward into the air. As she came down, she repeatedly slammed against the rock. In a matter of seconds, her descent stopped. Her anchors held. She swung about eight feet below the last one placed, a total fall of sixteen feet. Mentally she checked herself out. Her left shoulder throbbed, but nothing seemed broken.

Laying way back and facing the sky as she dangled on her harness, she flattened her feet against the wall, working to right herself and get her hands on the wall as well. She was back to the thin crack, giving her something that provided a decent hold.

Still dangling as she maneuvered to get back on the wall, Liv watched the rope slack go back through the anchor above her as Jennifer pulled it in from below. Liv stiffened. An anchor hung halfway out of position. The drag of the rope and her dangling weight were pulling it out the rest of the way.

"Stop! Jennifer, stop!" Liv screamed. Lunging, she scrambled to find hand holds.

Jennifer immediately braked the rope.

"The anchor!" yelled Liv, her voice echoing across the moraine. "It's coming out!"

Jennifer wanted to do something, but there was nothing she could do. She felt completely helpless.

Throwing her right hand into a narrow section of the crack, Liv tried to use the hand as a wedge to hold her to the rock. As she did so, her feet flew off the wall and the wedged hand became her only contact with terra firma.

Ping!

The sound of the anchor popping out did not achieve enormous decibel levels but in the silence of the wilderness, it exploded in the women's ears. The thin thread anchoring Liv between life and death had snapped.

With 16 feet of slack rope between Liv and the next anchor eight feet below her, she looked over her shoulder as gravity pulled her toward the ground. She would fall the eight feet to the anchor and then swing the length of the rope, 16 more feet below it. That would bring her crashing down with

24 feet of momentum into a large immovable boulder sticking out of the rock face.

As Liv's body jerked with the snap of the falling rope, Jennifer pulled hard on the rope from below, frantically trying to get as much of that 16 feet out of the rope as possible. If she could shorten the length, she would reduce Liv's fall, giving the younger woman a better chance.

In the crack 35 feet above, flesh shredded as Liv's clenched fist, ripping through the crack, scraped rock. She swallowed a scream. Suddenly, her left shoulder almost jerked out of its socket, her hips and side crashing against the granite. Her fist, caught painfully inside a very narrow section of the crack, suspended her safely on the rock face. Her fall had been broken.

As the weight of her body swung from it, the wrist felt like it would tear from its socket. The rope slack disappeared as Jennifer hastily hauled rope through the belay device. As the color returned to their frightened faces, the two women exchanged unstoppable smiles of relief.

Twisting around, Liv, her face contorted in pain, found another hold for her right hand. She wedged one foot in the crack below her and placed another on an accommodating small ledge to her right. Secure again, she carefully extricated a very bloody left hand from the crack.

"Come down," called Jennifer. She gripped the rope tightly. Her face dripped sweat from the exertion of the belay. Drops of blood from Liv's hand landed like hot rain on her cheeks and upper lip, intermingling with the sweat. She stepped to the side, worried the teenager might have a disabling injury. She needed to get her down and get all the way back to the SUV. Either that or wait for Aldrich security to find them and hope they were not part of Eldridge's coup. Or they could freeze to death.

"Liv, Can you hear me? Come down."

Liv did not answer Jennifer's call to retreat. Instead, she tried to open and close the fist of her left hand. It barely responded. She had no grip.

CHAPTER 17

Vern's Place: LaPorte, Colorado, northwest of Ft. Collins
December 23, 9:42 a.m. Mountain Time

Like orange and yellow beacons, the lights of Vern's Place shone as small, glimmering points through the driving snow, guiding the Clements into the lot. The black Volvo rolled over the fresh powder and up to the front entrance of the rustic, wooden-slatted building. On the way over, Dave updated Mel on Fr. Jim. He exited the driver's side, holding the door while Mel came around. She started to get in when Dave tapped her shoulder. He stepped around the door and hugged her.

Wrapping her arms around the blue cashmere overcoat she brought him, she buried her face in his chest.

"I love you, Mel," he said in the quiet that always accompanied a snowstorm. Only the rushing of the wind could be heard.

She rapped a fist into his shoulder and then squeezed him harder. "Why don't you hug me more often?" she said. "I miss it."

He did not answer. He did not know the answer. He only knew the hug felt good, comforting, to him.

Mel stepped back and looked at her watch. "9:43," she said. "Seventeen more minutes before they take attendance."

He looked around in the dark whiteness. "Feels like night," he said.

"It's beautiful. I wish we could enjoy it."

The door of the restaurant opened as two men in heavy coats came out. They hunched into the wind as they crunched over the snow toward a green pick-up. The smell of bacon, eggs, and coffee wafted out the door.

"Smells good," Mel said.

"Maybe you should eat. I'll explain to Jim why you need to be in the loop. He's a priest. He'll get it."

"Be careful with him. It's possible that Jennifer's story about a Vatican conspiracy is true."

"I doubt it, but if it is, then Liv may be in safe hands with Jennifer after all."

"If it isn't?"

"Father Jim can help us find them. He's been tracking Jennifer for three weeks. And he has resources."

Mel reached into her overcoat. She pulled out a small pistol case. She had taken it out of its hiding place between the sweaters on her closet shelf.

"What are you doing with that?" Dave asked.

"Take it."

"I hate those damned things."

"Bad enough to risk losing your life or Liv's without it?"

"Or yours."

"I'll call the police if I need to. You're the one that's having breakfast with an Irish priest linked to the IRA."

She unzipped the case and shoved the Ruger LC380 into his coat pocket. "There's a seven round magazine in it. Plus another round in the chamber. Hollow points."

"You chambered a round? Are you crazy?"

She reached into the case and pulled out a spare clip. "Seven more rounds. And the safety's on. So relax."

Mel's father had given her the gun several years earlier to replace an old .38 he had given her when she first left home. Mel talked Dave into joining her at the firing range on three occasions; he never got comfortable with it saying his biggest fear was that he might use it. Then, to his surprise, as Mel placed the spare clip in his pocket outside Vern's, he felt a little safer, more in control.

They kissed, a few seconds longer than their normal perfunctory smooch. They separated slowly and Mel dropped into the car behind the wheel. Dave placed a hand on her shoulder and she reached up and held it briefly. She put the car in gear. He closed the door.

As the Volvo crunched over the packed snow toward the highway, Dave approached the entrance. He noticed the credit card signs on the glass. He thought Vern's did not take credit cards. Of course, he thought.

He turned and raced back through the snow, catching the Volvo at the street and banging on the trunk. Mel rolled down her window.

"You scared the hell out of me," she called.

"I know how we can find Liv," he said, leaning into the window, holding the top of his coat closed. "Her credit card. We can check her spending online. If they're going any distance, they'll need gas. Jennifer hasn't used her cards in weeks because she doesn't want to risk being found."

"Unless that's just some other story she made up for us," Mel said.

"It's worth a shot."

"You do the online banking. What's the ID and password?"

"Same as usual."

She tilted her head with a look of disbelief. "For our banking? That's just dumb."

"Probably. Can we focus?"

"Do you have the app on your phone?"

"I never set it up. I do everything on the computer."

"I can do it," she said. "I'll download the app to my phone and see what I can find out."

"Let me know."

"I won't get it done until after I get to the high school. Hopefully, she'll be there and this will all be academic."

"I hope so."

"Good luck with the priest."

"He has to know more than I do."

Inside Vern's, Jim sat in a wooden booth by a large window. Snow piled several inches high on the outside of the window sill. Sipping coffee, he read a tiny black book of psalms that he used for his Divine Office, the psalms and prayers a priest reads at specified times throughout the day. To maintain his cover, he left his full Roman Breviary, which included a daily scripture reading and lives of the saints as well as the psalms, behind in Rome. He carried with him only this small, easily concealed devotional. This morning at Tierce, or the third hour of the day, he read Psalm 118.

"Bet you thought I'd never make it," Dave said as he walked up.

Jim put his coffee down, a grin crossing his face. He half-stood. They shook hands.

"Thanks for meeting me," Dave said.

"It's this or drink carbon monoxide fumes in traffic," Jim responded and then sat back down. "That avalanche clean-up is taking longer than they thought. The truck drivers in here say it won't be cleared until at least noon." The priest folded his hands on the table. "Any news?" he asked.

"Not a thing. I'm hoping you can help me think this through."

A waitress appeared. The conversation stopped. Dave ordered coffee. "How about a cinnamon roll, Jim?" he asked. "Runs neck and neck with Silver Grill for our local best."

"I'll do it."

After the waitress walked away, Jim leaned forward, his eyes boring in on Dave's. "I don't understand how your daughter fits into Claire's scheme."

"I think she may have taken Liv to leverage me somehow."

"Claire?"

"No. Jennifer."

"I thought they were enemies now."

"They still may be, but it turns out Claire and Jennifer were working together all along. Until Sheila was killed. We just found encrypted mails between them going back two years. Jennifer was giving her our confidential data."

Jim sat back in the booth and raised his eyebrows. "Wow. But then why did they want me to kill her?"

"Probably because Jenn figured out what they did to Sheila."

"What about your daughter? Why do they need leverage on you?"

Dave remained reluctant to share Middleton's information. "I don't know."

"What's your value to them?"

"I'm supposed to take over as CEO when Ed's Parkinson's gets too far along. Maybe they need me more compliant for some reason."

"They can always find another CEO. Might take a while, but Ed's still in place."

"It's a little different than that. I went through the hoops to get the malaria vaccine pilot set up as a World Health Organization Demonstration Project. I served on the board of the W-H-O working group that makes those decisions before joining Prodeus. They know me and they trust me. That helped get us the designation and will continue to be critical to getting outside funding."

"That adds up," Jim said. "With Evan Conger gone, what happens to their partnership with the working group at W-H-O if you go away?"

"The malaria pilot program probably goes back to square one."

"So they need to keep you on their side."

"I used to think that was a good thing."

"It is. If they need you, they're not going to hurt your daughter." Jim cut off a slice of bacon but did not put it in his mouth. "So if the Aldrich was doing everything on the up-and-up, they wouldn't have to be concerned about your loyalty, right? That means something else is in the mix that we don't understand. What's the main thing the Aldrich needs Prodeus for?"

"The PDNA I showed you in Lokoma. They need it to convince the locals in West Africa that there isn't some kind of plot to plant disease in them with the vaccine."

"The Nigerian polio thing. We talked about this with Chief Karanja."

"Right. The Nigerians thought the West introduced the polio vaccine to give AIDS to their people and sterilize their women."

"And your device provides a baseline. What I never understood is how analyzing the DNA tells you whether or not someone's got HIV. Or is sterile for that matter."

"It's a two-step analysis. The analyzer looks for HIV in the bloodstream. If it finds it, it analyzes its DNA. In that way, we know what form of HIV is present. If it doesn't find it at all, then we know the individual does not have the virus."

Dave picked up his phone to check the time. Not yet ten. Less than ten minutes had passed since Mel left. It seemed an eternity with no word on Liv.

"One of the problems with HIV," Dave said, "and particularly problematic in this situation, is that standard HIV testing does not reveal the presence of HIV until it is in the system for as long as 90 days. So if a person shows negative today, but positive again in two weeks through standard testing, it could look like we introduced it. But the PDNA can detect the protein pre-cursors that show the presence of HIV, allowing us to discover the virus before a standard HIV test would pick it up."

"What about the infertility thing?" the priest asked just before taking a bite of the bacon.

"We don't address that one. Hopefully, the HIV analysis will be enough to keep us credible."

The waitress brought Dave's coffee and refilled Jim's. Dave dribbled milk in the coffee and stirred it.

"How will they know your test isn't rigged somehow?" Jim asked.

"Until the last few days, I would've argued that our independence as a third party contractor guaranteed that. Now, it looks like our test may, in fact, be rigged."

Jim showed no surprise. "To show what?"

"That everyone who is HIV positive can benefit from the malaria vaccine. But that's not accurate. In excess of one-fifth of the population will either be effectively immune to malaria, something the PDNA detects, or have a DNA structure that will reject the benefits of the vaccine."

Jim narrowed his eyes, looking out to the snow, thinking. "I can't follow the connection," he said. "Why would they want that?"

"Maybe it's innocent. Maybe they're testing an HIV vaccine piggy-backed on the malaria vaccine." Dave sipped his coffee.

"What makes the Aldrich tick?" the priest asked. "If we think about their mission, maybe there's something revealing in there."

"Or how about their board?" Dave said. "Pamela Thatcher effectively controls it. She also is doing her damnedest to get control of our board. Somehow she's talked every other underwriter out of playing in our IPO, clearing an exclusive path for Thatcher Ripley."

Jim drummed fingertips against his lips as he thought. "Then, somehow you hold the keys to the kingdom," he said.

The plate-sized cinnamon rolls arrived. Each man sampled a small piece of the warm, spiced dough. Jim held out a hand and mumbled a quick grace.

"Very good," Jim said after the first bite.

"Mouthwatering," Dave said as the cinnamon, caramel and pecans rolled over his taste buds. He looked at the time on his phone again. Only four minutes had passed since he last looked.

"I need to tell you about what I uploaded to the Vatican," Jim said. "It doesn't seem to connect to the HIV-malaria match-up your guys found in the code. It looks more like something to generate spontaneous abortion. The fertility piece that your analyzer doesn't review."

Dave stopped chewing. "So the PDNA's a sideshow to keep the Leoneans from discovering the real problem?"

"Possibly. I wasn't able to study all the science myself. It's what I gathered from correspondence I found on Sheila's PC. Rome is reviewing the science, and there are a lot of graphics and formulas, to see what it really says."

"Nothing in the files about HIV?"

"Only that Sheila felt she had formulated a cure."

Dave folded his hands, elbows on the table. He looked directly into the priest's eyes. "So there really is a cure?"

Jim nodded.

CHAPTER 18

Prodeus Offices
December 23, 9:58 a.m. Mountain Time

Brian Middleton dropped his thin frame into a chair in front of Ed Hepp's desk. He just spent the last 30 minutes walking all over the plant trying to find Dave. The man had disappeared.

Dave had told Brian not to say anything to Ed, but this latest information could not wait. No matter how close Ed was to Claire, the man would want to act on this information. Without Dave around, Brian had to make a decision.

Ed listened receptively. His openness surprised Brian. Not once did Ed get defensive on behalf of Claire. Instead, he expressed tremendous concern.

"This is shocking to say the least," Ed said.

"I'm glad you think so, Ed. Dave thought you might defend Claire and make excuses for her."

"Not on something like this," the big man said.

"To be fair to Dave, he doesn't know any of the real juicy stuff. If he did, he probably would've brought you in the loop immediately."

"Well, don't tell him anything else until we find him. We need to sit him down in here and develop a plan together. No lone rangers on this one. And you know Dave..."

"Right. He likes to go off on his own."

"Not gonna happen this time, Brian."

"No, sir. Word is mum."

Ed ran his thick fingers back and forth over a pencil in his hand. "Other than Dave, there are just three of you in the loop. No one else?"

"No one. We've been very careful."

"You need to keep it that way."

After Brian left, Ed closed the door to his office. Staring out into the mounting blizzard, he called Claire's direct line at the Aldrich, his big index finger quivering slightly as it pressed the speed dial number.

"It's Ed," he said. "Things just got a little messier."

A few minutes later, Claire stood by her enormous fireplace at Cameron Pass. The heat from the flames warmed her. She could afford to have nothing leaked. Not now. Any interference at all could destroy everything. Too many puzzle pieces neatly laid in place.

She pressed the intercom button on her phone and dialed Mike Farley.

"Yes, ma'am," said the voice on the other end.

"We have a few loose ends to clip off. Come on up. And bring an updated weather briefing. We need to get some of your people down to Loveland."

"I can tell you that the weather is still not helping," Mike said.

"I don't care. This one's worth the risk of losing a few of your boys. Everything's on the line."

CHAPTER 19

Vern's Place
December 23, 10:02 a.m. Mountain Time

"You could confront her," Jim suggested. "If Claire knew that you weren't just guessing, she might let Liv in on the first trials."

"I've been down that path two or three times," Dave said. "She always denies it exists. And she gets a little huffy about it."

The priest slid the edge of his fork into the cinnamon roll, sawing off a small piece. "We have a few problems to solve," Jim said, letting his fork rest on the plate. "First and foremost is finding your daughter. Once we've done that, we need to get to Sierra Leone. Health Minister Tombu is a friend. The two of us need to convince him that he has to stop the inoculations until we can figure out what the subterfuge is all about."

"Call him."

"I called him about the fertility angle. I got his attention but he insists on evidence. He answers to the Leonean President. The President is determined to move forward with the project. He doesn't dare approach the President without evidence. They're not going to undermine his relationship with the World Bank and the IMF over speculation."

"Can Adrian Guerra get to their president? The World Bank certainly wouldn't want this to go on without clarification."

"I don't think Adrian's in our camp," Jim said. "Found his name in too many files. He's involved with whatever's going on."

Jim speared the slice of cinnamon roll and placed it in his mouth. He chewed, swallowed and took a sip of coffee while Dave waited. "Only way to sort this out is in country," he said after swallowing.

"To Sierra Leone? That's very risky for you. And what if Claire and Mike have figured out you're not really on their side of this? They could be setting you up."

The priest nodded agreement. "Getting me back in Sierra Leone provides an easily disguised opportunity to have me killed. I certainly have enemies there. Mike and Claire can hide behind that."

"Then don't go."

"I need to get to the bottom of this before I run from it."

"You can't get to the bottom of it if you're dead."

"God will provide. Aren't you going, too?"

"It's my job. They don't know that I'm on to them."

"But you provided sanctuary for Jennifer Winters. They know you're not going to tow their line."

Dave thought for a moment. "I don't have much choice, either, I suppose. My livelihood, my future and very possibly my daughter's life hang in the balance."

The ringer on his mobile played a few bars of synthesized Wagner.

"Mel?" he answered, "What did you find out?... Oh, hell... They must be going to the mountain lab..."

The priest's eyes widened. Dave continued to speak into the phone. "... They'll never get in. At least, I hope not... What's Jennifer thinking?..."

Of course, he thought. Claire and Jennifer have been in it together all along. Now, they had Liv. They must have known that it was only a matter of time before he suspected something, particularly with field data coming in. And Hepp? Either in on it or completely under McQuaid's spell – for the money.

Mel kept talking on the other end of the phone. Dave did not want to frighten her with his latest suspicion until he gave it more thought.

"They must have gone before the storm hit," he responded into the phone. "...Won't work. The road's still blocked. Nothing's getting by... I'll call you back... Two minutes... Mel, I have to go... I will. I'll call right back."

Dave placed the phone on the table. He lifted his eyes to the priest. "They've gone to the lab," he said.

"How do you know?"

"Liv bought gas at Ted's Place at the corner of 287 and 14 at 5:30 this morning. That's right at the foot of the canyon. Lab's the only place up there that makes sense. Jennifer's taking her in. To leverage me. It has to be."

"I'll call Mike," Jim said.

"Won't that endanger them?"

"No, Jennifer can drive right in."

"So why did she hide at my house?"

"We know my brother had her friend killed. I think Jennifer genuinely believed she could be next. What she didn't understand is that, in killing Sheila, Claire counted on getting Jennifer back to pick up the slack. She didn't cooperate so Claire had Hepp fire her, figuring she'd come running back to the Aldrich. When she still didn't come in, Mike had me come after her to kill her, but he wasn't about to let that happen. That's why he was there. He used me to convince her that the Vatican was up to no good. Making her frightened of a force outside the lab was designed to finally drive her back in."

Dave sighed. "So why didn't they just kidnap her? Why all the manipulation?"

"I don't know. Maybe it's because Claire just enjoys the game. Or maybe I'm all wrong. Maybe Claire meant for Jennifer to get inside your house."

"Why?"

"I don't know. To control you?"

"Through my family. Through Liv. They know about her HIV. They know I'm vulnerable there. Even if I found out about their software manipulations, they could probably keep me quiet by reading me in to whatever's going on. They probably wouldn't need to hurt me and risk the PDNA program."

Jim pressed a key on his mobile, dialing in to his brother's mobile. "Don't say anything," he said to Dave. "He can't know I'm with you."

Dave nodded agreement.

Jim spoke into the phone. "Mike, it's Sean…"

Sean? Dave's discomfort index skyrocketed. The priest held up his index finger, indicating that he would explain later.

"…Stuck in an endless line of traffic at the foot of the canyon… Might not be today… We need to figure that out… Jennifer left here in the middle of the night… Phone traffic between the Clements. They're panicked. She took their daughter…. I don't know I've been out of range of the eavesdropper since I hit this traffic… They found a gas charge at 5:30 this morning at the foot of the canyon. Looks like she's on her way in, but she should have been there by now… Why in the name of… Leverage?… That's bloody blackmail…"

He glanced at Dave as he listened to his brother rage about Claire working around him.

"…Then go see Claire, but find them, Mike. They should have been there hours ago… Later."

Jim folded his phone closed and held it on the table between folded hands. He thought for a moment, prayed briefly.

"Sounds like your daughter's become an insurance policy," he said.

CHAPTER 20

Rawah Wilderness
December 23, 10:17 a.m. MT

The distant whining drone of snowmobiles echoed over the moraine. Over a hundred feet below them, sitting on the rocks where she had started her climb earlier in the morning, Liv studied the burgundy scarf Jennifer had tightened around her wrist to stabilize it. At best, she had a bad sprain.

It had been a slow, careful process to lower Liv from where she had fallen. She had maneuvered with her feet and her one good hand, while Jennifer eased up on the rope. Clouds had moved in overhead and the wind had whipped up, making it more difficult as the combination of wind and rope buffeted Liv against the granite. Now, the two huddled together against the rock face, freezing. Across the moraine, they could see security vehicles surrounding their SUV.

The sound of a single snowmobile grew much louder as it approached and then slowed to an idle rumble almost straight overhead. Jennifer and Liv looked at each other, both unconsciously holding their breath. They leaned into the rock so as not to be seen.

"Are you all right?" a man's voice called from above.

Jennifer covered her eyes with a gloved hand. Liv shivered violently, tucking her face, bright pink from the icy chill, into her folded arms. With no place to run and no way to climb, they had run out of options.

Jennifer stood and looked toward the top of the cliff. "She's hurt," she shouted.

"We'll send help," the man yelled.

Turning off the snowmobile, the guard pressed his walkie-talkie. "Found them, Mike," he said.

CHAPTER 21

Vern's Place
December 23, 10:34 a.m.

The two Colorado Highway Patrolmen stood at the front counter, getting coffees to go. They did not have time to stop and relax. Accidents riddled the highways. Re-routings had created a need for emergency shelters.

"No, sir," one of them said to Jim. "287 north to Wyoming and 14 are both closed down now. Even if we get that rockslide cleared, the snow's too deep in the canyon for cars to pass. We'll be trying to get it plowed and sanded as soon as we can get in. For now, the snow's staying ahead of us."

"Thanks, officer."

Jim walked over to Dave who stood by the cash register paying the bill. He had expected to join Claire and his brother at Cameron Pass for a helicopter ride from the lab to Grand Junction where Thatcher's private jet would pick them up for the ride to Freetown.

"Guess you're not going on that trip after all," Dave said. He signed the receipt and took the yellow copy. "Mel will be happy to have you over," he said as he opened the door, letting in a gust of snow. He could not help but notice how fresh and clean the air smelled, one of the beautiful things about even the worst snowstorms.

"You have enough problems right now without company."

"What are we going to do? We're stuck like everyone else. At least, we think we know where she is. You may be our best hope for getting her out."

The two men began using their hands to wipe the snow off the windows of Jim's Taurus, the snow landing on it almost as fast as they took it off. Neither had gloves.

"So, if Thatcher Ripley, our IPO underwriter, is somehow involved, what does that mean?" Dave asked.

Jim shook out his bare hands, wet and red with cold. He tucked them in his coat pockets, feeling relief from the warmth. "I'll be blunt," he responded. "In this case, your company functions almost like an old-fashioned intelligence front operation. Everyone's in the dark about everything except their piece of the action. And no one, except for the people at the top of the food chain, knows the true objective. If Thatcher Ripley really is involved, if the code really is purposely misleading, and if people really are getting killed – there's a very big agenda here. They're not people you fight and win. You're probably a very carefully chosen and craftily managed pawn."

"I'm nobody's pawn."

"There's probably a better word. Semantics won't change the facts."

"What's the agenda?" Dave asked.

"You mean why would they want to sterilize hundreds of thousands of women? Not a clue. We've yet to figure out the whole story. For all we know, when the full truth is in front of us, we may actually like it."

"I don't know, Jim. They sure as hell feel like bad guys to me." Dave swept a hand down the driver's side windshield one last time. "That's the best I can do for now," he said, shaking out his hands. "The rental car company should give you scrapers with these things."

"There's probably one in here somewhere. I just couldn't find it."

"Probably in the trunk," Dave said, looking at a good foot of snow piled atop the back end of the car.

"So, if my daughter's up there, she's in real trouble."

"No. She'll be all right. They're just working you. They can't afford collateral damage with American civilians, particularly inside the United States. That's the plus side of bureaucrats being fixtures with job security. Your law enforcement agencies operate independently. It's a near certainty that this thing does not have broad buy-in across your government. Drawing the attention of the FBI or even the Colorado state police is too risky. They're just trying to keep you under control for now."

"Jennifer seemed convinced that Thatcher could manage the FBI."

"But not every agent in the field. She can cover up later, but she can't afford interference with the operation while in progress."

"What about Sheila?"

They entered the car and closed the doors.

"Not a civilian," Jim answered in the quiet of the car. "And if it's true, they had her in the lab under their control where they could manage the evidence. It's a game of mirrors. They had me convinced Jennifer killed her. But I know better now."

The engine roared to life with a burst of exhaust as Jim turned the key.

"Since we think my daughter's on her way to the lab, that's not very reassuring."

"They want her alive and well. Your cooperation at this stage of their program is essential. Without it, the risks of exposure and failure escalate. That much we know."

Dave cleared an area of condensation on his window and peered into the blizzard.

"We don't know anything," he said softly.

CHAPTER 22

Mountain Lab, Rooftop
December 23, 10:48 a.m. Mountain Time

On the building's roof, Mike Farley pulled weather radar printouts from his pocket and unfolded them. Pink, indicating snow, coated the thumbnail sized forecast maps on the page. It encouraged him to see periods of clearing anticipated in the early afternoon before the forecasted second phase of the blizzard swept in.

The rotors of the bright red single engine company helicopter, a sleek Bell 407, slowly began their rotation, causing the papers to flap and then bend back in Mike's hands. He looked to the narrow band of clearing sky overhead. Running from where Mike stood through an air corridor that almost perfectly paralleled Route 14 and the Poudre River Canyon into Fort Collins, the patch of blue offered a short window of opportunity. The thick gray snow clouds on either side could close in again at any moment. The wispy edges of white along the cloud banks indicated the winds aloft remained too dangerous for anything short of mission-critical helicopter flight.

Still, flying through the canyon would be much safer than trying to manage the winds over the peaks. The turbulence on the leeward side of the peaks on the descent into Fort Collins would be like a deadly high altitude cement mixer today, likely to smash any airborne intruders into the high mountain walls. The winds in the canyon might be very strong, but they would also probably be straight-line and more predictable.

Leaning into the hatch, Mike shouted above the din. "If you can't make it to the front range, at least set her down someplace where they can drive out," he instructed the pilot. "Route 14's a no-go, but 287 could work. Traffic's still moving this side of the Wyoming line."

He turned to the two men strapped into the rear seats. "We're counting on you."

Hands cupped to their ears, the men nodded their acknowledgment.

Mike started to back away from the chopper, glancing quickly to the sky and then back to the pilot. The pilot gave Mike a quick thumbs up and then slipped his headphones over his ears. He twisted the 407's throttle.

Saluting sloppily, Mike dashed away from the chopper as the rotation of the blades accelerated spitting wet gusts of cold, fresh powder into his face. With the wind behind it, the chopper rose rapidly, moving over the moraine behind the facility. In the deep snowbound silence that followed, Mike pressed the talk button on his walkie-talkie.

"Sanitation team's en route, Claire," he said.

On the plateau on the back end of the building, two snowmobiles, one pulling a travois bearing Liv, roared toward the rear entrance. Jennifer rode on the back of the other, her arms latched around the waist of the security guard. When Mike Farley's voice – and not that of Eldridge - came over the two-way issuing instructions for their rescue, Jennifer breathed much easier.

CHAPTER 23

Claire McQuaid's Office
December 23, 11:02 a.m. Mountain Time

"So what's the game plan for the girl?" Mike asked

"She's going to clear some interference for us." Claire paced in front of her enormous stone hearth, snow blowing again in front of both great windows that bordered it.

Mike walked to the small bar inset into the wall. He poured himself a cup of coffee, his eighth since 4 a.m. when he woke to start one of the biggest days of his life.

Claire spoke to his back. "Where's your little brother?"

"Stuck on the front range. There's a blizzard down there. We may need to go without him."

Alarm coursed through Claire. "We go nowhere without Sean."

Mike's eyebrows rose. "Sean? When did he become so important? He's done his job for Christus. They have the files we wanted him to send."

"He's proven capable of killing," she said more calmly. "You know that now. We need him over there."

"No, he didn't prove capable of killing. Wasn't that the point? To confirm he was still playing for the Vatican."

"You know better, Farley."

Mike sat back against the bar. "So," he said. He swigged the coffee, burning the roof of his mouth. Ignoring the pain, he slammed the cup down on the granite counter.

"...Who are we killin' now, your ladyship?"

CHAPTER 24

Eldridge Perry's Office
December 23, 11:14 a.m. Mountain Time

Jennifer, accompanied by two of Mike Farley's guards, did not feel dread as she walked into Eldridge Perry's dark office. She had been neither shot nor taken prisoner upon arriving at the lab. Claire and Mike had not targeted her. Eldridge Perry had, just as Mike said. Anger carried her into his office.

"Get up you sonuvabitch," she said, walking into the room.

A specter looked up from behind the desk, silhouetted by the computer screen. He did not stand.

"Welcome back, Jennifer."

"Farley told me about your little coup."

"It's tough to be a pawn." He nodded for the guards to leave.

Jennifer turned to the men. "You're supposed to stay with me." They ignored and left, closing the door behind them.

"What the hell," she said. She felt herself quivering with rage. She turned back toward Eldridge. "I'm no pawn."

"Not you." His answer came in at entirely the wrong angle.

"What's that mean?" she asked.

"Me. I'm the pawn."

"You? You had her killed."

"As part of my plot with the Vatican for a coup at the Aldrich," Eldridge confirmed.

Jennifer's grip encircled the metal rails of the black iron chair Eldridge kept for office guests. "So I'm told," she said

"Does Dave Clement believe it?"

"He doesn't know anything about you. He knows that a conspiracy of priests and IRA want me dead. One of your boys, an undercover priest, damn near killed him with a blow to the head. If Mike Farley hadn't been there, he would've killed me."

She saw a flash of white teeth, heard a snicker.

"I'll bet you were convincing when you told that story to Clement and his wife. You don't have to be a good actor when you believe the altered reality. Also offers a good explanation for your leaving their home right about now. Plays into the news stories we'll all be reading later in the week."

Jennifer dropped into the chair. She dropped her head into her hands. She got it. Finally, she got it. Claire McQuaid – the ultimate chess player. The woman always planned five steps ahead, intuitively able to anticipate each order of consequence further down the chain of prediction. And Sheila had died as part of all this intrigue.

"She was my closest friend, Eldridge," she said quietly.

Eldridge tilted his chair back, his hands folded atop his flat belly. "She'd become a major liability. And you and I both know you're not the kind of person who keeps friends. To you, friends are people who haven't lost their usefulness yet."

"I don't see any family pictures in here."

Eldridge did not answer. He opened his desk drawer and thumbed through a file. Pulling out a thin sheaf of paper, he slid it across the desk. Jennifer picked it up and tried to read it.

"I can't see in this ridiculous light."

"You don't need to. You just need enough to stimulate your memory. Those are your reports, encrypted e-mails. The ones warning us that Sheila had gone off reservation, that she was a threat to the project."

Jennifer's hands crinkled the edges of the paper. "But I never…" She stopped. She had known the potential consequences. Why did she think they would not play out? Maybe I'm entirely stupid, she thought.

"You did the right thing, bringing the kid up here," Eldridge said. "You can't leave her in Fort Collins to be typed with the new HIV mutation. All our work – all your work – would be destroyed. Millions of additional lives ultimately lost."

She did not look at him. She stared blankly into the murk, the reports now wrapped tightly into a scroll in her hand. Eldridge leaned forward, trying unsuccessfully to get her to look at him.

"What is this, Jennifer?" he said. "Some kind of ass-backwards Stockholm effect? This family, this little girl – tools. Remember? Means to an end. Losing her is a sad thing, but a very, very small price. Don't tell me that you of all people have lost your compass in this thing? You're our researcher turned biostatistician. The numbers person who just happens to understand the science as well as anyone. Our Spock. Compassion doesn't become you."

Bending the scroll in half with both hands, Jennifer sat forward and looked at the floor.

"We're soldiers in this one, girl. We can't have the whole picture. If there were leaks, Claire could never pin them down. The whole program could be shut down because of a single indiscretion. By compartmentalizing, by troops like us taking things on faith, we're able to handle a Sheila situation without hurting others who don't have the puzzle pieces she does."

"Did. Pieces she did have."

"Right. Past tense. But that's what we signed up for. It's why Claire gave us this opportunity to make the kind of difference few people ever get to make. We're true believers."

Eldridge smiled and sat down. "How long does she have?" he asked.

"You tell me. You have the data on the so-called homeless beneficiaries."

"What's her count?"

"Her mother said it's still below 300. She thinks she's already building resistance to the Fuzeon injections."

"How long has she been taking them?"

"About ten days, I think."

"I'd be very surprised if her HIV's already built a thorough resistance. The viral load is only going to crawl back for now. It should take at least the better part of a month for the mutation to completely neutralize the Fuzeon. So long as she stays on it."

Jennifer pursed her lips and inhaled through her nose. "It will turn on her again, then?"

Eldridge nodded.

"After that?" Jennifer asked.

"When did you introduce the mutator?"

"Three weeks ago today."

"How'd you do it?"

"Applied it to an open wound when she cut herself doing pull-ups."

"Cut herself?"

"She thinks she did, but I helped. How much time?"

"Probably 90 days out. Maybe a little more. That climb..." He shook his head in amazement. "...She must be a strong kid."

"Strong-willed for sure," Jennifer said. "So let's get her CEM15-D."

"You've been gone way too long, little missy."

"I don't understand."

"First of all, we need her to stay sick to keep her father working with us."

"By the time they realize she's cured, Dave will be too deep to get out."

"That's the plan."

"So what's the problem, Eldridge?"

"The biggest problem? There is no working CEM15-D vaccine. No cure for our mutated AIDS. Your little friend's not going to survive this."

Jennifer sat perfectly still. No vaccine? No cure. She studied Eldridge's face for a snicker, waited for a punch line. He held her gaze with a defiant look.

"You're serious. How can that be? The whole program fails or succeeds contingent on that. I never would have..."

"A detour. CEM15-D seemed to be working fine, but after several days in test patients, it stopped adhering to T-cells."

"Sounds like a fixable situation. What if we re-introduce the natural CEM15 protein as a patch until the adherence issue is solved?"

"Nothing's that easy, Jennifer. Vif-D overcomes the natural protein immediately."

"No lag? Not even a little to buy us time?"

"Days at most."

"How about Vif-D? Can it be removed?"

"No, once Vif-D is in the body, our only known fix is CEM15-D. By design. Keeps all the control with us."

"If we designed it in, we can design it out."

"Extremely unlikely."

She stepped forward, her forehead within a few inches of his nose. "Ok. So who's working on CEM15-D now?"

"No one. I'm using Sheila's back-up man for field work in Sierra Leone."

Jennifer's mind raced through the consequences of not having CEM15-D ready. "Don't you have the horse before the cart? What's the point of field work in Sierra Leone if we don't have CEM15-D to stop the mutation? That's the drug we're counting on to change the globe, the cure upon which this whole damned program relies. The miracle, Eldridge! Have you people completely lost your compass?"

"We're focused on the well-being of the whole."

"Eldridge, without CEM15-D, we're talking about tens of thousands of lives - "

"Maybe millions," he interrupted.

"You just... This...Dammit. Sheila was right."

"We have a job to do. You have a job to do. Mitigating that is in your hands."

"What the hell... Last spring, I injected an innocent kid with HIV. Three weeks ago, I accelerated it with Vif-D. You've made me a killer."

"Not if you get CEM15-D done in a hurry."

"How do I explain this to her? Hell, how do we justify this?"

"You don't explain it to anyone. That much is a given. Not if you don't want to be part of a collateral damage clean-up yourself."

She rolled her eyes. "Sure. I get it. But I can't just let her die. I can't just accept that I'm a killer."

"Chill. There's still a cure on the back end of this. We will be able to cure the mutation. It has accessibility characteristics that the garden variety does not, characteristics we can manage easily with CEM15-D."

"But you said it wasn't ready."

"Probably would have been if Sheila had not become so distracted." Eldridge studied his hands in the reflected light of the computer monitor. He sighed as he looked up. "Now you know why Claire wants your stubborn ass back," he said.

Jennifer flopped back in her seat. "She has a helluva way of showing it."

"You're the one who went paranoid. Claire's a master at the chess of all this. You lost your faith for a little while. Admit it."

"Is the Leonean press conference still scheduled for tomorrow?" she asked, a plan formulating.

"Absolutely. Christmas Eve headlines. Schedule is everything."

"Claire left yet?"

"Later today. When the storm lets up."

Jennifer placed the crinkled report on Sheila back on Eldridge's desk. She stood and walked out the office door. She said nothing until she reached the small infirmary where Liv slept soundly where she had left her.

Jennifer knelt beside here. She nudged her. "Liv. Wake up."

Her face pale and gaunt, the exhausted teenager opened her eyes. Jennifer took both Liv's hands, squaring off with her.

"How would you like to avoid the climb back down?" Jennifer said.

"Are we safe here?" Liv asked, rubbing an eye with the back of a small fist.

"I think we probably are, but we're not staying here."

"He gave you the cure?"

"No, it's not here. It's in West Africa."

"I don't understand."

"We're going to Sierra Leone."

CHAPTER 25

Fort Collins: Somewhere along LeMay Avenue
December 23, 11:36 a.m. Mountain Time

After Jim dropped Dave at the house, he drove away and called Mike. He explained that he had finally pulled out of traffic in the canyon because the police did not expect it to re-open today. Mike told him that flights at DIA had all been grounded. The schools in Fort Collins had just starting sending all the students home before the roads became completely impassable.

He instructed Jim to find his way to the Rocky Mountain High School football stadium at 12:15. A brief opening in the weather expected around that time would allow a helicopter into the area. From there, he would fly to Grand Junction to get on Thatcher's plane.

"So you spent all morning in traffic?" he asked.

"All morning," Jim lied.

CHAPTER 26

Clement Home
December 23, 11:38 a.m. Mountain Time

Dave's phone rang as soon as he entered the house. Mel hurried up to him. She waited anxiously as he answered the call.

"Oh, thank God," he said. "Hold on while I tell Mel."

He hit the mute button on the phone. "Liv's okay. It's Claire. They have her at the lab."

"Thank God," Mel echoed. "What in God's name is she doing there? With Claire?"

Dave unmuted the phone, "Did she say why she's there? I assume Jennifer is with her."

"That one should be charged with kidnapping," Mel whispered so Claire would not hear.

"They climbed?" Dave said into the phone, "What the hell? What were they thinking?... No, not with her CD4 count...It's damned dangerous..."

Mel looked at him with a combination of horror and anger.

"How do we get her back here?" Dave asked Claire as he hit the phone's speaker button. "I'm putting you on speaker, Claire. Mel's here with me."

On the other end, Claire offered a plan. "I wish we had found her sooner, Dave. We have a helicopter in the Fort Collins area, but the weather window's very small. There's not enough time to have it come back here and pick her up."

"Sounds like she'll have to spend the night," Dave said.

"Two nights with the canyon completely blocked."

"Maybe you can ferry her down tomorrow," he suggested.

"Forecast is for us to be socked in up here."

"She needs to come home, Claire" Mel said. "Her medications are here."

"I understand," Claire said. "She can't be without them, especially after compromising her immune system like she did this morning."

"I don't know what was going through her head?" Mel said. "I'm sure Jennifer had something to do with it."

"Listen, I have an idea," Claire offered. "We can turn this around into something constructive. What if you joined me on Pamela Thatcher's private plane?"

"How does that help?"

"Liv's done with school for the holidays, right?"

"Right."

"So why can't you and Mel just pack bags for yourselves and Liv, including the meds. Join us in Freetown for Christmas. Even better, we're stopping at

Tenerife on the way back for a little R & R at the beach. Your family can use it. On me."

Dave's face pinched in confusion. "Freetown's not exactly a garden spot."

"Think of it like a layover on the way to Tenerife where you can have a nice family Christmas in the tropics. Plus you get to be at the press conference and enjoy the product of your efforts."

"That's a very interesting offer, but I'm not sure I understand. We're snowbound down here. And Liv's up there with you."

"There's not much time with the blizzard, but if the two of you can pack in 45 minutes, we'll have the Bell pick you up in your cul-de-sac. But you have to be ready. The weather window is expected to close in the next 90 minutes."

Dave looked at Mel. "Claire, can I call you back?"

"No, wait," Mel said. "Let's do it. Under one condition."

"Name it."

"You talk to us about AIDS cures on the way over. Help us figure this out. We know you have more than you're telling us."

"How about on the way back? Or in the Canaries? Trip over has me buried in preparation."

"Is there something to talk about?" Mel asked.

After a short delay, Claire responded. "Yes."

Mel looked at Dave who nodded his concurrence. "Done," she replied. "We'll be ready in forty-five." She pressed the END button and handed the phone back to Dave.

"I don't trust her," Mel said.

"Then why are you willing…"

"The priest told you there's a cure. Jennifer told us there's a cure. No one at the lab killed Jennifer when they got there. Or Liv. But they have her. They're using the weather as an excuse to not bring her back to us. I'm not about to leave her alone with those people if we can be with her. Do you have any better ideas?"

With things spinning suddenly and entirely out of his control, Dave's anxiety bounded out of his stomach into his throat. His mouth completely dry, he mumbled, "Forty-five minutes."

Dave felt for the Ruger in his overcoat pocket. As he packed, he loaded two extra seven round clips. He shoved them inside his briefcase sandwiched between his laptop's battery charger and his international power adapter.

Not flying commercial had many advantages.

CHAPTER 27

Aldrich Mountain Lab
December 23 11:49 a.m. Mountain Time

Eldridge Perry escorted Jennifer and Liv to the elevator. Jennifer felt the hair stand up on the back of her neck, a chill racing through her. Though her entry had been brazen, it had been business as usual with Eldridge – like nothing disruptive had happened. The adrenaline rush of attempting to conquer the mountain carried her through the first hour. Now, raw fear threatened. Eldridge said the Vatican plot story and the plan to assassinate her were gambits to drive her desperation and keep her believable to the Clements. Knowing Claire, Jennifer felt certain other benefits existed as well. The woman never tired of using people as pawns. And no one could think as many steps ahead as Claire. At the same time, Jennifer never trusted Eldridge. Why would she start now? Maybe he was lying about all this. It all seemed too easy. Would they kill her, too? Would a hit team be waiting for her and Liv when they exited the elevator?

She attempted a weak smile for Eldridge. His lips tightened and he turned away, his eyes watching the slow progression from "G" to "2" above the elevator doors. She could hit him over the head or something. Knock him out and run. With what? She had nothing.

The doors opened. Eldridge waved her ahead of him. The corridor looked completely different than when she had last been here. A wave of panic rushed through her. She turned and stretched for the elevator doors, trying to stop them before they closed. Eldridge grabbed her arm.

"No. Let go of me."

"Slow down, Jennifer." He pulled her back into the corridor.

"Where are you taking me?"

"Claire's office."

"This isn't the way…"

Then the fog of pre-emptive panic cleared and Jennifer recognized the hallway in the back of the building. "Never mind," she said.

Eldridge held Liv back in the hallway and motioned Jennifer into the office. He closed the door behind her, remaining outside with Liv.

Upon entering the office, Jennifer found herself smothered in a motherly hug from her former boss and mentor, instantly putting Jennifer at ease. Claire stepped back and held Jennifer's hands in hers. "I'm glad you're back," she said quietly.

Nothing had changed with Claire, no new and overwhelming evil in place. The woman still had a hold on her.

"You are back?" Claire asked.

Jennifer did not answer. Of course, she was back. What other options did she have? From what Eldridge told her, she had confirmation of Sheila's contention that the program to save millions threatened to become genocide instead. Her program. Claire had given her the ball four years ago. Jennifer had the vision to see the benefit in establishing a third party, Prodeus in this case, to build a Trojan horse to facilitate delivery of the mutation, a horse whose builders would think had an entirely different purpose. Only she and Claire knew everything. Claire carefully compartmentalized all activities. Even Sheila only knew her own piece of the plan, at least until she got too nosy.

But what if Claire had kept elements of the plan from Jennifer? Until the last month, the thought would never have crossed her mind. Now, Jennifer wondered if Claire had genocide in mind all along.

"Jennifer?"

"Yes. I'm back."

"Thank God. We need you.

"On the CEM15-D program?"

"Yes."

"I'm a statistician, Claire."

"You were also our best research scientist before you decided to try your hand at numbers. And you know how to run a drug development team."

Suddenly, Jennifer realized that many, many lives depended on what she did next. She walked away from Claire toward the oversized stone fireplace. She turned and touched one of the wing chairs.

"May I sit down?" she said, even as she eased herself into the chair.

"Please," Claire said as she sat in the matching chair across from her.

"Eldridge told me about the problem with CEM15-D," Jennifer said. "I should be able to fix it."

"Good," Claire said. She reached over and placed a hand on Jennifer's forearm. "You don't want Dave's kid on your conscience, do you?"

"No. No, I don't."

"So what do we do about her and her father in the meantime."

"I told Eldridge we'd be bringing Liv on the plane this afternoon."

"Perfect. Just what I had in mind. I've already talked to her parents. They'll be joining us as also."

"Interesting. Well played, boss. That will certainly help explain how a Colorado girl acquired a unique West African mutation should her father or anyone else figure it out."

"The least the kid deserves after that heroic climb is a little tropical adventure. You have to tell me why you made the climb? You put Liv in grave danger. If anything happened to her, it could have made things very difficult. I wanted you back, but I do understand why you didn't drive up to the front gate."

"I bet you do."

"Sorry. But the climb was madness. We thought a little theater might be helpful to maintaining your cover with the Clements. Dave and his wife needed to buy in. I was concerned that you were so close with them that they would figure things out if you weren't really frightened. I never figured you'd try to climb a mountain with a sick 15 year old."

"Probably the only thing you didn't anticipate. What about the Vatican assassin?"

"He's a priest all right. But he's Mike Farley's younger brother - "

"The missionary to the Lokoma? What the hell. How can the world be that small?"

"I'm afraid we tested him with you as the target. You were never in any danger. Mike was there throughout. Right?"

"So it was all a big game."

"Not all."

"And you genuinely need me to finish out the vaccine?"

"Yes."

"Then, Claire, let me tell you something. You're frigging insane. I've been with you for seven years. I trust you. How could you put me through this?"

Claire stiffened and stepped closer to Jennifer. "I love you like a daughter, Jennifer, but you are nothing in the greater scheme of things. There are things going on here that you will not understand until they're finished. We have taken the fate of the world in our hands and I will do whatever I have to do, no matter the price to you, me or any other individual. The last thing I'm going to do is wait for your concurrence to manage the seemingly infinite range of permutations I deal with. Some things you need to take on faith."

Jennifer scrutinized Claire's face. No emotion showed. Just calm commitment. And her emerald eyes looked completely icy now.

"Ok," Jennifer said. "So now what? Dave's going to figure this out after today."

"It looks like he probably will. Makes our precautions look wise since we need him inside Prodeus for at least the next year. Ed Hepp's Parkinson's is getting much worse and he'll need to step down right after the holidays. A replacement other than Dave won't have Dave's clout with W-H-O. And a fresh face might sniff around more than we'd like. There is also one other new problem, though."

"With Dave?"

"Yes. It looks like Middleton's finally figured some of this out. He told Dave about our encrypted emails this morning, including the last thread with Sheila."

"How'd he figure it out?"

"You left your encryption CD in your PC when you left the company."

"Oh, hell." Jennifer placed a hand on her forehead and closed her eyes.

"Not great tradecraft on your part, but you can relax," Claire said. "We're covered. Thanks to your work in their home. Dave Clement can't separate himself from the crime since he harbored you for the last month. He'll figure that out pretty quickly. Between that and his daughter's problem, he'll stay solidly in our camp. A replacement wouldn't have that useful baggage. You've managed to co-opt one of the more ethical executives I've ever encountered. It's a remarkable achievement." Claire offered a smile of approval.

"But, Claire. Dave will try to figure out a way to do the right thing. He could eventually turn on us."

"That would take many months."

"And what changes in those months?"

"The new AIDS vaccine with CEM15-D will be delivered with your help. The Prodeus firmware will be updated to delete our routines on all the PDNAs in the field. Vif-D will be removed from the malaria vaccine. We will leave behind no trace of our role in introducing the new clade. It will look like it spontaneously arose from the Leonean bush. If Dave tells the true story after all those things fall into place, it won't be hard to demonstrate that he had some kind of psychotic break."

Jennifer looked down, tapping her foot. Claire had thought of everything. In turn, things had moved according to plan. Except that now tens of thousands would die from the mutation before the second stage of the vaccine was delivered. "Why don't we wait to deploy the malaria vaccine until the AIDS vaccine is ready?" she questioned.

"Timing. The longer we wait, the more likely that someone will put together enough data to show that our HIV clade did not exist until we delivered the malaria vaccine. For the moment, we've been able to eliminate anyone that pulled together enough data to be dangerous. Our luck can't hold out forever."

"So we let thousands die for our profit?"

"There's so much more to it than that, Jennifer." Claire stood, placing an arm on the younger woman's shoulder and taking her hand. "Profit is a necessary way to support the cause. And be prepared for the number to be in hundreds of thousands, not tens."

Jennifer groaned audibly. "That's genocide, for God's sake."

Claire let go of her. She stepped up to the stone wall and petulantly pounded a fist on it. "These people are dead anyway," she said. "Their sacrifice will make their world better for the next generation."

Jennifer walked up behind her. "That's not our call, not with this many deaths."

"According to who?"

"I don't know about this, Claire. We never envisioned anything like it."

"Well, you had better. This is no time to get short-sighted over emotional issues. With or without you, this program will proceed."

"An offer I can't refuse?"

"This is your plan, Jennifer. Your strategy. You own it and you can't turn from it. Not now. You knew the human cost could be high."

Jennifer looked past Claire to the snow falling lightly outside the large window. As the storm again lessened in intensity, she could make out the faint gray outline of Mt. Clark in the distance. Beautiful but desolate, alone at its altitude in the Rawah. Now, Jennifer sensed desolate loneliness emanate from the mountain, overwhelming her.

"Playing God's not as easy as I thought."

"That, fortunately or not, is our destiny. Over 100,000 people have already been vaccinated. It's done. You can't turn back the clock."

100,000 vaccinated, Jennifer thought. With Vif-D. She felt the energy rush out of her. Breathing came in conscious gulps. Her forehead felt numb, as though she might pass out.

"Jennifer? Are you with me?" Claire called through the fog as she paged Mike Farley on the intercom.

Jennifer felt hands guide her back into the enormous wing chair. Claire's medical training kicked in and she dropped to one knee in front of her protégé. Fingertips pressed against the artery in her neck. Another hand pressed against her forehead briefly before it felt for the temperature on her wrists.

"Your vitals seem okay. When was the last time you ate anything?"

"I don't remember."

"Before that asinine climb?"

"Mm-hmm," she affirmed.

Claire turned to find Mike Farley holding a glass of ice chips and an orange wedge. She put the wedge in Jennifer's mouth. Jennifer's teeth weakly tore the flesh off. Sitting back on her heels, Claire said, "You came up to try to save the program and that kid both, didn't you?"

Jennifer shrugged her shoulders. While still numb and a little nauseous, she already felt better.

"Maybe it's not so hopeless. Maybe if you can find some way to accelerate the sampling from the Leoneans, we can get phase two of this vaccine done in time to give her a chance. Her and thousands more like her."

Mike turned away before rolling his eyes.

"What do you say?" Claire asked as she gently squeezed Jennifer's hands with hers.

"I'm in," Jennifer responded. "I'm all in."

After Jennifer and Mike left her office to pack Jennifer for the trip, Claire dialed Pamela Thatcher's mobile.

"Aunt Pamela?... We're ready to go here. A few hiccups. Nothing we can't handle…"

CHAPTER 28

Lokoma Village
December 23, 7:17 p.m. GMT

Jacob could not remember the road to Lokoma ever being this smooth. Fresh asphalt and rock filled all the big ruts and bomb craters. Only the smallest potholes remained. He stayed parallel to the road much of the way from Freetown; the roadwork had covered the entire distance. He wondered who did it and why.

He planned to hide in the village. No one would look for him there. He did not think anyone saw or recognized him in Port Loko, but he had work to do and could not afford to be caught. The fear he felt after the assassination attempt had turned to pure contempt for Fela, Adrian Guerra and the Leonean government. Together, they had schemed to take the family land, to take away his mother and father. He would get the land back, single-handedly – like Rambo.

He hefted the sling of the AK-47 onto his shoulders. After ditching his weapon in Port Loko to keep from being discovered, he secured another one from a cache he hid in the jungle a few miles southwest of the city. His neck already hurt from carrying similar weapons, but a callous had formed on his right shoulder where only days before the remains of a large blister had been. Another blister existed just below his left shoulder blade where the weapon's magazine scraped as it bounced with each step. He could have removed the magazine, but did not want to risk losing the precious seconds it took to re-insert it in the event of an ambush. The rebels had taught him that.

Reaching around, he scratched the itchy malaria vaccination scab on his left arm. He touched the drug scar on his temple. It also itched. He wanted some of the rebels' medicine to make the itch go away – and to help him sleep, to chase away the dreams that haunted the few hours of rest he had managed in the last few weeks. More than anything, he wanted to see his mother. He wanted Ani to hold him, to make everything all right. Maybe his father would let her be his wife again. No new man would take her with only one foot. The priest had been killed. His God had lost to the gods of the jungle, driving the family into the camp. Why should Hamara not have more than one wife now?

He approached the village near dusk, the smell of cooking fires warning him of the presence of others. The mine workers, he thought.

Circling through the jungle so as not to be seen, he came to a huge new clearing where long evening shadows from the rainforest stretched across the fresh gray asphalt that covered the plateau behind the village as far as he could see. An increasingly loud rumble heralded the approach of a jeep occupied by four armed men in uniform. Jacob ducked back into the trees, unslinging his weapon. He did not recognize the soldiers' uniforms, but he recognized their Abo dialect as they passed near him; they boasted loudly to each other about sexual conquests.

Fela's men. Why were they not in the Leonean uniform like the ones in Port Loko? He raised the Kalashnikov, sighting them in. The smell of smoke. Cooking fires. There would be more of the soldiers close by. He dipped the barrel of the weapon, watching the men drive over a distant ridge.

He needed to remain hidden until he found the leaders. Fela and Guerra. But, just like Rambo discovered, someone else had to be giving them orders. He would find Fela and Guerra again. He would follow them and see who they met, see who led them.

He approached the village -- still abandoned. The smoke swirled up from a camp of soldiers several hundred yards across the plateau. Hiding in the village no longer seemed like a good idea.

But why had the soldiers camped here? To protect the miners? Jacob saw no evidence that the miners still existed.

He returned to his grandparents' hut. There, he prayed to them, asked them if Jesus was with them, asked that they reconcile the angry spirits of the jungle with Jesus. He curled up in the corner of the hut on a beige straw mat covered with dark rust-colored stains. Chewing coffee beans helped him stay awake for the night ahead.

Beneath him, the dried blood of his grandparents formed the stains on which he rested.

CHAPTER 29

Lokoma Village
December 23, 10:47 p.m. GMT

In spite of the coffee beans he chewed, Jacob dozed off, a restful sleep brought about by the peace he felt as he nestled in the imagined presence of Nona and Poppa. When he awakened, he stuck his head through the hanging beads that formed the doorway. He found a moonless, star-filled night filled with the rhythmic sound of insects clicking and chirping in the blackness. He could still smell the cooking fires, giving him hope that he had not slept too late; he wanted to catch them while they enjoyed their post-dinner conversation. The rebels that captured Jacob sat around smoking marijuana and talking after their evening meals. Jacob assumed that these Abo soldiers would share the same habit.

He left his boots in the hut, knowing he could move noiselessly without them. He contemplated the Kalashnikov. It would slow him down, make him less flexible in maneuvering through the forest. Without it, he could easily lose the soldiers if they gave chase. He secured his knife in a scabbard on his waist. That, his speed and his wits would be his lifelines.

Entering the jungle near the hut, he stepped on to trails he first traversed as a naked toddler roaming free in the jungle. Monkeys would playfully taunt him, sometimes throwing dirt and pieces of fruit at him. Jacob had fed them bananas he found on the ground, making fast friends who glided along on the branches and vines above him.

This childhood nirvana existed before the civil war turned his parents paranoid, restricting Jacob's wandering. The behavior of the monkeys and the other animals did not change, but a new danger threatened. The rebels and the soldiers clearly differentiated themselves from the animal kingdom; they mutilated and murdered for sport. Only lions, rare now in this part of Sierra Leone, consciously sought out human prey. Even then, they only killed enough for a meal. Rebel bands occasionally treated themselves to a meal of human meat, but not for lack of food; instead, they sought to intimidate their enemies and impress their peers with their audacity. Rambo never ate anyone, Jacob thought.

Approaching the soldiers' camp, he discovered that some of them lived in new huts instead of in tents or on the ground; they planned to stay in the area. Avoiding the light spilling over from battery powered lanterns and the fires, Jacob slipped to the jungle floor. He slithered through the grass and dirt to a well-camouflaged spot near the edge of the clearing. The high, thick green canopy kept the sun out, inhibiting the growth of ground cover under that canopy; however, the sun could reach those areas near clearings, its light spilling in from the sides, creating a shield of tall grasses, weeds and thick bushes along trails and clearings. Here, precariously close to the soldiers, Jacob found his hiding place.

"What you do wid da bitch, mon? Have your way wid her first?" The teenager put the joint back in his mouth, sucking in deeply while waiting for an answer.

"Hell, no!" said another teen. "I killed her and had my way wid her den."

"What da hell you did dat for?" said a third teen.

"'Cause they be tight like virgins when you do 'em like dat, mon."

The boys cackled, high-fiving each other all around. Jacob thought of how Ani had been mutilated by her captors. He envisioned her wet eyes as she hobbled to Freetown with him, saw the inflamed oozing rawness of her stump as she lay unconscious in the camp clinic. He felt for the knife on his waist, looked at the weapons carelessly laid to the side by the soldiers. He could do a lot of damage before they stopped him.

Then he heard the nun's gurgling again. Felt her mercy. He touched the cross hanging from his neck.

His mind flashed to his friends lying dismembered on the trail, while he quivered over a jammed weapon. He again saw soldiers scramble as his bullet missed Fela in Port Loko. He pulled his knife. Rambo would have no mercy. He could take them all.

Things can go wrong, he thought. Who would warn Hamara about the Abo alliance with Guerra and the government if the soldiers killed him?

Waiting for the breeze to shake the trees so as not to be heard, Jacob quietly sucked in a deep breath to suppress his rage. His fingers dug into the rich loam under him.

"So when da French coming?"

"Not French, mon. Middle Africans."

"De one who come here last month, he sound French. Dat all I know."

"Nope. Middle African. Dey jus' speak French, not Krio or English."

"Dey could not come too soon. Been so damn long since I seen a woman, you boys gettin' to look good to me,"

"Somet'ing big is in da next days. I hear dat Abo soldiers are on da move to da big hotel on the hill over Lumley Beach."

"Freetown?"

"Rich Americans at dat place."

"Why don't we go?"

"We waitin' for da French, mon."

"Middle African, I tell you."

The conversation devolved into more talk about abusing women. Jacob's mind raced through the information. Fela planned to attack Freetown. He did not know why; he just knew it could not be good news. If they captured Freetown, his family would be trapped in the refugee camp. The Abo soldiers would show no more mercy than they had in the past, particularly to the family of Chief Karanja. They would all be killed.

Jacob slithered backward from under the cover. Once out of range of the light from the camp, he stood and ran, enjoying the feel of bare feet on his home soil. Back in the hut, he re-slung the AK-47 and pulled more coffee beans out of the pouch on his waist. He tied his boots together, hanging them around his neck by the shoestrings. Dropping to his knees, he said a last prayer to his grandparents.

"Nona and Poppa. I pray you are with Jesus and in the favor of the jungle spirits. The Abo intend to kill our family. I know this. Pray to Jesus for me so that I am strong. I am going to Freetown to warn them …"

When he finished, he shrugged the sling of his weapon further down his shoulder. Tugging on the sling for tautness, he stepped out of the hut. Looking up to the stars, their view now clouded by the smoke from the campfires, and then to the darkness in the jungle surrounding him, he listened – for anything that would reassure him. The loneliness hurt, physically hurt, biting at his stomach and drying out his throat. The sounds of animals and insects calling in the vacuum of the night only deepened the recognition that he stood entirely alone.

"A boy," he mumbled quietly. "Just a boy. I'm not Rambo. I want my mother, my family." Tears drizzled down his cheeks.

He began walking slowly through the dark village, each vacant hut calling to him, reminding him, threatening him with danger – threatening with memories. Movements of creatures in the darkness, movements to which he had once grown accustomed – been comforted by -- in the presence of his family and neighbors, now lurked ominously in the shadows.

Approaching the road to Freetown, his pace slightly faster with each step, he called on his grandparents and all the ancestors of the tribe to protect him from the spirits angered by the priest. His legs suddenly stretched into a run, arriving at a pace he determined to maintain for the more than 30 miles to Freetown.

Sheer exhaustion from the effort would bring a new calmness to him within only a few hours when, 10 miles from the village, he would stumble into a thicket, his pouch of coffee beans long since exhausted. He fell asleep behind a stand of short palms while tiny, wide-eyed colobus monkeys watched quietly over him from their hiding places.

CHAPTER 30

Thatcher's Private Plane, Freetown airspace
December 24, 10:38 a.m. GMT

Liv pressed her nose against the window as the plane descended into Freetown. Beneath her, the tropical city cascaded over lush, green mountains into clear blue ocean. Whitewashed buildings with red tile roofs made up much of the man-made landscape. Christmas lights, decorations, and nativity scenes showed up in backyards and open green areas below. How could this be such a troubled and dangerous place?

Fuzeon and the new meds accompanied by a long nap on the flight seemed to have boosted her energy. She felt like herself again. Only she had climbed a mountain. And she would be landing in Africa in a few minutes. On Christmas Eve. She turned to her mother who, like her, had been taking in the view out the plane's window. She tilted her head into her mother's shoulder. Mel pulled Liv close, stroking her hair.

Further forward in the plane, Dave, Pamela Thatcher and Claire discussed the day ahead. Once at the hotel, the team would clean up and meet back in the conference room for a final briefing with Minister Tombu at 12:30. The press conference started at 1 p.m., timed to be featured on the morning news shows back in the US, the top feel-good story for the holiday. Dave looked at his watch. 10:38 a.m. in Freetown. 3:38 a.m. in Colorado. He had slept very little. The events of the last 24 hours kept churning through his mind. It amazed him to find himself sitting at a table across from Pamela Thatcher on her private plane.

The woman charmed him. Never had the word seemed more appropriate. Depending on which survey and which year, Pamela often surfaced as the wealthiest woman in the world. Now, Dave basked in the glow of her celebrity, feeling like a schoolboy. He tried to keep in mind the suspicions he and Fr. Jim harbored, but dismissed them as paranoia in the presence of Thatcher's charisma. Jennifer's story that Jim actually operated under the auspices of some Vatican plot to disrupt the vaccine project seemed a little more plausible now. Decades as a loyal Catholic seemed unable to outgun the cultural weight of celebrity.

And now he had access to both power and wealth, like never before. By the time the press conference ended, this team would have established his product and his company on the world stage as the leader in the conquest of malaria.

The potential price taunted his conscience. Middleton's reverse engineering is flawed, he rationalized. Half a million lines of code could easily be misread. To be fair, the team did the work in their spare time, unable to actually test the outcomes in a live environment. The statistical anomaly on true readings in the Sierra Leone trial? Just that. An anomaly. Not that extreme in the first place. Small sample.

Claire discussed the ongoing rollout of the vaccine. Thatcher listened intently, glancing at Dave occasionally for confirmation. Dave nodded, made short polite comments on automatic pilot.

Father Jim's story bothered him, but Jim admitted he did not understand the technical language or diagrams in the files. Dave thought that Jim may have seen what he feared seeing. Or what he expected of an enterprise that involved his brother. Sheila? Jim told Dave he knew they killed her. "They." Who are they? Dave wondered. What about the hit on the head? He only had Jim's word that the priest had not slugged him. Yet he admitted being in the house. To kill Jennifer.

Dave turned around, saw Jennifer huddled over paperwork, trying to catch up on what she missed during the weeks in hiding.

So why is she here? Alive. Involved.

"They're nice people, Dad," Liv explained earlier when Dave and Mel joined her and everyone else in Grand Junction. "Mrs. Thatcher said she thinks there are things they can do to help me."

Jennifer cornered both he and Mel in the airport lounge, apologizing profusely. "I went off the deep end. The only manipulation here was meant to get me back to work in the lab. I'd been so stubborn that they leveraged Ed to fire me at Prodeus. A normal human being would have called Claire right away, especially since she already offered me a job a week earlier. I freaked instead. Because of Sheila."

Mel looked hard into Jennifer's eyes. "Sheila was killed, wasn't she, Jennifer?"

"My God, yes. It's so horrible, but the lab didn't have anything to do with it. No one knows for sure, but Claire thinks it has something to do with a guy Sheila had been seeing. Thinks they rendezvoused in Walden and something happened."

"But she, your best friend, never mentioned this guy."

"Maybe that's why she wanted to see me at the Silver Grill that Saturday. And she did mention him. Sort of. The tattoo I told you about. I bet it was his phone number."

"What was it?" Mel asked. "Rocky 2 something?"

"Rocky 28714. I'll never forget it now."

"Someone should tell the police."

"Police already know. It's no longer in service. Hasn't been for years, which makes this ex-boyfriend of hers all the scarier."

Dave did not tell Jennifer about the priest's claims. He decided to hold that information back. If the priest was right, Dave could endanger his family by telling Jennifer what he knew. If the priest was wrong and if there really was some kind of Vatican-linked conspiracy, disclosure of the priest's confidence might cause the Aldrich people to think Dave was somehow in collusion.

When they were alone before boarding, Mel told Dave that Jennifer's sudden turnaround seemed very suspicious.

"Trust me," he said. "It is. She either thinks we're fools or she's one herself."

"I don't know," Mel answered, "She knows we're savvy. I don't think she cares what we think. She believes we can be controlled."

Dave did not respond. For one of the few times in his life, he felt nearly completely helpless. He touched the Ruger in his jacket pocket for reassurance.

As the plane soared over the Atlantic, Pamela reached over and took Dave's hand, squeezing it warmly between her two hands. "The work of your team is about to change the world, Dave. You have every reason to be very proud."

She smiled, a wide comfortable smile filled with perfect white teeth. The blue in her eyes glittered, drawing him in.

"Thank you, Pamela."

"No. Thank you. I can only imagine the hours and stress you and your team dedicated to this effort over the last few years. Millions and millions will owe their lives and ultimately their lifestyles to your efforts."

Dave's shoulders straightened, his chest puffing up. Despite his suspicions, he liked being flattered by this powerful woman. With all the false humility he could muster, he said, "It's all about partnership. Claire and her team. My team back in Loveland. None of it happens without all of them coming together in common cause."

Pamela released his hand and sat back, her hands now folded in her lap. "Humility," she said. "It's very becoming. Even if overplayed." She winked at him.

He glanced over his shoulder, hoping to exchange a smile with Mel and Liv, but the two focused out the window, very much enamored of the view of the approaching West African coastline. Dave smiled a satisfied smile. A lot had happened in the last 18 hours. A lot that brought hope to his family, hope for a cure for Liv and re-kindled hope for the kind of business success that would bring him financial independence.

All the paranoia of the last few weeks may, in fact, have been a bizarre cascade of misunderstandings. Jennifer's paranoia had driven all that. He found himself unconsciously glaring disdainfully across the table at her, but shook it off as soon as she turned his way. She meant well, he told himself; the death of her friend and her firing had traumatized her. And Claire and Pamela did not seem to harbor any ill feelings toward him for his own behavior. More importantly, Liv had now surfaced on Claire's radar screen as a participant in future trials for an Aldrich AIDS cure. Certainly Jennifer's misguided actions had helped bring that about.

In a seat near the rear in his role as security, Fr. Jim alone among the passengers held unflinchingly to strong suspicions about Claire McQuaid and Pamela Thatcher. Emerging from a men's room in Grand Junction as Pamela's plane refueled, he thought he overheard Claire call Thatcher "Aunt Pamela" in the hallway. When he approached, he did not hear the "aunt" again. Was it some kind of pet name? He asked Mike; he claimed he had never heard Claire refer to Pamela as "aunt." Mike insisted that Jim must have mis-heard. Jim felt certain he had not. Claire had, indeed, called Thatcher "Aunt Pamela." A small point, maybe, but one about which the priest now obsessed. These women had an invisible agenda into which he, his brother and Dave Clement had no insight. His mistrust of Mike prevented him from sharing his concerns.

For inexplicable reasons, Claire's emerald eyes kept crossing his mind, floating like a vision. But they were not cold as he'd come to know them; they were warm and inviting. He tried to shake it off, but the vision kept coming back.

Dave checked his seat belt clamp as the plane approached for landing. He pressed the button in his seat that restored it to the "full and upright position." He caught Jim looking his way. Dave nodded very slightly in acknowledgment; the priest lifted a finger to acknowledge him.

Briefly in Fort Collins, Dave had fallen under the priest's spell. Now, under Pamela's spell, he chose to believe all the paranoia amounted to an incomplete understanding of the facts. The kind of stories confided to him happened only in the movies. Vatican conspiracy? No. If nothing else, the bureaucrats and holy men in the Vatican would not have the audacity. And they would never kill to get their way. So why had the priest told him his bizarre story about Aldrich conspiracy? Maybe the priest, too, had gone over the paranoia brink. He had been sent to look for something so he made the facts add up to a story that satisfied that need, but not the real truth.

And if the priest had summed the facts up accurately, if Middleton's paranoia about the Aldrich code proved out, if Claire had Sheila Stratemeier killed... Incredibly unlikely, Dave thought. Pamela and Claire wanted to help people and make a little money doing it. Just like him. Committing the kind of acts of which Fr. Jim accused them could only work against their own interests. If somehow it all were true... Dave remembered the gun tucked away in his coat.

As the plane descended, Dave glanced again at Mel and Liv. He felt very uneasy again. He did not know why, just that something still seemed very wrong.

Upon deplaning, the entourage found itself greeted by Minister Tombu, Adrian Guerra, and a military escort. Both Claire and Pamela took turns hugging Adrian, clearly not a first meeting. After introductions all around, Tombu and Adrian directed everyone into large black SUVs. Dave chose to ride in the last one with Mel and Liv. He crossed the tarmac carrying his sport coat, careful not to let the gun fall out of the pocket.

"This is so cool, Daddy."

Mel reached across the seat, hugging her husband. "I love you," she whispered in his ear.

Over her shoulder, Dave noticed Minister Tombu hand Jim a letter-sized envelope. Behind them, Adrian's eyes watched the transaction.

CHAPTER 31

Kimtumani Hotel, Aberdeen Peninsula, Freetown
December 24, 1:07 p.m. GMT

Dave felt a little uncomfortable in the presence of the press corps with all its lights and cameras, but soon overcame that with an enormous swell of pride during Pamela's introduction. She read from prepared notes.

"Mr. Clement and his organization have dedicated nearly all their waking hours, risking careers and families, to complete a working portable DNA analyzer. The PDNA allows us to bring the world's most sophisticated diagnostic tools to the world's most unreachable areas. The fruit of the partnership between The Aldrich Institute and Prodeus will alter the course of history, reversing the advance of disease in the Third World by making drug discovery viable for poorer nations.

"The PDNA has allowed us to more broadly deploy a new malaria vaccine, testing for efficacy before administering the vaccine, not wasting the vaccine on those who genetically can either not respond to the vaccine or whose genetics make them extremely unlikely to get malaria. In this way, we are able to not only implement a working malaria vaccine, but we are able to deploy it much more effectively, saving tens of thousands more than we might have otherwise because of finite supply, skilled personnel and limited funding. Every time a person is identified as an inappropriate candidate for the vaccine, another appropriate candidate receives the vaccine – another appropriate candidate is spared the ravages of the disease."

Pamela removed her reading glasses and now spoke extemporaneously. "And, as if Providence chose to directly intervene at this moment in history," she continued solemnly, "and further prove the value of this work, I have just today been made aware of a significant discovery made possible by the PDNA. Even Mr. Clement, perhaps the leading champion of this program, is not yet aware of this finding. You will not find this in your press packages…"

On the dais, Dave looked out to Mel and Liv, shrugging as he flashed his eyebrows. Jennifer looked to Claire who acknowledged her with a tight grin.

"…Through the PDNA, we have been able to isolate a new mutation, a new type of HIV. Because of the field diagnostic capabilities, we have been able to identify this new clade as more virulent than any seen before…"

This was not good news. The press buzzed.

"…However, again because of the PDNA and the Aldrich software embedded in it, we are in a position to achieve rapid drug discovery and stop the advance of this, ultimately saving hundreds of thousands, if not millions, of lives here in West Africa."

Pamela immediately began recognizing members of the press to answer questions.

"What do you mean by more virulent?"

"Dr. McQuaid can best answer that."

Pamela stepped away from the mike, making room for Claire who stepped up to the dais.

"Virulence, in this case, measures acceleration and drug resistance." Claire said. "The clade discovered here thus far seems resistant to any of the current pharmaceuticals employed to combat AIDS. It also appears to kill within six months of initial infection."

Mel took Liv's hand and pulled her close. Thank God she doesn't have this, thought Mel.

"I don't understand what you mean by a clade," shouted a woman from the BBC.

"A clade is a major mutation group," Claire explained. "In most of sub-Saharan Africa the HIV-1 clade C dominates, but in Nigeria clade G is dominant. In the United States, HIV 1 clade B dominates, and so on. Our team back at the Aldrich headquarters in Boulder, Colorado, has reviewed the data from the PDNAs round the clock since testing began nearly one month ago. In the last 24 hours, they presented their initial conclusions to me. This mutation, HIV-1 clade L, has never been seen anywhere else in the world. It may be unique to West Africa. So far.

"Premised on the available epidemiology in the country and the data the genetic material itself reveals, the mutation is less than five years old, but has somehow completely overtaken the HIV-2 that had been the dominant form here before the civil war first reached Freetown in the late 1990s."

Claire pointed to a man from CNN.

"What's to keep this clade from spreading throughout the region?"

Claire hesitated and sighed, deliberately building a moment of drama. "First, due to the nature of the PDNA readings, we believe we can manufacture a cure on a fast track, one that we could bring here for testing within months, as opposed to the normal cycle of years. Minister Tombu and the government have agreed to stand down on any inhibitions to early testing, not subjecting potential cures to the normal cycle associated with the FDA in the United States."

"Why are you so certain?" the CNN reporter followed up.

"We're not prepared with diagrams today, but the very virulence that makes this clade so dangerous also makes it vulnerable to new and more effective pharmaceutical pathology."

"That still doesn't answer the question about it spreading further in the meantime."

Pamela stepped up to the mike. "Minister Tombu and the government have no choice but to quarantine the areas of outbreak," she said matter-offactly. "We also believe we need to deploy PDNAs in such a way as to encircle the area of infection and determine the boundaries of this epidemic. I'll let Minister Tombu explain the details of the quarantine."

Dave quickly did math in his head, calculating the increased sales of PDNAs, manufacturing capability and company valuation. Then, he grew very distracted by another set of numbers. He recalled from the Aldrich reports the rate of HIV infection thus far encountered in the PDNA testing. Hundreds of thousands would be dead in Sierra Leone alone within the next year. If the mutation had spread or did spread over the borders, the death toll could readily top a million within the same period.

Maybe Middleton's team saw this in the firmware, he thought. The Aldrich may have already factored the new clade into the software and Dave's engineering team did not know what they were looking at. He made a mental note to find out from Middleton which firmware rev the team had reviewed.

Across the room, Jim scrutinized Pamela and Claire. Every instinct in his body told him they had just lit the fuse for a bomb that would decimate the population. He looked to Dave who seemed preoccupied elsewhere though his eyes stared at Claire behind the podium. Then, Jim looked at Mel and Liv. He knew Claire brought the whole family for leverage.

The priest thought about the suburban execs he knew in his Atlanta parish years earlier, before Christus recruited him for the missions. He remembered how little backbone they had, how much their comforts drove them to compromises. He hoped Dave Clement's soul held more tightly to principle. He hoped and prayed that his faith would be strong when true difficulties arose.

Jim feared that within a few hours that desperate hope would be tested.

CHAPTER 32

Kimtumani Hotel, Freetown
December 24, 5:55 p.m. GMT

Dave waited patiently for the dial-up connection to link with his e-mail. As the modem whistled, the little green progress bar struggled from left to right at a painfully slow pace. He envisioned an enormous phone bill. Internet service providers had yet to set up local international service in Sierra Leone forcing Dave to connect with an international call.

He sipped the warm club soda, tempted to walk down the hall and get ice while he waited. He decided exposure to the local water through the melting cubes would be a bad idea. Liv and Mel had gone for a walk along the bay below the hotel, a needed bonding opportunity. He had not mentioned it to Mel, but he now worried that exposing Liv to West Africa might be a mistake, a concern he thought only minor when they left Fort Collins. He suspected that in order for a mutation to explode as rapidly as the Aldrich claimed, something more than sexual transmission must have entered the picture. After the press conference, he asked Jennifer to provide a model for the course of infection in the region premised on the aging available through the PDNA analyses. After teasing that she no longer worked for him, she squeezed his arm and assured him she would make it a priority.

Brian Middleton's name scrolled up in the sender column as the laptop's monitor finally refreshed. Dave clicked on it, but it did not take. He waited a moment longer and tried again. This time, the e-mail opened – slowly, but it opened. Middleton had more information. He had investigated Jennifer's emails. In an encrypted e-mail, Sheila had warned Jennifer that Claire and Eldridge seemed intent on some kind of genocide, that they would implicate the Catholic Church, make it the patsy. Jennifer wrote back reassuring her that could not be true. If it were, she would fight it alongside Sheila. Brian explained to Dave that he felt compelled to bring Hepp into the loop if he could not reach Dave soon.

Dave closed the message. God knows what's really true, he thought. Maybe Sheila was completely off-reservation. Maybe her paranoia had driven all the rumors, all the accusations of unlikely plots.

He quickly wrote Brian back. "Do NOT tell Ed," he wrote. "Consider this an order. Will explain when we talk."

Dave knew Ed would tell Claire. He still felt that could be dangerous.

He scrolled down to a message sent later by Ed Hepp. He double-clicked. His breath caught as he read the brief message.

"Oh, dear God, no," he mumbled.

He dialed Fr. Jim's room. When Jim picked up, Dave blurted out, "My engineers that cracked the Aldrich code -- they're all dead."

CHAPTER 33

Catholic Refugee Camp, south of Freetown
December 24, 10:12 p.m. GMT

In the darkness, only cooking fires lit the area inside the fence. People came and went as they pleased through the main gate, the fence apparently more as a defense to keep people out than as a means to imprison the refugees inside. Just inside the fence, white lights surrounded a small nativity crèche the nuns had put up with spare wood and papier-mâché figures the children had made in class.

Fr. Jim and Dave sat in a rental car outside the main gate. Coincidences had begun to pile up. Neither believed the deaths of Middleton and his engineers to be accidental. Hepp said witnesses saw a large SUV hit them as they crossed the street to the sandwich shop near the plant. The SUV took off. In the blowing snow, no one had been able to read the license plate.

"It's odd that all four men died at the scene," Fr Jim speculated. "How does an SUV take out four men at once? You'd think there would be different degrees of injuries - and a survivor or two in the hospital."

"Hepp's taking his orders from Pamela or Claire," Dave responded, though part of him remained in disbelief.

After meeting in Jim's room earlier, Dave and Jim decided they needed to find Hamara and the PDNA Dave had sent to him months earlier. Dave hoped to get hold of it before it could be tampered with by firmware downloads from Colorado. If he could take it offline before tonight's online update, it could confirm that the firmware was designed to give false data, that the Aldrich had deliberately tampered with the code to produce misleading outcomes.

The Lokoma's PDNA might be the last chance to prove it. Now that Claire knew Middleton's team successfully cracked the Aldrich firmware – why else would they have them killed? - Dave had little doubt that the Aldrich would change the firmware with tonight's download to hide its tracks. Even with the men dead, Claire would take no chances.

"So what are they hiding?" Dave asked.

"Has to be this counter-fertility Trojan horse. What I sent the Vatican from Sheila's lab computer supports that the vaccine probably contains the counter-fertility drug. Your PDNA, without data being falsified by the firmware, would reveal it."

"There's more to this, Father. I don't see how Claire and Thatcher benefit from mass sterilization."

"It's all we have to work with."

"We're missing something."

"I might have something to help us in the morning. I'm expecting files from a priest in Nova Scotia. The Vatican had him send them directly to me via DHL. Evan Conger had them with him when he died."

"What would Evan have known?"

"Only thing they told me is that Evan left a message that he thought his plane had been sabotaged. And that he was the target."

"How do they know that?"

"His phone survived the crash."

The men agreed to meet in the morning as soon as the package arrived. They exited the car and approached the gate. Two guards armed with short rifles with long banana clips stepped out, leading with the barrels of their weapons. Jim pulled identification, explained to the men who he was. Even though the camp was run by the Catholic Church, the men remained unimpressed until Dave handed them ten American dollars each. The men smiled and waved the two inside.

Following the directions provided by one of the guards, Jim led the way through the camp's muddy alleyways. Fetid odors of sickness, decay and human sewage assailed them. Only the smoke from the cooking fires helped moderate the odors. The sound of drumbeats and chanting came from several areas of the camp. Some of it seemed mournful. Still more of it sounded hopeful here in the midst of what amounted to a hell on earth.

Wasted time could prove costly. The PDNAs automatically uploaded data at 11:30 local time every night. During that communication, downloads also could take place. Dave's team had designed that feature into the system so that improvements and patches for any flaws could be added to the boxes without having to deploy expensive field repair personnel. If Dave's hypothesis was right, Hepp and the Aldrich would want to eliminate the renegade code until the suspicions of Dave or others melted away. Once new firmware entered the boxes, no evidence of the old firmware's detail would exist, only the log record of a firmware update, a fairly common event for patchwork.

It was 10:25 now.

Approaching a hut not much larger than the walk-in closet in Dave's master bedroom, the men heard a child coughing inside. Sara, thought Dave. Jim walked ahead of him, stopping at the strings of beads that acted as a door to the hut.

"Chief Karanja?" he called through the beads. A moment passed. "Hamara. It's Father Jim Reilly."

Seconds later, a hand pulled the beads back. The chief, his bearing erect and regal, stepped through them. Unsmiling, he studied the priest's face. After several seconds, his eyes crinkled over a broad grin.

"Thanks be to God," the chief declared, placing his hands on Jim's shoulders.

Jim reached out and pulled the smaller man to him, wrapping him in a bear hug.

"Everyone thinks you're dead," Karanja said as they separated.

"The bad guys nearly made that happen, but the Lord apparently had a little more work for me. I can explain all that later. How is your family?

"Come in. See for yourself."

"First, I brought a friend." Jim stepped aside, revealing Dave behind him.

"Dave," the chief said. "Another surprise."

The chief reached out to shake hands with Dave. "You are both welcome in my home. Come in, please." Hamara led them through the beads.

A small oil lantern provided the only light in the hut. In one corner, two slender children slept under a thin blanket cuddled atop what looked like a crib mattress.

Two women stood to greet them, one leaning precariously on a crutch, her right foot missing. Jim hugged the women who both grew tearful.

"How is Sara?" Jim whispered, not wanting to wake the girls.

"Not well," Mariama said. "She has AIDS. Jacob brought medicine, but it doesn't seem to help."

"I'm so sorry."

Mariama knelt beside the children's bed and stroked the hair of each girl. "They have strong spirits, Father. I tell them stories of Jesus every day."

"Is Emma sick, too?"

Ani hopped once to maintain her balance. "Just tired. She plays hard."

"But we feel a little safer thanks to the blessing of Dave's malaria vaccine," Mariama said as she stood. "At least, we don't have to worry about that. Except for Hamara. He made sure everyone else got the vaccine first. By the time his turn came, they ran out. Can you imagine that? The chief, the most important member of the village, and he refuses to take proper care of himself. He calls it the right thing to do. I call it irresponsible."

"The doctors will take care of me when the next shipment arrives."

"Pray God that it will be soon," Ani said.

"Where is Jacob?" Jim asked.

The women looked to Hamara who visibly stiffened.

"They captured him. He is a boy soldier now."

While Mariama and Ani prepared tea, Hamara had the men join him in sitting on a large mud cloth spread over the dirt floor. He explained the events that led to their present situation. With each passing minute, Dave glanced at his watch, finally interrupting at 10:55 p.m. The firmware updates would start in thirty minutes.

"We came to get your help, Chief. There is something we need to do before 11:30. A lot of lives may be at stake."

"How?"

"Do you have the PDNA I sent you?"

"Yes, of course."

Dave breathed a sigh of relief. "May I have it? We need to take it with us."

"It's not here. It's in the clinic. The doctors have been using it for the malaria vaccine testing."

"We need to get it back."

"Why?"

"We think it may have purposefully been changed to hide important information, information that could save lives."

"I haven't had the vaccine, but I think the machine is in one of the exam rooms."

Dave's eyes lit up. "Of course," he said. "That's it. Chief, how many others in the camp have not had the vaccine."

Jim pondered Dave curiously.

"Very few of us," Hamara answered. "The doctor in charge would know."

"Jim," Dave said, "we need to see this doc and get him to work with us. We have a control group in this camp."

Tilting his head, Jim squinted at Dave. "I don't understand."

"They're using the PDNA to distort the results. We have samples of everyone but Hamara and a handful of others. If we can get samples of their blood pre-vaccine and pre-PDNA, we may be able to find what changes are being created by the PDNA and the vaccine."

"Almost my entire tribe has been vaccinated," Hamara said. "Are they in danger?"

"I doubt it," Jim said, jumping in quickly. "The results are being distorted for other reasons, probably financial. There's no financial benefit in hurting your tribe. These people don't waste motion."

The three men exchanged glances, searching for a next step.

"Father," Dave said, "can you use your priestly credentials in a Catholic camp to get the doc to quickly collect and preserve blood from Hamara and a sampling of the other unvaccinated people."

"Let's find out," he said.

At 11:05, they awoke the doctor. In his two years of service in Sierra Leone, the doc had personally witnessed thousands of deaths, unnecessary deaths in his mind, from malaria. He gladly helped the man who had taken steps to stop this scourge. As the doctor led them down the hall of the clinic to the PDNA, Dave explained, "Somebody may have hacked our equipment. The distorted data could risk lives."

"Who would do that? What kind of people…"

The doctor's voice trailed off. Dave guessed he had seen enough cruelty to draw his own conclusion.

"What can I do?" the doctor asked.

"We need to take this thing offline right away."

"What about the other vaccinations?"

"Don't give them," Dave said. "But we need a big favor in that regard. We need you to collect blood samples from the un-vaccinated and preserve them. Make sure half are HIV positive."

"I don't have a lot of space for long-term refrigeration. I might be able to store 25 or 30."

"That should be enough. It won't be for long. Where possible, it would be better to have blood from those who have family that did receive the vaccination."

"That means you'll need names?"

"Yes. It's the only way to correlate the data."

The doctor knew that the Leoneans had been promised complete confidentiality about the genetic results. He weighed his request. These men had come down in the middle of the night for this. And Hamara vouched for them. Among all the village leaders, Hamara had impressed the doctor as having the coolest head.

Ten minutes later, the men walked out the front gate of the camp and crossed the street to a burned-out convenience store. Hamara peeled back a set of floorboards and jumped into the crawl space. Jim handed him the PDNA, now inside its vinyl case. Bending over, Hamara disappeared, returning empty-handed a moment later.

Back at the main gate, the men said their good-byes and Hamara started to head back to his shack.

"Wait," Dave said. "Would you like to get your family out of here for a few nights?"

"And go where?" Hamara asked.

"Come stay at our hotel. There's hot and cold running water and three buffets each day. It would be a wonderful chance to heal in a more sterile environment."

"I can't take your money."

"You can't turn me down. It's an American tradition."

"Is this true?" Hamara asked, looking to Fr. Jim.

"It would be bad luck to turn down our friend," Jim said, a small grin on his face.

"Consider it a Christmas present for your family," Dave added.

Half an hour later, the group piled into a taxi outside the gate, the trunk and their laps filled with all the possessions they had left. At 1 a.m. Christmas morning, Dave checked the Karanjas in for their first night ever in a hotel.

He arrived in his own suite to find Mel and Liv sound asleep. He kissed each one on the cheek and whispered Merry Christmas. He found a candy cane on his pillow with a note on hotel stationary that said, "Merry Christmas, Daddy. Coolest Christmas ever!"

CHAPTER 34

Catholic Church, downtown Freetown
December 25, 5:52 a.m.

Peering through the pre-dawn darkness, Fr. Jim studied the smoke-stained clapboard structure before him. The note Minister Tombu handed him at the airport said the church south of the State House. This had to be the one. From the outside, it looked more Protestant than Catholic, its front columns, rotting from moisture and disrepair, calling to mind a Georgian mansion. Brown bags of burned out Christmas luminaria, set there for midnight Mass the evening before, lined the steps leading to the entrance.

Only candles lit the inside of the church. One on a long brass candle holder stood watch beside a makeshift nativity crèche. Jim knelt in the fourth pew from the front on the left side, just as instructed. He ticked off two decades of the rosary on his fingers before another priest knelt beside him.

"We've missed you, Fr. Reilly," the man said.

Jim turned to see Tim Mazewski, assigned to the archbishop's staff here.

"Maybe I'll stay this time."

"Seems you have more important work. The files you sent the Vatican reveal a plot targeted at the Kono district, heavily Muslim. The vaccine shipped there apparently has been modified."

The Vatican had confirmed Jim's reading of the plan outlined in Sheila's files.

"In what way?"

"Something in it will cause infertility and risk spontaneous abortions among women receiving it. That could approach 5,000 women in that region."

"I have to stop it."

"You don't have much time. The schedule in the file you sent says vaccinations begin tomorrow in the Kono Clinic."

"I have to get there today then."

A clatter behind him indicated that someone had joined them.

"Now, how ya gonna do that, boy-o?"

Jim stiffened. Mike. Jim turned expecting to see a gun. Instead, he saw a smile.

"Jennifer and I have a few caseloads of replacement vaccine in the pick-up outside."

"How did you know that I'd be here?"

"My security's very good, little brother. Why do ya think the bastards hire me?"

"You knew I was coming?"

"Yes. And we intercepted the instructions to Fr. Tim here. I don't know who at the lab is behind this, but we can't let it happen. No matter what else I may be, I still respect Holy Mother Church. And I know you do, too."

"Is Claire behind this?"

"No. She's our ally on this. She secured the replacement vaccine for us. I'm thinkin' it's Eldridge. Claire and Jennifer agree."

"Why?"

"That's a mystery we get to solve when we return to Colorado. C'mon, boy-o. We have a jeep out front and a helicopter at the airfield. We can be in Kono by 10:30."

Jennifer drove them back to the airport in the jeep. There, they loaded their cargo on to the helicopter. With Mike as the pilot, the two headed south down the coast and then southeast toward Kono, a hundred miles inland.

Jennifer stayed behind in Freetown. A knot twisted in her belly. She finally figured out she really liked Mike. Now she feared she would never see him again.

CHAPTER 35

Peninsula Mountains, South of Freetown
December 25, 7:11 a.m.

Flashes of sun cut through the leaves, awakening a hungry Jacob. He reached for his pouch, remembering it was empty as soon as he touched it. A mango lay to his left, its rind pulled back to reveal its intact flesh. As he picked it up, a colobus chattered gleefully from its hiding place in the brush. Jacob tipped his head in thanks, biting off a piece of the mango and placing it between himself and the monkey. The monkey stared back and forth between Jacob and the mango for a moment. Then he shook his head aggressively in acknowledgment. He lunged for the mango and shoved it in his mouth as he bounced back into the brush. Jacob laughed.

As he finished his portion of the mango, Jacob glimpsed blood in the dirt under him. Turning his feet upside down, he saw that his soles had cuts all over them from his long run. Today, he would wear his boots, seemingly heavier on his feet than around his neck.

Crawling quietly through the brush to the road, he searched for an indication of where he had stopped. A tree reaching across the road in a great arch, the underbelly of its branch gnarled with a giant knot, told Jacob how far he had to go – fully a long morning's walk by road, longer in the jungle where Jacob would remain hidden as he paralleled the highway. He listened for vehicles or people. He heard only the morning song of birds and the chatter of waking monkeys as he pulled his boots over his feet. He hated them for the blisters that often formed on his heels, but the bottoms of his feet needed a break.

Slipping further into the jungle, he motioned for the colobus group to follow him. He smiled the broad smile of a boy who viewed monkeys as personal friends. The rebels often used them for bushmeat, a delicacy for officers. Jacob killed the officers; he could not bring himself to kill the colobus.

Two hours later, the rainforest thinned out as it rolled down the west-facing slopes outside Freetown. Bombing, poverty and ill-considered development had produced a rock and concrete wasteland strewn with unmanaged weeds. Here, the natural camouflage that hid Jacob on his long trek fell away. He thought he might blend in, but knew that the Kalashnikov over his shoulder would make a ten year old stand out. Like Rambo, he chose to move behind the shacks and rundown wooden buildings of the poor community that heralded the entry to the capital. The blister on one of his heels howled with every step. Seeing three boys, two roughly his size, kicking a half-deflated soccer ball over the weeds and stones, he noted their sandals, nothing fancy but exactly what Jacob needed to protect the soles of his feet and to keep the blistered heel from rubbing.

Unslinging his weapon, he ran toward the boys, pointing the Kalashnikov. The boys froze. Just like Rambo, Jacob put a finger to his lips and motioned for the boys to move against a wall.

"Da shoes," he said.

Two of the boys cried now. "Please don't shoot us, mister," one whined.

The third boy argued. Jacob had motioned to his shoes. "Dese be my only shoes," he said stubbornly, "I need my shoes. You have shoes. Better shoes. What for you need mine?" Jacob lifted the butt of the rifle and started to swat at the boy. The boy's eyes widened and he threw his arms in front of his face as he ducked away. "No, mister, no!" The boy crumbled to the ground.

Jacob withheld his blow. Balancing his weapon in the crook of his left arm, he bent down with his right and pushed off his boots. He threw them at the third boy. Poking the boy in the side with the barrel of the rifle, he said, "Da shoes. You take mine."

The boy looked at him confused. Jacob kicked the boots closer to him.

"Yours," he said." Now give me mine."

His eyes never leaving the barrel of Jacob's weapon, the boy pushed off his sandals. He placed them carefully at Jacob's feet.

Jacob pointed the barrel at the boots again. "They're yours now," he said.

The boy looked curiously at the boots, He warily reached for them. He pulled them over his feet and stood up. A grin spread across his face as he eyed his two companions. "I never had boots before," he said.

"Happy Christmas," Jacob said as slipped on the sandals and then slowly backed away from the boy and his companions. He finally broke into a run as he turned the first corner.

An hour later, distant fireworks drew Jacob's eyes northwest toward Lumley Beach. Smoke curled to the sky. More blasts. This time from due west. From his hiding place in an abandoned shack on an eastern hill, Jacob could see fire explode from the windows of the State House, its whitewashed walls quickly overcome with black soot and licking flames. His focus shifted to the south, the Catholic refugee camp. No explosions there. No smoke. His family had thus far been spared.

CHAPTER 36

Kimtumani Hotel, Freetown
December 25, 11:40 a.m.

Screams and smoke alarms filled the hotel rooms and corridors. Chairs and tables smashed through windows as people sought air and exit. Desperately, some jumped. If they survived the fall, automatic weapons fire cut them down on the hotel lawn. An advance contingent of the attackers had been careful to take certain individuals hostage first, intent on protecting them from the randomness of the firefight.

Pamela Thatcher remained calm throughout, demonstrating her seasoned leadership skills as others struggled with a cocktail of panic, fear and anger. The Abo attackers sequestered her in the suite where she had been attending an afternoon reception. Pamela's capture promised to draw worldwide media attention to the Abo cause in a much more effective way than mutilations and massacres of Leonean nationals ever had.

Dave Clement nearly had escaped from the same reception, but a gunstock slammed against his neck stopped him cold. He lay on a couch still half-dazed with Jennifer Winter administering an ice bag to the base of his skull. He mumbled that he had to get to Mel and Liv, but Jennifer assured him that they would be safe, that it would only hurt them if he risked his life any further.

Claire stood over Jennifer, nodding her head in agreement, encouraging Jennifer to keep Dave calm.

Upstairs in the hot tub in the ladies' dressing area of the hotel's modest indoor spa, Mel and Liv entertained Ani, Mariama, Emma and Sara Karanja. Amidst the roar of the whirlpool engine and the gurgling of churning bubbles, all of them laughed a lot for the first time in a long time. The Karanjas had never experienced this kind of luxury. Emma and Sara, emanating life as though she had never been ill, giggled uncontrollably as they leaned into the hot jets of water and splashed at the bubbles.

Suddenly, metal lockers crashed from the other side of the door to the wet area, Mel reached for her towel. A loud report nearly deafened her and the others as a bullet ripped it from her hand.

"Get down, lady," said a rebel as he rushed through the door. "All of you stay dere."

Three companions followed the soldier into the room. Their weapons at port arms, they stepped to the edge of the hot tub and peered at the women and girls dressed only in underwear or bathing suits.

"We been blessed with wonderful Christmas presents here," said one of the rebels, running one hand through the hot water until it caressed Ani's shoulder. He placed a hand under her arm and attempted to yank her from the tub. She resisted and the other soldiers, no more than teenagers, helped him. When her flailing footless limb surfaced, the soldiers let go.

"Who been doin' dis to ya?" one asked. "We don't want damaged goods."

"You come willin' now or you end up like her," another said to all the women and girls.

Ani rolled over the side on to the tile, pulling herself upright. Mariama followed, pulling her girls up behind her. Liv and Mel, submerged in the foaming water up to their chins, exchanged glances. One of the soldiers started to raise his weapon. Mel futilely placed a hand over her nipples peaking through her soaked white bra. She pulled Liv to her with her free hand. Liv mimicked her mother's hopeless camouflage. As they stepped on to the tile, red with embarrassment, stooped and contorted in a senseless attempt to preserve their modesty, the soldiers burst into loud laughter.

Ani, seeing their horror, reached for two towels and threw them to the women. Liv and Mel, both shivering, each mumbled "thank you" as they wrapped the towels around themselves. The soldier nearest Ani angrily kicked her in the backside, knocking her into a hamper. Mel started to go to her aid, but the hot barrel of an AK-47 seared her midsection, halting her progress.

Hiding behind Mariama, Emma began whimpering, big tears rolling down her cheeks.

"You shut her up, mama," said one of the teens, "or I'll kill her sure."

"She's only three years old," Mariama protested as Sara wrapped her bony body around her little sister to calm her. The whimpering grew quieter as Emma buried her mouth in her sister's chest.

Using their weapons as prods, the soldiers pushed the women toward the door of the spa.

"We need our clothes," Liv said.

"White girl, why you t'ink to hide your bony ass?"

"Speak fo' y'self, man. I might like some o' dat."

"Better get your t'ings, den," the first one said. "Bring dem along, but no dressing 'til we get where we go."

The women and girls scrambled to get their clothes and purses from the lockers, wrapping pieces around themselves as they stumbled down the hotel corridor behind prodding weapons. Stumbling to the ground, Sara struggled to get up, starting Emma crying again. Liv raced forward and picked both tiny girls up in her arms, carrying them and whispering.

"Everything's going to be okay, girls. Just be cool. Be very cool."

Mel put an arm around Liv to help her stay up as they tumbled into the elevator.

In a large conference room on the hotel's mezzanine floor, the members of the press found that their captivity entailed certain unusual liberties. The

Abo officers encouraged them to roll their cameras and report the events of the assault, detailing the names and status of all the hostages, making it clear that the hostages would be killed should there be any resistance to the revolution. Within an hour after the hostages had all been corralled into a large ballroom, an Abo officer presented an overhead presentation, a particularly unusual offering from a West African rebel force. Complete with handouts, the slides, projected from a portable projector linked to a laptop, detailed the names of each hostage, each name accompanied by a brief description. "Hotel guest" showed up most frequently as a descriptor, but appellations like "prominent American investment banker" and "world's wealthiest woman" did not need to show up more than once to guide the lead of the stories being filed.

CHAPTER 37

Freetown near the State House
December 25, 12:25 p.m.

Hiding across the road from the State House in the ruins of a restaurant not yet rebuilt from the last invasion of Freetown, Jacob watched as the Presidential guard, having hardly fired a shot, marched on to the State House grounds with their hands behind their heads. The armed rebels surrounding them, clearly Abo, seemed very methodical, barking commands as they organized the prisoners into platoon sized units. They stepped back from their charges, lighting cigarettes and waiting.

Within a few minutes, a cell phone rang and shouted commands went down the line. The rebels stomped their cigarettes out in the grass and returned their full attention to the prisoners. A bus loaded with press and driven by a rebel soldier pulled up on the street between Jacob and the grounds. Rebel soldiers formed a phalanx between the press and the prisoners, roughly knocking down any member of the press corps who crossed an invisible line on the edge of the grounds.

Rifle barrels selected three prisoners from each platoon and prodded them into an open area just behind the phalanx. The prisoners, hands still behind their heads, dropped to their knees. The rebels opened a view line for the press cameras, shouted more commands. The press frantically jockeyed for position, cameras banging off each other as they settled into place. An Abo officer, one of the few older men Jacob had seen, watched until the jockeying among the press had stopped. When satisfied, he turned back to his soldiers and shouted something.

Then, silence. All movement stopped. A series of rapid pops followed, blood erupting from the heads of the kneeling prisoners as they collapsed wide-eyed to the ground. The rebel phalanx fell back, allowing the press in for close-up shots of the dead bodies. Attempts to interview the rebels themselves met with forceful gunstock blows, the press corps quickly getting the hint.

Having seen as much cruelty as he had, as much death and mutilation, Jacob thought this scene should not have bothered him. Instead, it re-awakened the terror that had been de-sensitized in him by the bloodshed in the hills and the jungle. The Abo, sworn enemies of his father and his tribe, emitted a power Jacob had not seen. He could only conclude that the spirits betrayed by the Karanjas' conversion to Jesus had concentrated all their might behind the Abo. A yearning to see his father swept over him. Hamara would know what to do, how to stop them – or where to hide.

Racing out the back of the burned out restaurant, Jacob maneuvered from city block to city block, careful not to encounter rebel soldiers. He needed to get to the refugee camp, warn Hamara, and even somehow rescue him if a warning proved too late. After twenty minutes of this, he realized there were no soldiers, rebel or government. He had not seen a soldier since he left the State House area. What kind of war is this? he wondered.

At the refugee camp, Jacob learned that his family had not been seen since the prior evening. Someone said they had left with two white men. Had they been warned? Had they escaped?

Starving and exhausted, Jacob found a rundown soccer bar, one of those dreary places filled with smoke where men drank beer and watched soccer by satellite dish all day long, following the sun around the globe. He put Leones down on the bar and asked for a sandwich. In years past, a bartender would have laughed at a ten year old reaching over a bar with cash. But this boy carried a Kalashnikov and had the weary, hollow glare of a killer. The bartender reached into a case, pulled out a sandwich and pushed it, with Jacob's money, across the bar to the boy.

"I didn't pay," Jacob said.

"You a soldier?" the bartender asked rhetorically.

"Yes."

"Soldiers don't pay here. They protect us. And it's Christmas."

Puzzled, Jacob tilted his head, studying the man. The bartender nodded toward the TV. Instead of soccer, video of the State House and of the Kimtumani Hotel filled the screen.

"You part of this?" the bartender asked.

Jacob thought a moment. "I don't know yet."

Then a listing of hostages began scrolling over the screen, like credits at the end of a movie, video of executions running under them.

"...Pamela Thatcher, managing partner of Thatcher Ripley... David Clement: American business executive... Melanie Clement: wife of American executive... Olivia Clement: daughter of American executive..."

"Dey don't know what dey be about," said a man at the bar, a cigarette dangling from his mouth. "You don't be takin' bigshot Americans prisoner."

"You be right abou' dat," said another. "American Marines will be here in no time."

"You don't know dis thing," said the bartender. "Americans are busy wid other things. Dey don't have no soldiers to send here. Maybe we finally have some smart rebels..."

Jacob stopped listening. His eyes followed the most recent names as they rolled up and out of the screen.

"...Hamara Karanja: Lokoma paramount chief... Ani Karanja: wife of paramount chief... Mariama Karanja: wife of paramount chief... Sara Karanja: daughter of paramount chief... Emma Karanja: daughter of paramount chief..."

The methodical, heartless executions on the State House grounds replayed behind the names. Jacob stuffed the last half of his sandwich in his shorts. He said nothing as he hurried through the hanging beads that acted as the bar's front door.

CHAPTER 38

Kono, Southeast Sierra Leone
December 25, 12:53 p.m.

The chopper set down in a clearing behind Kono's small one-story regional hospital. Mike Farley adjusted the stick and turned the rotors off. Waiting a moment to be certain the shutdown completed, he nodded to Jim. The priest half-smiled. The brothers, both unaware of the violence that had befallen their associates at the hotel, finally had united in an effort to do good, saving instead of taking lives.

"Would ya say God has his ways, big brother?" Jim asked.

Mike grinned. "I'd say he might, young Father Jim. It's a special Christmas."

A surge of warmth rushed through Jim. Not since their mother died had Mike allowed himself to be anything more than agnostic; never had he allowed that, even if God existed, he might play a benevolent role in the lives of human beings. Long faithless, doubt had finally crept into his being.

Jim slapped a hand on Mike's shoulder. "I suppose we Irish boys should be unloadin' some fresh vaccine for these folks."

"I suppose so," Mike rejoined.

The two hopped out of the cabin. They opened the rear compartment, each grabbing an ice chest. Adjusting the chest in his arms, Jim sucked in a giant breath. The air tasted good here, the Leonean air to which he had grown accustomed over nearly a decade. Mike passed him, navigating the palm fronds that interrupted the stone path to the concrete block clinic. Jim marveled that his brother, the killer, had come all this way to save the lives of strangers.

Jim looked to the sky. Not a cloud disturbed the pure blue. Maybe it was a sign.

"Thank you, Lord," he prayed quietly. "Our Father, who art in heaven..."

Finishing, he followed the path into the clinic. There, a French physician and a Leonean nurse listened as Mike attempted to explain that a bad batch of vaccine had inadvertently made it out of manufacturing. From the doorway, Jim saw Mike shove his ID back into his front hip pocket.

"We have this," Mike said, slapping a hand down on the cooler he had placed on a folding table, "and nine -"

Jim entered. He placed his cooler beside Mike's.

" - make that eight more ice chests in the back of the helicopter. This is good vaccine. 4,800 doses. We need to destroy the old vaccine and use this instead."

Jim interrupted. "Have you begun inoculations yet?"

"First thing tomorrow morning," the doctor said in barely accented English, the only detectable French showing as he swallowed the r's in the word tomorrow. "What went wrong with the old?"

Mike looked to Jim. Under no circumstances could the brothers tell anyone of the murderous plot. Jim hesitated; even after two months undercover, lying did not come readily to him.

Mike spoke. "The recipe went awry on these. Something about sedimentation and the aluminum adjuvant in the formula. The sediment means the ingredients aren't bonding and the elements for an immune reaction aren't in place. Innocuous actually. Just not a malaria vaccine, making it no more helpful than water."

"Let me see the bottles," the doctor instructed.

Mike undid the clip on the ice chest.

"Bring me one of the other bottles, Biana," the doctor ordered the nurse.

The woman disappeared through an interior doorway, returning in a moment with a bottle of bad vaccine.

Holding one good bottle and the bad bottle side by side, the doctor examined them. The two vaccines looked identical in that they were clear like water. He shook both vigorously and re-examined them.

"I don't see any sedimentation," he said.

Mike and Jim exchanged a concerned glance. "It must be microscopic," Mike said.

The doc studied the brothers. "I'll have to take your word for it," he said finally. "I'll help you unload."

The three men headed out to the truck. As soon as they cleared the doorway, Biana grabbed a bottle of the replacement vaccine and placed it in her pocket. She walked through the interior doorway again, entering a corridor that took her to a small office. She picked up the phone.

"It's here," she said in French. "Don't worry. I'll be certain the old bottles are not destroyed. "

CHAPTER 39

Kimtumani Hotel
December 25, 1:32 p.m.

"What's wrong with her?" Liv asked Mariama.

They sat lined up against a wall in the hotel's large ballroom where only a day earlier Liv's father stood triumphant before the press. Little Sara's energy evaporated quickly after the rebels corralled them into the ballroom. So had everyone's in some ways, but Liv feared that Sara had more going on. The little girl had no meat on her at all. Every breath seemed labored. Two small lesions on Sara's right cheek looked very much like lesions Liv had seen in pictures. She had expected to find AIDS in Sierra Leone. She had not expected it in a five year old.

"She's very sick," Mariama said.

"Is it AIDS?" Liv asked.

Mariama fixed her gaze firmly on Liv. "Yes," she said as though daring Liv to find fault with the answer. "Many children and adults have it here. It's not like your Glee TV show or your Orange County housewives. We have real problems."

"Most of America's not like those TV shows," Liv said. "They're not real life for most of us."

"So what's your real life?" Mariama asked, trying to repress the challenge in her voice.

"It's a good life. I have my problems, but it's a good life."

"What kind of problems you have? Your father is rich and famous. Your friends are rich and famous. You could probably fit our entire family compound in your American home."

Liv had intended to tell her about her own AIDS, but now it did not seem appropriate. Why did poverty always trump difficulties for the well-to-do? I'll die every bit as alone as Sara, thought Liv. Don't feel sorry for yourself, she chided.

She looked away from Mariama, breathed back a snivel. She looked back at Sara, the little girl's eyes wide as her younger sister Emma counted her toes, struggling to remember what came after six.

Liv slid across the floor next to Mariama. "Mrs. Karanja, does Sara have medicine?"

Mariama snorted in exasperation. "Yes, but it stopped working. Look at her. For two weeks, she seemed to be growing stronger, her energy lasting later and later into the day. Now it's gone before midday. Others in the refugee camp have died within a few weeks once they reached this point. That's not an Orange County problem, is it?"

Liv opened her purse. She pulled out her needle free injector and two small vials, one with sterile water and the other with the Fuzeon powder, one of the fourteen sets of vials her mother had brought with her. It was enough to last for two weeks.

"Give her this. It's the best thing so far for fighting this."

"What is it?"

"Fuzeon. It's for AIDS."

"Why do you have it?"

"It's mine, ma'am."

Mariama leaned back. She studied the white girl. "You look well."

"I feel well."

"So why do you have this drug?"

Liv swallowed hard and blinked back a tear of self-pity. "Because I have HIV. The Fuzeon restored my strength. Now it can restore Sara's."

Mariama studied Liv for several seconds before thrusting the injector and vials back into Liv's purse. "I can't take this from you. You need it."

Liv placed an arm around Mariama and placed the medicine in her lap. "Take it. I have my strength. Your little girl doesn't. There's plenty more for me when I return home."

Liv reached into her purse and took out the plastic bag containing the remaining vials, disposable needle free syringes for the injector, and alcohol pads. She placed it in Mariama's lap. Then she stood and walked away. Mariama grabbed the medicines from her lap and stood to force them back on Liv. A guard seeing the commotion stepped in her direction and she dropped back to the floor.

Mariama scooted over to Sara. She contemplated the confusing array of vials and syringes, trying to read an instruction pamphlet that was in the plastic bag. She looked back at Liv and then back at the medicine. She pulled Sara close and closed her eyes for a few seconds. Then, she called to Liv. "Can you show me how to use this?"

Liv turned back smiling. Surrounded by the threat of death from the rebels, maybe she could at least save this child.

Across the room, Mel huddled, watching the interaction between Mariama and her daughter. As soon as Mel figured out what had happened, she started to jump to her feet. Dave yanked her back down. He and the others at the reception had been brought downstairs at gunpoint.

"No sudden movements around these guys, Mel." He knew the guards would not hesitate to shoot.

The effort aggravated Dave's headache. For the second time in a week, he had taken a hard blow. He had to concentrate to keep from seeing double.

"She's giving away her medicine, her lifeblood."

"Looks like it," he said.

"She'll die."

"We all might before this is over."

"Do you think they plan to kill us?"

He hesitated before speaking. "No. We're all going to be fine. And Liv will get home and get a fresh prescription. Meantime, maybe she's brought hope for Hamara's little girl."

Mel studied his face. "You're scared, too."

"Yes. Yes, I am."

She cuddled up against him, latching on to his arm and tilting her head to his shoulder. She watched Liv instruct Mariama on how to mix the Fuzeion and use the injector. After a moment, she looked up to her husband. "What if they hold us hostage for a long time?"

Dave pondered for a long moment. "Then maybe we take the medicine back," he said.

Together, they watched Liv for another moment, watching her light up as she brought hope in a syringe to Sara and her mother. "I doubt Liv would let us," Mel said.

He reached into his sport coat pocket and felt for the small Ruger.

"I still have the gun," he whispered to her.

"I thought you left that at home."

"No, I have it."

"What if they find it?"

"I'll use it."

"Dave, don't you dare. That thing won't last five seconds against them. They have automatic rifles for God's sake."

"I won't be stupid."

She sat up and glared at him. "But you will," she said. "You will be stupid. I know you."

"I promise I won't," he said, pulling her back into his arms.

CHAPTER 40

Plateau Beside the Karanja's Village
December 25, 1:45 p.m.

In all the years of turmoil, the Abo soldiers had never seen such an impressive display. C-130 cargo planes swooped down to the airfield, landing like a flock of giant birds, quickly lowering their ramps, expelling troops, helicopters and assault vehicles. Putting down their joints and cigarettes, the young men cheered the arrival of their new allies from the Middle African Democracy, running on to the field to offer assistance. Most of them discovered the betrayal only when they felt the impact of the bullets. The last to die heard the gunfire first, saw their comrades cut down, but did not have enough time to both assimilate the information and move finger to trigger. A giant earth mover from one of the planes churned them into the ground in the quick clean-up that followed.

CHAPTER 41

Freetown, Halfway House for Child Soldiers
December 25, 2:05 p.m. GMT

Jacob knew of the halfway house. Almost all of the boy soldiers did. They would talk about it, how it sat on the beach in Freetown, how they had all the food they needed and how there were no drugs or guns. Out loud, the boys made fun of the halfway house and referred to anyone who would go to be a "halfway man." Privately, almost all the boys entertained the tempting possibility of asylum there.

Jacob always thought he would walk in to become part of the home, never that he would come to break others out. He walked in with a two cartons of cigarettes he took from an abandoned market near the fighting at the State House. Passing out packs of cigarettes to the boys playing along the beach outside the halfway house, Jacob quickly made new friends. Whether the boys smoked or not, the cigarettes could be as good as currency during civil uprisings. Already the boys talked about the new fighting in town. Jacob told them the soldiers were Abo, a tribe more widely despised by other tribes than Jacob anticipated.

He quickly recruited a dozen boys to join him in fighting them. They ran up the beach away from the house. Seeing Jacob's weapon, knowing that the new fighting might soon reach the beach, the halfway house managers did not try to stop the inevitable, especially not when the young recruiter wielded a loaded Kalashnikov. Jacob led the boys a half mile southeast where he armed them with automatic weapons and cartridge belts from a cache hidden in the hills. As they climbed through the rainforest over the city, they heard and then saw loud cargo planes in the distance. The planes turned eastward from the sea, seeming to head in the direction of Jacob's village. Jacob thought they brought more Abo troops.

Returning to the city, the boys moved house by house through the streets, careful not be seen by either government or rebel troops. Armed without uniforms, the boys could easily be construed as enemies by either side. Crossing the narrow bridge to the peninsula would be the biggest challenge. The rebels would surely have soldiers stationed there. Walking across would be a sure invitation to a gun battle against superior firepower. Four of the boys claimed to know how to drive. Two of those could sit high enough to see over the steering wheel.

When they saw the government army Humvee parked halfway over a curb, they argued the merits of taking it. The keys dangled in the ignition; it seemed too easy. Inside they found grenades and more cartridge belts. The original owners of the Humvee must have left suddenly; they or their pursuers would be back. The rebels would automatically shoot at them whether or not they jacked the Humvee. If the government troops caught them, they would assume they were rebels, but they would assume they were rebels under any circumstances. The truck had bulletproof armor and could withstand small arms fire and indirect mortar hits. Its undercarriage had been built to withstand land mines. They could drive right through a roadblock.

Jacob did not know these details for certain; the Humvee's legend merely accepted as fact. He quickly achieved consensus to brave the bridge in the vehicle, the very idea of having this much military muscle around them too tempting for the boys to resist.

CHAPTER 42

Kimtumani Hotel
December 25, 2:45 pm GMT

Liv stroked Sara's hair. Mariama had called her back over to sit with them.

"Mama said you gave me your medicine," Sara said.

"You needed it."

"Will you die now, too?"

"We all die someday, but you and I will both live a long time."

"I don't want you to die. You're too pretty to die."

Liv's grin widened. "Not as pretty as you."

"I'm too little to be pretty. Big girls are pretty. Can I touch your face?"

Liv placed Sara's hand on her cheek.

"Soft. You're so pink and white. Like an orchid."

Liv did not know what to say.

"I look like chocolate. Good enough to eat."

Liv giggled. "And I'll bet you're very sweet, too."

"I'll call you my pink orchid girl."

"And what should I call you?"

Sara thought a moment. Her eyes lit up. "Sweet chocolate girl."

Liv blushed. "How about I just call you Sara and you call me Liv. Those are good names."

"Okay. Do you know how to braid hair, Liv?"

Pamela sat with Claire.

"No chance we'll get killed in a botched up rescue operation, is there?" Claire asked.

"A lot of money is at stake for these boys. They won't screw up."

Claire looked around the room, studied the gunmen at the doors. "I thought we were supposed to be in a separate room," she said.

"Well, that is a screw-up."

"You're not helping my confidence."

"Adrian won't let anything happen to us," Pamela said.

"He was supposed to be here an hour ago."

"Speak of the devil."

At that moment, five rebel officers walked into the ballroom escorting Adrian Guerra and Fela, the Abo chief. Fela wore a full dress military uniform, Guerra his usual tropical weight white shirt and khaki slacks. A cameraman trailed them taking video of everything.

One of the officers called for silence in the room. As soon as the hubbub subsided, Fela spoke.

"This is Adrian Guerra. He speaks for the United Nations."

Guerra waved his arms. "Everything is being done to secure your release," he said. "Chief Fela has presented a list of demands that UN negotiators are reviewing urgently."

"How long will we be here?" demanded one man.

"You won't be here long at all if you're not careful, sir," Fela said, intimidating the man into silence.

"Listen, we've agreed to appoint a team of three hostages to help negotiate for your freedom. When I call your name, step forward and join me. Pamela Thatcher, Dave Clement and Claire McQuaid. Would you please join me immediately?"

Pamela nudged Claire. "I told you to trust him."

Across the room, a surprised Dave kissed Mel on the cheek as he got up. "Nothing stupid," she said into his ear. "Please."

"Nothing stupid," he said. "I love you."

As the group formed, Fela's eyes fell on Hamara Karanja. He grabbed Guerra's arm. "Wait a moment," he said.

Fela walked up to Hamara. "What a surprise," Fela said. "This must be my birthday."

"It's the birthday of Jesus, Fela," Hamara said, his face determined.

"Well, it's certainly Christmas. I seem to be getting everything I wanted. The country. And now you. I thought I would have to track you down."

"You stole my land, Fela. What else do you need?"

"I need all of my ancestor's enemies to die. Just like you, I'm sure. The Lokoma tribe has no place in my country."

"It's the 21st century, Fela. I thought you were more enlightened than all this."

"I'm not exactly someone who dwells in the light."

Fela walked up to one of the officers, whispered something and then left with the hostage negotiation team, Guerra and his bodyguards.

As the door closed, a soldier smashed the stock of his gun into Hamara's chest, knocking him to the floor. Other soldiers grabbed Ani and Mariama, tying ropes around their waists. They knocked out ceiling tiles and threw ropes over ceiling beams, hauling the women into the air upside down. Wrapping separate lengths of rope around one leg of Mariama and another around Ani's bad leg, they tied the other end of the ropes to Hamara's ankles. Pulling on the ropes, they hauled Hamara into the air upside down, all his weight pulling on Ani and Mariama. They then tied lengths of cord around each woman's neck and tied them to Hamara's neck. As they swung in the air, the already tight cords squeezed their windpipes making it difficult to breathe. The three, determined not to give the soldiers any more satisfaction than they had to, struggled to suppress their moans of pain, terror and rage.

Sara cried into Liv's shoulder. Mel held Emma in her arms, pressing her face against her breast so that the little girl would not see her parents' suffering. The soldiers waved the barrels of their weapons around the room, threatening anyone who protested their actions. The ropes slowly cut into the flesh of the women as the combined weight of themselves and Hamara caused them the ropes to constrict more and more tightly. Blood rushed to their heads and they gasped for breath. Each time they struggled, the ropes around their necks tightened further as well. Ani began to mumble the Our Father. Hamara and Mariama joined her.

The soldiers consulted. One walked up and jammed the stock of his rifle into Hamara's solar plexus.

"No prayers," he said as Hamara's body jerked, causing the three of them to swing on the ropes, making the cuts deeper.

"They'll die," Mel said.

"That's right, lady," said a rebel officer. "Want to join them?"

"Why are you doing this?"

Liv pulled her mother backward. "Shut up, mom," she said.

"Sit down, lady, and do as your girl says."

Mel sat. Liv held on to her, wondering if they were next. The soldiers taunted the Karanjas and the hostages in the room looked on helplessly as the minutes ticked by.

Kimtumani Hotel Parking Lot

Prodded by rebel gunbarrels, Dave followed Claire, Pamela and Adrian to a helicopter in the hotel parking lot. As he boarded, he heard tires skid and saw a military Humvee drive through a small rebel contingent by the lot's main entrance. He could barely hear the gunfire above the churn of the helicopter's rotors, but he saw bodies dropping.

"They're not waiting for negotiations," he shouted above the noise, but Pamela placed a hand on his shoulder and pushed him down into his seat.

"No, Pamela," he shouted as he jumped back up. A rebel soldier tried to shove him down, but he reached into his sport coat pocket and pulled out the Ruger, waving the man off.

"Dave, don't!" Claire yelled. "You don't understand what's going on here."

He ignored her and moved to the exit. A rebel at the door readied to fire on him, but Claire knocked the man's arm toward the sky and the shot went off harmlessly.

Dave jumped to the tarmac where a third soldier knocked him to the ground.

"No!" Pamela ordered the rebel as Dave rolled over to see a rifle barrel pointed toward his head. "Get me his damned peashooter."

The rebel tore the Ruger from Dave's hand.

"Now get aboard, Dave," Pamela commanded.

The soldiers helped him up and pushed him back into the chopper.

"Be patient, Dave," Pamela said, tugging on his coat sleeve.

As the aircraft started to slowly lift off, Dave leaned toward Pamela and shouted to be heard.

"It's my family, Pamela." He jumped eight feet to the pavement, falling on to his side as he hit and rolled. He looked up to see Claire and Pamela both restraining trigger happy rebels. The helicopter kept rising. He ran toward the hotel.

Ballroom

Inside the ballroom, blood filled the heads of Hamara, Ani and Mariama Karanja, their eyes bulging.

Suddenly, a young Nigerian businessman threw a shoe across the room. The clatter caught the rebel's attention. They ran to the corner. The man ran toward the door on the opposite side of the ballroom. His hand gripped the door handle when a crossfire of automatic weapons fire cut him down.

Liv, Mel, Sara and Emma cuddled more closely together. A rebel placed the barrel of his weapon in Ani's mouth.

"You be half dead anyway, lady. How about we take your head off to match your leg."

Ani tried to pull her head away, but the teenager shoved the barrel deeper into her throat until she could be heard choking. His finger moved toward the trigger.

"Let her alone, you coward!" Hamara shouted.

The barrel still in Ani's mouth, the boy turned toward Hamara. "What you goin' do, old man? Spit at me."

All of the rebels laughed.

"Maybe slow is better. Maybe we should start with matching legs."

The rebel withdrew the rifle and pulled a machete out of a scabbard on his waist. His face contorted in some deep-seated rage, he lifted the machete behind his shoulder and started its sweep forward.

Glass exploded through the long drapes on the far side of the room. The Abo soldier checked his swing, sparing Ani's other leg for now, his focus on a Leonean military vehicle that drove into the scattering crowd.

The rebels poured fire into the Humvee, surrounding it only to find it empty. Suddenly from behind the Humvee, a rain of automatic fire exploded. The rebels' bodies twitched in every direction, collapsing to the ground in bloody heaps.

More rebels burst in through the main door of the ballroom, but Jacob's boys already had turned their fire in that direction.

In the hotel lobby, Dave heard the gunfire in the ballroom. He followed a handful of rebel soldiers racing to help their comrades. As they arrived at the smoke filled doorway, bullets cut them down at Dave's feet. He flung himself to the floor. Sooty smoke from the AK-47s filled his lungs and the bitter, sulfuric taste of gunpowder coated his tongue as chunks of plaster pelted him. He threw his hands over his head to protect it. When the gunfire seemed to move in a different direction, he crawled toward the ballroom entrance. He looked into the room and saw his wife and daughter standing in the middle. He started to race into the room when the doorway around him erupted as the gunfire from within the room re-trained on it. Bullets flung two rebels into him like weighted ragdolls, knocking him back to the ground.

Hostages poured through the hole in the ballroom's wall of windows to get outside, but Liv and Mel stayed. Amidst flying bullets, they wrestled with knots to loosen the ropes on the Karanjas. Sara and Emma stood behind them crying and calling to their parents.

Jacob raced out of the smoke, grabbing one of the machetes from a dead rebel. He went to his parents. With the machete, he sliced the ropes as Mel and Liv slowly let their friends down to the floor.

"We have to get out of here," Jacob said. "There will be more of them."

"Who are you guys?" Liv asked looking down to her diminutive rescuer.

Jacob nodded at Hamara who unknotted the last of the ropes. "His son."

Hamara, his head still spinning from the ordeal, caught Jacob's eye in acknowledgment. Both tilted their heads slightly in that instant before they returned to the task at hand.

Putting the Clements and the rest of his family into the back of the Humvee, Jacob put his father in the driver's seat. "The boys are a little short to be very good drivers, Papa."

Hamara nodded, a proud smile crinkling his mouth. Jacob called to the other boys. They rolled grenades toward the now empty ballroom's doors and raced for the vehicle. As the grenades started to explode, Jacob shouted at Hamara who gunned the engine in reverse and bounced back out into the hotel parking lot.

"What about Dave?" Mel yelled to Hamara from her seat in the back.

"We'll come back for him."

The Humvee raced between parked cars and scrambling hostages. Mel and Liv looked out the window for Dave in the chaos. As the vehicle flew over a speed bump at the parking lot's main entrance, Hamara depressed the gas pedal even further, accelerating toward the causeway that would take them to the heart of the city where they could hide. As they raced down a hill with the causeway in sight, the thump-thump of a dozen military helicopters sounded overhead. As the helicopters descended, the noise grew deafening. The boys trained their rifles on them until they realized they were not after them. Instead, they flew past them in the direction of the hotel.

"Whose are they?" Hamara asked, his eyes fixed on the road as he accelerated the Humvee to over 80 miles per hour.

"Can't tell. Not government. Not American. And not Abo. It's a flag I've never seen."

Suddenly, two tanks pulled into the road at the causeway entrance, blocking it entirely. Hamara drove to the side of the road, only to see water straight ahead of him. He swerved back toward the center of the road and the vehicle tilted precariously to its left. Hamara struggled for control. He tried to turn away from the roadblock, but the steering wheel would not cooperate. When he had no other choice, he stomped on the brake, the Humvee skidding sideways toward the tanks, the squeal deafening.

CHAPTER 43

State House, Freetown
December 25, 3:52 p.m. GMT

Within hours, Joseph Mossoumou found himself in Sierra Leone's State House, occupying the President's offices. The President and his wife had been assassinated by the Abo in the family quarters of the building minutes earlier.

An armed escort brought Fela in.

"Happy Christmas, Chief," Mossoumou said. "Ah, that's right. You don't celebrate Christmas."

"But it has been a day for gifts," Fela said.

"I agree. The operation has been quite successful. Please, sit down."

"I need to stand, to pace. What we've done is incredible, the speed of execution never seen before."

"You're very proud."

"Not a shot fired. Except for a few executions for the benefit of the world at large."

Mossoumou opened the president's humidor on the desk. "What about the 15 men killed by boy soldiers in the ballroom. That was an unplanned wrinkle. How did that happen?"

"I still don't know where they came from. At first, I thought it was your troops so I ordered my men to stand down outside the ballroom. For a few moments, I thought you had betrayed us and were killing my men."

"Interesting that you would suspect that of your closest ally, Chief." Mossoumou reached into the humidor. "Cigar?" he asked.

"Yes, we deserve at least that, don't we?" Fela responded.

"I heard, too, that you decided to carry out a little bit of a personal vendetta in the ballroom."

"That's my own business. Nothing to do with us."

"It is when you endanger our operation for private entertainment. I'm told that the presence of the Lokoma chief brought the boy soldiers to you. Why was he there?"

Mossoumou walked toward the balcony that hovered over the gardens looking across to the ocean, the smoke from the battle clearing on the wings of a sea breeze that carried it into the mountains behind the city. Fela followed him.

"It's over, Joseph," Fela said, looking up to the bear-like Mossoumou. "It all worked out. I secured Lokoma for your troops."

"You're right. That worked out. The Lokoma plateau provided a viable place to land our troops and equipment. Freetown's airport is over 4 hours by land. Government troops would have seen us arrive and had more than enough time to react. Lokoma put us within 90 minutes on the road you paved for us. And no one even knew we'd arrived."

"So I'll expect rich reward."

"You have the Lokoma's bauxite reserves, Fela. And a few new diamond mines."

"And you have the country and its oil reserves onshore and offshore. After such a fine performance, I thought you might consider sharing some of the royalties."

Mossoumou stretched to his full height, expanding his enormous chest. "The personal vendetta in the hotel was not a fine performance. By no means."

"Joseph. Please. I just needed to clean up some loose ends. The opportunity presented itself."

Mossoumou relaxed his body. He sucked on his cigar. "The view is beautiful." he said, "Something about the taste of a cigar and a breath of salt air…"

He gestured for Fela to stand on the balcony next to him. "Can you taste it?" Mossoumou asked, pushing Fela gently toward the balcony rail.

"I only taste the cigar. A very good cigar."

"Take the cigar out and inhale more deeply," Joseph said.

Fela did as asked, sucking in a gulp of fresh sea air. The fragrance of the blooms in the palace garden were already overcoming the smell of gunfire. "It's the taste of a new future," Fela said, holding his cigar out to the side.

The heel of Mossoumou's left hand landed between the Abo chief's shoulder blades. He stumbled over the edge of the balcony rail, starting to right himself as he felt Mossoumou lift his ankles off the ground. He tried to reach back for the rail but he was too far out. He had fallen halfway to the gardens before he realized that Mossoumou's word could not be trusted after all.

CHAPTER 44

Kono Regional Hospital
December 25, 4:13 p.m. GMT

The district administrator, a local chief, insisted on a meeting with Fr. Jim and Mike before they left, but he had other priorities to attend to first. He posted guards around their helicopter to make sure they did not leave. When Mike expressed concern about getting the helicopter back to Freetown before dark, the man grew adamant about the courtesy of an hour's meeting. Late in the afternoon, he finally brought them to his office in a new one story concrete block structure that looked like it had been built from materials left over from the hospital construction. He sat them at a conference table adorned with an early supper of palm wine, yams and rice. After brief courtesies, the conversation turned to the discovery of the tainted vaccine. Neither brother would reveal their source so they explained that they only acted as friends of the pilot project, doing what was asked of them without question.

"Are you not head of security for the Aldrich Institute?" the administrator asked.

Surprised that the chief knew any details about him, Mike shifted in his chair, suddenly wary. "I am," Mike answered.

"So you should know how this vaccine problem was discovered."

"I'm not a scientist. The vaccine is a technical issue that I wouldn't understand under any circumstances."

The chief steepled his fingers and sat back in his chair, the only cushioned one in the room. "And what about you, Father? Do you know more about this?"

"No," Jim responded. "We learned of the problem and hurried down here to fix it. We didn't take time to ask why."

"Blind faith, Father?"

"More or less."

"In the same way that you insist on the rightness of your beliefs and ignore the Koran?"

Fr. Jim and Mike glanced at each other. "We should be goin' now," Jim said, rising from his chair.

"To where?" the chief asked.

"We're expected back in Freetown," Mike said.

"How will you get there?" The chief's words seemed more like an informative statement than a question.

"What's going on?" Mike demanded.

"Your helicopter is under armed guard. A precaution to keep away vandals. Unfortunately, the men guarding it do not know you and might mistake you for vandals."

Jim looked through the wooden slats of the window shutter. Soldiers stood at the entrance to the offices as well.

"Are we prisoners?" Jim asked.

"No, of course not. You're just being detained."

The chief's phone rang. He picked up and glared at the Farleys as he listened. Putting the phone down, he stood up.

"Please follow me," he said.

"Where?" Mike asked, but the chief did not respond.

Instead, the chief led them outside to where soldiers rushed up and attempted to arrest them. The brothers resisted, trying to push the soldiers away and run for the helicopter. Fists and rifle butts viciously knocked them to the ground. Mike's demand for an explanation met only angry cursing and name calling – in French.

Amidst the rain of blows, Jim found his instincts completely disabled. All his conspiracy thoughts about the Aldrich involved Mike, but Mike seemed as much a victim as him.

Mike continued to fight back, an arm breaking free long enough to grab one of the men's testicles. A rifle barrel swung like a baseball bat landed on the side of his neck, knocking him out. Hands jerked Jim's arms behind his back and clamped handcuffs on him. Two men rolled Mike over and placed cuffs on him as well.

Fingers dug in behind Jim's clavicle. Just before he passed out, his long dormant French helped him understand instructions from the group's apparent leader.

"Remember, she wants them well," he said. "She needs them alert later, capable of feeling everything."

CHAPTER 45

State House, Freetown
December 25, 5:05 pm GMT

Adrian Guerra, Pamela Thatcher and Claire McQuaid all sat at Joseph Mossoumou's newly seized conference table. In the center, Mossoumou had placed a small Christmas tree commandeered from another part of the building.

"Happy Christmas, my friends," he said. "We have much to celebrate. Everything went as well as we could possibly have hoped. "

"The choice of Christmas was brilliant, Mr. President," Guerra said. "No one anywhere was prepared to react, except us."

"It's not over," Pamela said.

"Why would you say that?" Mossoumou asked.

Pamela placed her wineglass down. "Caution, Joseph. The White House has not spoken officially on the matter yet. No one, not even your old classmate, the under-secretary, knew how far this would go. No doubt some of them are privately delighted at the prospect of a more business-oriented presence in Nigeria. Some of them, on the other hand, will focus on it as a violation of international law, an unprovoked attack on a peaceful nation."

"And, without real US objections to our invasion," Mossoumou interrupted, "the world will sit back just like it did when you invaded Iraq. We'll see a lot of posturing, but in the end, they'll all send emissaries to do business with me."

"With us," Pamela said.

"Of course."

"You cross me on this, Joseph, and you'll be dead in days."

"Pamela, you took months to track down Saddam and you controlled the country. What makes you think you'll be able to get to me?"

He laughed a deep, sinister laugh. Pamela turned in her chair, fixed her eyes on his. She did not move another muscle. "This is not Iraq," she said. "You don't know who your friends are. No one with the kind of power you now have ever does. Don't make the mistake of thinking you do."

Mossoumou looked at Adrian and Claire, their faces fixed in freeze frame, eyes wide. He puffed up his chest.

"Have you not seen all the dead bodies around here? Have you forgotten who holds the power now?"

Pamela sat back in her chair and shook her head. "Save the manhood check, Joseph. We both know what you need to do. You're not stupid. And neither am I."

Mossoumou pondered her briefly. He gulped down the contents of his wine glass. Claire had expected the large African to laugh, to defuse the situation. Pamela and Adrian knew better.

"You're right, Pamela," he said, "This new power's more intoxicating than this wine could ever be. I need old friends like you to keep me from self-destructing."

He stood and walked around the table, pouring more wine into each of his guest's glasses and then finally into his own. He raised his glass toward Pamela and nodded. She returned his nod.

"To the wonderful sweet crude in the Sierra Leone trench," he said. "And to a profitable partnership."

CHAPTER 46

Kimtumani Hotel
December 25, 6:57 p.m. GMT

The lights of Freetown glimmered on the dark bay along Lumley Beach, its small waves lapping gently at the shore along the short boardwalk below the hotel. Mother and daughter held hands as they pondered the scene, the cooling sea breeze refreshing after the muggy afternoon.

Alive, Mel thought. Barely. The Humvee had stopped within inches of one of the tanks as Hamara regained control of the vehicle near the bridge. The tanks and more than 20 men with large weapons directed them back to the hotel. One of them leaned into the passenger window and told them in French-accented English. "We are soldiers of the Middle African Democracy. We are for you. Go back."

At the hotel, the MAD soldiers herded them and the other hostages into the parking lot. Under guard and under intense tropical sun, the families watched as Mossoumou's troops rounded up or killed the last of the Abo and secured the hotel. As the sun began to set, a MAD soldier escorted a tattered man across the lot toward the hostages. Covered in drywall dust and blood, the man scanned the hostages. Liv saw him first.

"Daddy, here!"

She and Mel ran to him. As they drew closer, they hesitated, noticing the blood all over his clothes.

"Not mine," Dave said. "It's dry, but it might be wise to wait for me to change before we hug."

"Dear God," Mel said as she and Liv both threw their arms around him.

Jacob held tightly to Ani throughout, the killer of less than an hour earlier clinging like the little boy he was. Finally, the victorious soldiers announced the siege was over and waved the hostages back into the hotel. Jacob and his children's squad quickly disappeared and could not be found when Hamara, Mariama and Ani sought them out.

Now, just three hours later, Mel pondered the sea and said, "Thank God it's over."

"A very bizarre Christmas," Liv responded.

"Horrifying."

"Do you think they would have killed us, Mom?"

Mel nodded affirmatively.

"Why?"

"Those boys didn't need a reason, sweetheart."

Liv remembered the noise, the confusion of people running in all directions. The smell of gunfire. And how suddenly people went from alive to dead.

"Jacob's not my little pen pal project anymore. He's a ten year old grown up. He saved his father and mothers. Maybe more than that."

Mel remembered the small wide-eyed boy that led a band of other wide-eyed little boys. So surreal, she thought. "Their guns were bigger than they were," she said.

"Do you think they've killed a lot?"

"I think so."

"Are they like the rebels? Would they kill without a reason?"

Mel, feeling numb from the day's trauma, pondered the water as it lapped on to a narrow strip of sand at the edge of the boardwalk. The steady pulsing of the tiny waves calmed her.

"Probably with very little reason," she answered. "I think people faced with the constant threat of violence can be very dangerous."

Mel reached down and slipped off her sandals. She stepped down on the sand strip and let the cool wavelets submerse her feet with each new inflow. Liv studied the water from the boardwalk. It looked dark, forbidding.

"Do you think little Sara will be okay?" Liv asked from her perch on the boardwalk.

Mel looked over her shoulder. "Put your feet in the water. It feels good."

"What if there's something in it?"

Mel smiled. "Liv, you're dealing with AIDS every day. What could there possibly be in the Atlantic Ocean that even compares to what you already face?"

Liv shrugged, kicked off her sandals and stepped down. She cringed as she stepped into the water. The wet sand felt soft. The water cooled her feet.

"Mmm. This is nice."

They enjoyed the next few moments silently, walking slowly along the narrow beach.

"You did a very selfless thing for Sara," Mel said.

"She looked a lot worse than I feel."

"Your medicine may be her only and best hope. I just wish…" Her voice trailed off.

"I'd kept it for myself?" Liv filled in the blanks.

"Maybe. I love you. I'm scared to death that something will happen to you."

"We'll be home in a few days and I'll get it refilled. A few days won't kill me."

"Sweetie, your immune system is very fragile. These few days could be costly to you."

"I knew that when I gave it to her. To stand by and just let her die would be too horrible for words. She seems so helpless."

Mel pulled Liv close and placed an arm around her waist. Liv tilted her head, resting it on her mother's shoulder.

"You're very precious, sweetheart. God really blessed us when you were born."

Liv said a short prayer in her head, praying for a miracle for Sara Karanja.

CHAPTER 47

Kono District, Sierra Leone
December 25, 7:25 p.m.

Firelight reflected off the mud-brick buildings that surrounded the small village square. The flickering orange light cast silhouettes of two men tied to posts staked in the ground. Djembe drums beat the steady ceremonial rhythm of execution.

Hands and feet tied behind him and the pole, Fr. Jim licked the sweat that dripped over his lip, a futile effort to quench his thirst. The scorching heat of the bonfire just a few feet away combined with the jungle humidity to squeeze the fluids from his body. His hands were tied to a peg high up on the pole so that he could barely keep the balls of his bound feet on the ground.

"Mike," he croaked.

Only ten feet away and strung up just like his younger brother, Mike had been stripped of all clothing and beaten black, blue and bloody, strips of skin ripped off by the spiked clubs used – just like Jim. Whenever exhaustion caused their footing to slip, their bodies sagged, scraping the raw skin of their backs against the exposed nails hammered halfway through the posts from the other side. The excruciating agony of the beating refreshed itself each time that happened.

Mike appeared to be half-conscious, unresponsive to Jim's calls. Somehow, Jim remained fully alert, only wishing he could drift out of consciousness to make the searing pain go away. His shoulders, back and calves strained and cramped from the effort to keep his body from rocking back into the nails on the post. As long as he could maintain just a little muscle tension, he could tilt away from the poles, keeping the pain almost tolerable. But each time he slipped, the excruciating agony resumed.

"Mike," he croaked again.

Still, Mike did not respond, his eyes closed. Jim prayed intermittently trying to mumble a rosary, but his thoughts kept drifting. Who was the woman the captors had referred to repeatedly? "She" wanted them alive – "for now." He tried to recall who in Sierra Leone might have wanted to do him so much harm. But the set-up? The vaccine? Someone had made them think they were helping. Someone who wanted to frame them – and the Church. Jennifer? Had she known? If Jennifer had been involved, then certainly Claire had something to do with it.

What about Sheila's files? Had the Vatican misread them? Or had they been planted? At a break between the meetings, Mike confessed that Claire had confided that she knew Jim continued to serve the Vatican all along, that Pamela had a plant in Christus that had actually managed the scheme from the inside.

Yet Mike hung here beside him. If Claire or the lab were involved, they had betrayed Mike as well.

Jim drifted back, his flayed backside bouncing off the pole. He started to scream but re-formed the effort into a screeching prayer as his feet scrambled to regain their footing.

"Our Father, who art in heaven, hallowed be thy name, thy…"

His voice rose and fell as the long howl of pain came out as words – words he did not have to prepare with his pummeled brain. On a parallel mental path, he thanked God for rote prayer. Never had he imagined this benefit.

Finally, back on the balls of his feet and pushing away from the post, the pain moderating, Jim, head hanging down, watched long shadows reach across the ground toward him. A soft hand touched his face, lifting it by the chin.

"Oh, thank God," Jim gasped.

Claire McQuaid smiled a small smile and held his eyes in hers. "God is just," she whispered.

Jim saw several soldiers come up behind her. "Look out!" he warned, but the soldiers stepped past Claire.

She stepped backward, joining Pamela Thatcher, the two standing to the side of the bonfire, arms folded. The soldiers wrapped rope around the chests of both men, yanking them into upright positions on the stakes, the spikes now lined up and pressing into them. As Mike and Jim choked back screams, their captors wrapped another shorter rope around their necks, pulled up such that the men were forced to gaze straight ahead.

Claire stood before them. "So, boys, ya never knew, did ya?" Claire spoke in an Irish brogue.

Jim thought she came to help. Why was she mocking them?

"I've been with ya all along," she continued. "Your worst nightmare, ya Taig bastards."

Jim had not heard "Taig" since he was a boy in Belfast. The Protestants used it to insult Catholics.

"What the bloody hell are ya doin'?" Mike managed to gasp. "Help us, for God's sake."

"No Pope here, boys. I'm helpin' by doin' the Lord's own work, sendin' ya off with the banshee to hell."

Dressed in a pair of shorts that reached to her knees and a long-sleeved khaki shirt, buttoned at the wrists, Claire unbuttoned the wrists. She moved her hands up to her collar. She unbuttoned the top button and continued until the shirt hung open. She pressed a clasp and dropped her bra.

As she dropped her shirt off her shoulders and to the ground, both men flinched.

"Not pretty, is it, boys?"

Claire's upper body had extensive burn scars and grafts, deforming her breasts into odd lumpy protuberances without nipples. One side of her stomach had a large crater in it with an irregular bulge just above her waist line. She had no belly button.

The djembe drums beat louder.

She unzipped and dropped her shorts, revealing further scarring on her hips, an ugly burn scar where pubic hair should have grown.

Standing before them as naked as they, she walked first up to Mike.

"Look at me, Mike Farley. Memorize every inch." She pressed down on the top of his head, forcing his chin against the restraining rope to make him look down. She stepped back again.

"Are your memories workin' yet?"

"Dear God," Jim mumbled. Suddenly, he knew. The emerald eyes. Of course. Her accent did not mock them. She grew up with that brogue. Brilliant, he thought. So brilliant. And so right.

> *The girl looked toward Sean just before ducking into the car. Her mouth twitched into a small smile; later, his memory would struggle to separate fact from illusion, feeling the flash of her glowing emerald eyes seek out his soul in that split second, pulling him into her.*
>
> *Frantic, he squirmed to break his brother's determined hold.*

"The car bomb," he said. "Joanne. Joanne Paisley."

Claire reached a hand toward Jim's face, gently caressing his cheek with her fingertips. "Good lad," she said.

"What kind of hell have we put you through?" Jim said. "My contrition could never be enough."

She dug her nails in, slowly scraping skin off his cheek. He winced, but did not try to turn his head away; instead he looked straight into her emerald eyes, just as he had done decades earlier. This time, he saw only anguish and rage in them. In his mind, he thanked God for giving him this chance to be offered as retribution, his full penance here at last. He reminded himself that Christ suffered worse for doing nothing, for the sins of Jim and all of mankind. He prayed for Claire, that she might finally achieve peace in her soul, that God forgive her for her violence.

Claire turned toward Mike. He strained at his bonds, but his captors knew their business; every move he made caused him more pain. As Claire stepped in front of him, she saw recognition in his eyes, recognition of the pretty, freckle-faced, strawberry blonde teenager.

"Figure it out, Mike?" she asked, her face now inches from his.

"Bitch," he spat. "That's thirty years ago. You're fuckin' crazy."

She jammed her knee into his groin, air exploding from his mouth just before a scream of agony escaped. She stepped back to watch him squirm.

"You're hideous!" he shouted. "With all your money, could you not even try to fix those damned scars?"

Claire put her nose within inches of his. "Go ahead. Spit at me again. Or maybe you should be smart and conserve every last drop of water in your body."

She placed a hand on his mid-section and shoved him back against the nails. He screamed. She did not release the pressure of her hand for several seconds. When she did, he gasped, struggling to get words out.

"You've... left nothin' of yourself... just to hurt us," he said. "It makes no sense."

"Not just to hurt you. To get perfect justice. Justice worthy of my family. I swore in the hospital that I would carry the reminders of my mother and my sister until I avenged them. Weeks turned to months. Months to years. Years became decades. Decades to develop the most appropriate retribution I could imagine."

Pamela stepped up to Claire, putting a robe over her shoulders and covering her wounds.

Claire shoved Mike back into the nails one more time. She lifted a leg and kicked him full force in the groin, the nails penetrating deeply into him this time.

Mike's wails cut straight to Jim's heart. "Why you, Pamela?" Jim asked, blinking sweat back from his eyes.

Thatcher stepped closer. Mike's screaming tapered to whimpers.

"Claire's mother was my niece," Pamela said. "You killed her and her baby. And nearly destroyed the life of my great niece."

"And you waited this long for revenge?" Jim asked.

"No. I lived to see Claire whole again. For justice for her, Father. From you and the Church that gave you sanctuary."

"The Church did you no harm."

"It gave you a hiding place. It denied closure to my niece. So that it could feel good about itself and protect killers. Forgiving when it wasn't its place to forgive. The Church had no right. That's unforgivable sin."

"You're wrong. The Church merely offered compassion."

"It sinned against my family. It will pay for its sin."

"Like this?"

"Here's what you've done for your Church, Father. Because of you, the world will see that a group deep within the Church plotted mass murder against the Islamic people. They even used an undercover priest experienced in terror and knowledgeable about Sierra Leone. That's why they sent you to the Aldrich lab in the first place."

"They'll know none of that's true."

"The winners write history, Father Jim. Or should I call you Sean now that your secret's out."

Claire stepped into Pamela's arms.

"Please forgive me," Jim said. "For your soul's sake."

"To save your life, Sean?" Claire said.

"No, you're wrong about the Church. I forgive you for what you're doing to me. I understand it. But for your sake, forgive my brother and I so that you might have peace."

An unexpected tear dripped down Claire's cheek. "I may never have peace," she said. "But I can find companionship in my suffering." She looked up to Pamela. "I'm done here," she said.

"I forgive you," Jim said one last time, resigned to the imminence of death.

Claire exploded. "Forgive me?!" she shouted, "You have no right to forgive me!"

She flung off her robe and began swinging wildly at him, pummeling his face and upper body. Pamela watched, her eyes wide. But she made no move to stop her niece.

As the blows accumulated, Jim's vision blurred and then blood dripped into his eyes, partially blinding him. I'm ready, Lord, he thought.

Then Claire stopped. Jim blinked open a clear spot in one of his eyes. Pamela had finally pulled her back.

"The plan," Pamela reminded her. Pamela studied both men, making sure they still could hear her.

"Now, boys. The moment we've all been waiting for. All this has been prologue. To balance the ledger, the soldiers here will carry out your sentence. One of you will receive the burns of my niece, Claire's mother. And the other will be blessed with the burns of Claire."

Two men with welding torches appeared beside Pamela and Claire. Jim prayed for strength. Mike struggled with his bonds.

"These men do excellent work. They've studied photos of both women. They intend to be precise. One of their primary objectives is to keep you conscious as long as possible, to pause from time to time to let you contemplate the pain and the smell of your burning flesh."

"Ya damn bitch! Both o' ya! You'll burn in hell for this!" Mike shouted.

Pamela turned to Claire. "Have you decided whether you want to stay and watch?"

Claire took a long look at the two helpless men. "You're angry and you're frightened," she said to Mike. "I like that."

She turned to Jim and held his eyes. "I don't like you. You should be as angry and frightened as him. But you pretend to be peaceful. You piss me off." She back-handed him across the face. He began mumbling an Our Father, his eyes looking upward, no longer focused on Claire.

A man appeared beside her with a digital video camera.

"No, Aunt Pamela. I won't stay and watch. I'll review the video later." Holding the robe closed, she scooped up her clothes. The two walked into the night beyond the bonfire. As they did, they heard the whoosh of the welding torches lighting. They heard cursing and shouting from Mike. And then screams, loud high-pitched screams.

CHAPTER 48

Kimtumani Hotel
December 25, 7:54 p.m.

The sea breeze brushed over Jennifer's skin, soothing her as it cooled the moist droplets of sweat induced by the evening's humidity. She kicked off her sandals, their thongs cutting painfully into the abrasions between her toes. Barefoot on the thick grass beside the hotel pool, she slid her feet through the silken green carpet.

Approaching the edge of the pool, she looked around and saw no one in the darkness. Unwrapping her skirt, she dropped it on a webbed lounge chair. Careful not to rip it, she wriggled her blouse over her sweaty body, finally achieving liberation as she peeled it over her head. In a lacy, teal thong and a black dress bra, she sat on the edge of the pool and slipped into the clear water. Putting her hands at her side, she pointed her toes, sinking slowly to the bottom. Eyes open, she witnessed the emptiness of the water, moonlight shimmering along its surface, reflecting small waves of light against the submerged white plaster walls.

Surfacing, she pushed the water off her face and shoved her wet hair back in one move. Her feet slowly pedaling, she bobbed on the surface, arms making barely perceptible circles in the water to keep her buoyant.

But this baptism did not purify her; innocent blood clung to her soul. She had seen the fruit of her work in the false hope on the face of Sara Karanja, in the anguished concern of Mariama, in Liv's misplaced trust.

All this to save lives, she thought. All this and, so far, only more death.

She stopped her pedaling, again dropping her arms to her side. As her toes touched bottom, her open eyes burning slightly from chlorine, she pondered not re-surfacing. Pondered the peacefulness of an underwater tomb. Pondered the urge to hurt herself. The anger with herself. The rage exploded from her mouth and nose in a sudden bubble of air. Within seconds, her lungs ached for breath. Mild panic replaced the rage.

With a series of flutter kicks, she reached for the surface. The pure air atop the water quickly relieved the pain in her lungs. She rolled on to her back and floated slowly under the night sky, barely perceptible motions of her arms and legs keeping her afloat.

She thought about Liv. Jennifer thought she could control the girl's father, suck him into her web, especially after she detected the tension between Dave and Mel. She did little things to aggravate the tension, like the pinhole camera in Liv's closet that she used to stalk the girl and make her parents think she hallucinated. Cruel, but kind of funny – until she came to know Liv, until her own heart ached at the sight of the cumulative pain she inflicted on the teen. She did other things, too, like intercepting Dave on his way out of the office to make sure he was late getting home or to a school event. She designed it all to pump up the tension between Mel and Dave, and to ultimately cause him to seek inappropriate comfort with her.

Now, Jennifer recognized that wishful thinking may have influenced her decision-making. Clement's vulnerability proved to be neither money nor infidelity with a woman 15 years younger. He wanted the money, she felt certain of that, but day in and day out, he demonstrated principle in dealing with financial temptation. She arranged for three suppliers to suggest kickbacks to Dave, substantial kickbacks. He spurned them every time, cutting one off cold.

Even after that, she remained confident that she would entice him into an affair. After Mel threw him out of the house, Jennifer thought he surely would latch on to the bait, but he persisted in rejecting her. It not only rattled her confidence; it hurt her – more deeply than she could have imagined. She came to see what lay beneath the man's nascent love handles and slightly receding forehead, a man deeply in love with his wife and daughter, the kind of man for whom Jennifer herself longed.

In that strength she so admired, Jennifer identified his greatest vulnerability. Discussions with Claire supported Jennifer's conclusion that she had no choice. Eldridge engineered the infected micro-dart. Jennifer planted it with an injector disguised as an expensive ballpoint pen while seated beside Liv at the company's Fourth of July picnic. Liv swatted at her leg when it happened, the sting slight and similar to that of a mosquito or a small housefly.

That strategy bound the insurance policy they needed to keep Dave in check. It exponentially escalated the tension in a fragile Clement household, the HIV diagnosis clearly a player in Mel's decision to show her husband the door. It opened the door for Dave to turn to Jennifer for solace. It also enhanced his hunger for a big pay day through the IPO, sharpening his focus on the mission and making him more pliable for Claire. Jennifer had no qualms about her action. Standard HIV in the form she gave Liv with the dart six months earlier was a burden, but very treatable.

Then came Mike's visit at the Clements' home after she had been fired by Prodeus. She had been alone that day and thought he had come to kill her when she saw him at the Clements' front door. Instead, he embraced her and confided the story about Eldridge plotting with the Vatican to overthrow Claire, a story she later found out to be a lie designed to somehow test her and control her. Mike told her that orders to kill Sheila came from Eldridge, not Claire. He said the stakes had escalated and Claire needed to be able to trust her. Jennifer needed to prove herself trustworthy and she needed to follow orders unblinkingly, including Claire's orders to implement the final Dave solution. She had no choice. If she did not do it, Claire would find another way to do it anyway. And Jennifer would lose her protection against

Eldridge and his Vatican cohorts. The contingency for dealing with Dave had been out there all along, but Jennifer never expected it to be necessary. She had been nervous, expecting the Clements to catch on at any time. It amazed her how effectively the web of deceit worked.

When she cut Liv's arm while they did pull-ups that night in the garage, she had been particularly anxious. She had never deliberately hurt anyone in that way before. But Liv trustingly let Jennifer pour a so-called healing gel into her fresh wound. Jennifer slept like a baby that night, glad to have pulled off the assignment undetected.

But Liv kept surprising her. Her view of the teenager changed from a spoiled brat to a good kid, facing a tough problem – a problem created by Jennifer and the Aldrich - in a remarkably unselfish way. Then, during the hostage siege, she watched from across the room as Liv passed the Fuzeon to the little refugee girl. Jennifer felt certain that Liv knew she placed her own life in jeopardy by doing so. Liv had no way of knowing the futility of the gesture. She did not know that only the Aldrich vaccine, a drug that remained incomplete, could keep Sara Karanja alive past the spring. Jennifer could formulate it. The design existed. Since the Aldrich created the mutation, it fundamentally had launched a controlled experiment, one that Jennifer could take to its next planned step. With a lot of intense work. With just a little luck.

She envisioned masses of Africans, Asians and Latin Americans, faces contorted in pain and pleading. Millions and millions that she once thought would be thankful for her efforts to save them. Now, instead, many of them would die early because of the plan's detours.

In Liv, she could save one person, one person she could touch directly. So much better than anonymous millions anyway. If she could do it.

Back from their walk, Liv and Mel joined a cleaned up Dave in the hotel bar recounting the day's events, the horrors and the ultimate triumph. The restaurant did not open tonight in the aftermath of the battle, its windows shattered, so the family made due with bar food.

Other patrons had tuned the big screen TV to CNN's coverage of the events in Freetown. Report by report, the bigger picture came into focus. Mossoumou's troops quickly descended on Freetown in response to a desperate call from Sierra Leone's president just before his assassination. Fearful that the rebellion would throw the country back into the darkness of the 1990s and early 2000s, both the United States and Great Britain quickly sanctioned the intervention, the US President disrupting his Christmas to make a brief announcement..

Only hours later, without US sanction, MAD invaded Lagos, Nigeria. Mossoumou's troops quickly seized the city while the main force of the Nigerian army fought both Chadian invaders and Islamic rebels 900 miles to the northeast. The Mossoumou regime called the Lagos incursion a police action requested by the Nigerian government as Boko Haram insurgents threatened to overpower the oil port's remaining defenders. Nigerian officials could not be reached for comment.

In the United States, Under Secretary of State for African Affairs Tony Wayne briefed the press, reassuring the world that Mossoumou would only act in the interests of West Africa and that the US would not overreact to the Nigerian crisis. The CNN commentator noted that Wayne and Mossoumou had been college classmates.

Mossoumou himself remained silent, according to the reporter, but tweets and other social network reports coming out of the region showed the MAD troops had arrived none too soon.

Dave noted that carefully worded press releases came out every few hours. He guessed that the social network commentary came from dedicated teams delivering pre-planned messages, all timed like exquisite choreography to modulate world reaction to hour-by-hour events. He wondered if he would have been cynical enough to recognize that just a day earlier.

After feeding its guests flat sodas, burnt hamburgers and stale buns, the hotel, in recognition of the day's hardships and to show some respect to Christmas, comp'd ice cream desserts to the Clements. The ice cream's still slightly soupy consistency showed that it had melted almost completely during a three hour power outage that shut down the freezers during the midst of the invasion.

As the family began to enjoy the sweet coldness of the dessert, CNN issued a fresh bulletin: "Troops of the Middle African Democracy entered Sierra Leone's Kono district this evening to quell an uprising. Kono is in the southeastern part of the country along the Liberian border. US Under-Secretary of State Anthony Wayne said that MAD is doing what needs to be done to avoid a border rupture with already troubled Liberia. Simultaneously, Wayne said the US has received assurances from President Mossoumou that the Nigerian incursion will be short-lived.

"The Kono uprising erupted spontaneously in the primarily Islamic region when local officials discovered what they claim was an attempt by two Vatican terrorists to taint the supply of a malaria vaccine. Officials in Kono report the terrorists altered the vaccine to cause spontaneous mass abortions and infertility in women.

"One of the men is a priest, Fr. James Reilly, a missionary to the region until his alleged kidnapping there four months ago. The other is Mike Farley, a known IRA terrorist. Both are thought to be in custody in Kono, although other reports indicate they may have been killed fleeing capture."

"Dad?" Liv said in a gasp, her eyes glued to the screen. Mel grabbed Dave's hand. All three unconsciously held their breath.

"According to a Vatican insider, James Reilly is an alias for Sean Farley, Mike Farley's younger brother. Sean, himself an IRA terrorist wanted by the British government for thirty years, is part of a group calling itself Senior Vindex or The Lord's Avengers."

Puzzle pieces clicked in place in Dave's head as CNN's report shifted to Rome where Monsignor Stanley Zabinski stood under camera lights on Rome's side of the border outside Vatican Square. Armed carabinieri stood vigilantly in the background.

"I walked out of the Vatican today, never to return," Zabinski said. "The horror attempted today in Sierra Leone is part of a systemic arrogance that puts the Church above the law, both that of man and that of our Lord. For two years now, I have been on the board of Christus. When recruited, I thought we deployed non-violent, but militant, missionaries. In the last few weeks, I have discovered that I have unknowingly been part of a compartmentalized system of covert and violent activities designed to fight the perceived enemies of the Church through means that violate the very core tenets of Christ's teaching. This system is Senior Vindex."

"Are you concerned for your own safety, Monsignor," a young woman reporter asked.

"What becomes of me is in the Lord's hands. I am prepared to be martyred for the true faith. That said, I am grateful that the Italian government has seen fit to provide protection and, soon, a place of hiding."

The reporter turned to the camera. "There you have it," she said. "An astounding turn of events with confirmation from a high ranking Vatican official, a turn that may shake the very foundations of western culture."

The screen returned to the CNN studios in Atlanta where a white-haired veteran manned the anchor desk. "Thank you, Eleanor Ragusa, in Rome. Reaction is pouring in from throughout the world. Demonstrations throughout the Islamic world are..."

Dave drummed his fingers on the table.

"So Jennifer was right," Mel said. "The Vatican has been up to no good."

"I don't think so. I don't think so at all. And Father Jim would definitely not be the delivery boy of any kind of evil. Something's very wrong with all this. And I'll bet Jennifer knows that. I have to find her."

"What..." Mel started, but Dave rose from his chair and headed for the hotel lobby.

"I'll be back," he called, "Whatever you do, don't leave."

"Where are you..."

He disappeared around the corner into the lobby.

Determined to demonstrate confidence with his request, Dave approached the front desk with jaw set and a firm step.

"Father Reilly's mail, please."

The desk clerk, neat and well-dressed in dark coat and tie in a lobby covered in dust from the day's action, smiled broadly. "May I see your ID, Father?" he asked.

"I'm not Father Reilly. I'm his friend. He asked me to get his mail."

"We can only give Father Reilly's mail to him."

The young man either had not seen the news or had not connected Jim Reilly, hotel guest, with the Kono events.

"Father is nursing a sprained ankle. He tripped while running from the gunmen."

"One moment, sir." The clerk picked up a phone and dialed. He held it to his ear. "There is no answer in his room, sir."

"He's probably in the bathtub soaking his ankle. Just let me have his mail. I'll have him call you when I get up there."

"I can't do that, sir."

Dave tried to remain patient with the young man's polite intractability. "You know…" He looked at the man's name tag. "…Samin, it's not wise to disappoint a priest. The whole religion and spirits thing and all."

If he did not feel silly enough when he heard himself say it, Samin locked it in for him. "I try not to disappoint, sir. Most of all, our guests would be disappointed if I gave their mail out to just anyone."

Desperate times, thought Dave. He had seen it done on television; he slid a twenty dollar bill across the desk. Samin slid it back.

"Sir, I have not helped you. It would be wrong to accept a tip."

"More?"

"Sir, my employer and my guests place a trust in me. I will not violate it."

Dave felt completely belittled by Samin's principle. "I'm sorry, Samin. You're right."

Dave shoved the twenty back in his pocket. Heading for the elevator, he devised a new course of action. First he went to his room where he grabbed a hand towel. Arriving at Jim's room three doors down the hall, he calculated the width of the framing on the side of the threshold. He eyed a spot on the wall that he felt certain would be outside the framing and, in turn, hollow. He wrapped the towel around his hand. Taking a deep breath, he smashed his hand into the wall, cracking the drywall. He hit it again and the drywall split open.

He quickly stood in front of the hole, hiding it behind him, waiting for someone to come out to see what the noise was. No one came. After a moment, he bent down and looked into the space. He had clearance for four inches to the drywall on the other side. He swung again, completing the hole. Reaching through the gap, he twisted the doorknob and let himself in.

He closed the door behind him. Walking to the night table, he picked up the phone. He rehearsed before dialing. "'ello, this is Fatha Reilly in room t'ree-oh-t'ree," he said. God, that's terrible, he thought. Half cockney and half Irish with a touch of middle America. Samin would never fall for that.

"Hello, could ya send me mail up to me room." Still sucks, he thought. He put the phone down. He needed a few minutes of rehearsal. He tried to remember the priest's lilt.

Then, he saw it. He had walked over it when he came in the door. Covered in drywall dust, a thin yellow and red DHL envelope sat just inside the door, probably delivered before all hell broke loose earlier in the day. He grabbed the cardboard envelope and sat on the edge of the bed. He unzipped the cardboard. Inside, he found a single page note from the priest in Nova Scotia and a thumb-sized flash drive.

The letter said the flash drive contained password protected files the Canadian priest had copied from Conger's phone but had been unable to open. The flash drive also contained two unencrypted files, one a note from Conger that said the encrypted files contained critical information that could not be shared with American authorities. The other simply said, "Check the ink." It made no sense to Dave.

Dave pondered the flash drive in his hand, a key with files he could not open. Not a key at all. What the hell am I supposed to do with this? he thought.

If it was about the Aldrich, where would Evan have found the information? Not Claire. Not Jennifer? Sheila? Sheila. Of course.

He wondered what the "ink" note was about. Something stray that Evan had written? Then why would he include it in the folder with the files he wanted delivered. Did ink have something to do with it.

Dave hurried to his room and opened his computer, shoving the flash drive into one of the laptop's USB ports. He clicked on one of the files and a login box appeared on the screen asking for a password.

Dave did not know where to start. He typed in variations on Evan Conger's name and the names of Evan's wife and children. He did not know any of their birthdays, but was able to find Evan's in Wikipedia. Still no solution. He started trying combinations with the word "ink". Nothing.

Then it occurred to him that the password might not be Evan's, that it might be Sheila's. So he typed variations of her name in. Then, he tried variations of her name with the word "ink". He typed, "SheilaInk." Then, it dawned on him. Ink. Sheila. The tattoo!

Dave typed.

Rocky 28714

An "incorrect password" message flashed on the screen.

"It has to be it," he said into the empty hotel room.

RO 28714

He typed it like an old-time phone number. Still no luck. Thinking of the priest in Kono and the betrayal by Claire, Dave slammed his fist on the desk.

He inhaled deeply to calm himself.

"Maybe it's not a phone number," he said. He grabbed a message pad and pen from the nightstand. He wrote down the full tattoo. Then he wrote the numbers individually.

2-8-7-1-4

Nothing, he thought. Next, he grouped them in different ways.

28 71 4

2 87 14

Then he saw it. Fourteen! Route 14, he thought. "And Route 287," he said out loud. 287 and 14: the two highways that came together at the foot of the Poudre Canyon. Where Liv bought gas on her way to the lab.

"It has a name. What the hell's the name of that place?"

He closed his eyes, envisioned it. "Ted's place!" he said. He typed it in without punctuation.

tedsplace

The contents of the flash drive appeared on the screen.

"Brilliant, Sheila!" he said.

The first of several files opened. It was empty. He opened the next of six files. Only one had content. He quickly scanned it and then found himself shocked and mesmerized, reading more carefully as he struggled with disbelief. The file described a plan by the Aldrich to deliver a Trojan horse malaria vaccine, designed to both immunize against malaria and cause mutation of the HIV in existing victims. The mutation accelerated the onset of full-blown AIDS, typically within 60 days. It was fundamentally immune to known HIV medications because of its virulence and means of mutation. Once full-blown AIDS set in, victims could be expected to die within three to six months.

There's been no discovery of a new mutation, thought Dave. The bastards created it. And he had helped them deploy it.

He read more.

Sheila had cooperated in the development because no one was expected to die from the mutation. The mutation, in fact, had been designed to create a pathway within HIV cells to destroy them. The Aldrich scientists claimed their mutation would not mutate any further, causing their proposed cure to be applicable on an ongoing basis. Moreover, the shorter incubation period and the very virulence of the mutated disease minimized the further spread of the contagion. Victims either received the cure or they died. They did not linger for years, much of it in a healthy state unaware of their HIV positive status, spreading the disease to others.

Dave lay back in the bed. "Wow," he said to the ceiling. "So there's a cure. This is good, damn good."

The report went on to explain that the real problem expected with the cure lie in the first step. In order to be cured of AIDS, patients had to first receive the mutation, putting them at greater short-term risk for death. Using the Prodeus portable DNA analyzer, the scientists expected to quickly identify any unique amino acid formulations in the genetic properties of the patients, thus finalizing the CEM15-D formula designed uniquely for each major group of patients. The Aldrich expected there to be no more than eight major amino acid profiles among patient groups.

But that's where both Sheila and Conger had an enormous problem with the Aldrich tactics. The subtleties of those formulations could not be known until a large enough sample of mutation victims had been analyzed.

Sheila argued that the implementations should be on terminal patients and only after she advanced the designer chemistry to a point where the final drug design could be completed within a few months if not weeks. Claire McQuaid, on the other hand, insisted that the program go ahead immediately and be done across a significant population in West Africa, delivered as a Trojan horse within the malaria vaccine.

Dave surmised that Sheila must have confirmed this plan and passed the information to Evan Conger. Then, within weeks, both she and Conger died violently.

Dave blew the air out of his lungs and dropped his hands to his side. It started to add up. It explained why the Aldrich wrote the PDNA firmware to falsely identify every HIV victim as susceptible to the malaria vaccine. It ensured that everyone who was HIV-positive received the vaccine and, hidden inside it, the more deadly HIV mutation.

And there was the announcement by Claire McQuaid and Pamela Thatcher that a new HIV mutation had been discovered in West Africa. A disguise for their real work. If they controlled the data at every level, they could indeed convince the world a new mutation had been discovered. And since they designed it, they were likely to reap the profits of discovering the "cure" for it. Huge profits. Billions of dollars. Once successful in Sierra Leone, the idea of deliberately giving people the mutation to enable the cure would cause the Aldrich vaccine to become ubiquitous, stopping the epidemic cold.

Except that, by Dave's rapid estimate, hundreds of thousands could easily die from the mutation before the introduction of the cure. Moreover, not every nation could afford enough PDNAs to do the amino acid profile to identify the appropriate formulation for its citizens. And the drug would have to be expensive. If the mutation spread worldwide, not unlikely premised on what Dave knew of gene flow, tens of millions could die within a few years instead of a decade. Enormous wealth and infrastructure would be needed to fight it.

In its misguided plan to sacrifice the current generation to protect future generations, the cure amounted to genocide.

The idea of deploying tens of thousands of PDNAs within those two years rushed through Dave's thoughts. Prodeus could easily be worth billions of dollars, if not tens of billions. With five percent of the company stock, Dave could easily look at a personal net worth approaching one billion dollars after a public offering of the company's stock. That would certainly take care of any future worries –

Except for Liv's HIV, the mystery of its source still unsolved.

But it could be fixed now. Once the Aldrich finished the designer cures, Liv could be given the mutation and her HIV wiped out. She would be well. And she would be among the first to get it. When Claire said she thought she might be able to help Liv, it was not idle speculation. She knew she could.

The people in Sierra Leone would give up their lives, but in a great cause, perhaps one of the greatest in history. And only existing HIV victims would be lost, people ultimately doomed in any event. Unlike the US where HIV medications were readily available, the people of sub–Saharan Africa suffered constantly with HIV, most living with no hope. Misery filled their lingering deaths and drained their families spiritually and financially.

If the Aldrich really could turn the designer cures around quickly, the long-term death toll would be dramatically mitigated and AIDS nearly eradicated within a few years. What could be wrong with that?

Lots, he thought. It came down to playing God. But leadership amounted to playing God sometimes. He thought about Middleton and his engineers. Maybe Claire did not have them murdered. Maybe… "No," he said out loud. "Claire had them killed. And Ed Hepp facilitated it somehow."

He stood up. He looked through the window across the bay to the lights of Freetown. The city looked beautiful in the darkness, the reflection of its lights shimmering in the bay, its scars invisible. The spacing between the distant street lights grew closer and closer as they moved away from Dave to their vanishing point. Like enormous stepping stones covered with glowing spots of white light, buildings climbed the closest hill in Freetown. In the blackness, headlamps flashed as cars drove up and down the hill passing unlit trees and buildings unseen by Dave in the darkness. At the top of the hill, the blackness became a dark moonlit gray silhouetted with tall palm trees as Freetown bumped into the night sky.

Dave knew that, in that quiet Christmas night, people prepared to sleep, thankful they had survived one more bloody day. But he knew, too, that thousands of them now slept with a rapidly ticking time bomb, their peace soon to be shattered once and for all. He needed to confront Claire, to ferret out the whole truth. He could not yet fully discount the possibility that Claire, in the end, was one of the good guys.

Jennifer's reverie ended when she heard Dave calling to her. She straightened in the water, looking around. Grabbing on to the side, she looked up and saw him leaning over a balcony six floors up.

"Wait there," he called before heading back inside.

Jennifer pulled herself out of the pool. Her soaked bra was essentially now see-through. She thought anyone but Dave Clement would view that as an opportunity. Dave would make her feel like a tramp. She rubbed herself down with a towel and then wrapped her skirt around her waist, hoping it would not stick too awkwardly to her backside. Dave arrived at the pool before Jennifer finished buttoning her blouse.

"Kind of pointless," he said.

She looked down and saw that the wet black bra showed right through the white sheer blouse. She let go of the buttons.

"You still have a chance," she said.

"No, you've played me for the last time."

"I'm not playing you."

"Come with me," he ordered.

She followed him across the pool into a dark area behind the building.

"What do you know about Jim Reilly and Mike Farley?" he asked, cornering her against a wall.

"What am I supposed to know?"

Dave appeared sinister in the dark, towering over the much smaller woman. "How did you do it? How did you frame them with the fake vaccine in Kono?"

"That's not me, Dave. I don't know what's going on down there. I only did what Claire told me to do."

"And what's that?"

"I went with Mike to meet Jim at a church early this morning. We brought vaccine Claire told me to provide."

Dave folded his arms. He looked like he wanted to hit her. "Why did they think you brought the vaccine?"

"To replace tainted vaccine in Kono."

"They thought they were fixing a problem?"

"Yes."

"Did you know they weren't?"

A gust of wind blew in from the bay. Jennifer shivered. "I'm cold in these clothes."

He grabbed her shoulders in a vice grip. He did not shake her, but held her steadily in his gaze. "Take 'em off. I don't care. You're going to tell me what the hell is going on."

Jennifer's shivering worsened. "You're hurting me."

"Answer my question."

"Yes, I knew. I knew I'd given them tainted vaccine."

"You set them up? Why?"

"Orders. That's all I know."

"Do you realize what's going on down there? What's going on around the world? Everyone thinks the Vatican has assassins, that it's killing Islamic babies."

"Yes. That's what she wanted."

"Claire?"

"Yes."

"So the whole thing is true. This isn't about malaria at all. The new HIV mutation. It's in the vaccine."

Jennifer shrank away from him, leaning against the concrete wall.

"You knew about it, too. You knew that the firmware would yield a false result on HIV-positive people, making sure they received the vaccine. And you're profiling their amino acid structure through the PDNA."

She said nothing, waiting for him to strike her.

"Answer me, Jennifer. Is what I just said all true?"

Her teeth chattered between blue lips. He grabbed her by the shoulders again, this time yanking her away from the wall.

"Answer me, dammit."

"Yes. Yes, Dave. It's true, but you don't understand."

"The hell I don't."

"No, you don't. You couldn't possibly. This will save lives. Tens of millions of lives over the next twenty years."

"And how many will be lost to accomplish that dream?"

"You're bigger than this, Dave. You have a worldview. You understand the kind of tough decisions that have to be made to lead mankind. This is one of those. You have to understand it. You have to think of the bigger picture."

"What does pitting Muslims and Christians against each other have to do with stopping AIDS? There's more to this. More than you're telling. Maybe more than you know."

"You're right. I don't know all of it. I don't know anything about the politics. Like this thing with the priest. It's a separate agenda that Pamela and Claire have. I have to trust them. And you should, too."

"You, Jennifer, are going to fix this before more people are massacred."

She pulled away from him. "The hell I am. They'll kill me."

"You should've thought of that before. We're going to find the press and you're going to tell them you planted the vaccine with an infertility drug on the priest and his brother."

She folded her arms defiantly. "And the firmware?" she asked. "The HIV mutation?"

"You bet."

"The press won't believe one conspiracy theory, let alone two different ones running at the same time. Let's see, Dave. You want me to tell the press that we framed the Catholic Church with a tainted vaccine in Kono to make it look like Catholics wanted to kill little Islamic babies? Why would we do that? That's a real stretch."

"It's the truth. I don't know why, but it's the truth."

She moved her face closer to his now. "Sure. And then for a nightcap, you want to me tell the world that, on a separate agenda, we didn't really discover a new mutation. Instead, we planted it in a malaria vaccine in order to kill millions of West Africans and make a lot of money. Really? C'mon, Dave. Get real. You're in the middle of all this now. Do you think you'll even believe something so outrageous after a good night's sleep clears your head?"

Dave stared at her, feeling very calm and empty of emotion. "I can prove it. I can show the world the code you planted in the PDNAs."

"No you can't. As soon as Middleton's boys reversed the code, we set in motion an update. All the PDNAs received new firmware as of 11:30 last night. The old code is gone without a trace."

"There's still firmware back at Prodeus," he said.

"Not any longer. Hepp took care of that. And he's moving control of the firmware back to the Aldrich to manage future updates. This will die down and we'll re-implement the program in a few weeks, if not sooner."

"Who will the public believe, Jennifer? Especially after we tell about the way you framed the priest."

"You can't do that, Dave. You have no evidence. Worst you can do is raise doubts. That will cause us a great deal of aggravation. Might even cause some extremists to commit a violent act or two in retribution. But you won't even slow down our program"

She stepped up to him, leaning her wet hair into his neck. "Plus you don't want to hurt me, Dave. Liv won't like it. Neither will you and Mel. You definitely do not want any angry Muslims or Catholics killing me."

"I'd love a ringside seat." He pushed her away, but she stepped right back into him.

"You know, of course, that I'm the only one up to speed on the vaccine to stop the mutation. If I go away, it could add the better part of a year to the project. Millions more will die."

"Not if the vaccine is stopped now."

"That won't happen. President Mossoumou has over a millions doses on hand. We supplied them. He won't stop. It will interfere with his plans."

"I thought you didn't know about the politics."

"I know enough."

"You're bluffing," he said. "Claire would not deliberately keep killing like that."

"Of course, she would. I know that now. But I have a hard time comprehending big numbers. Maybe we can make this about just one person." She stood on her toes and placed her lips to his ear. "Why do you think none of the drugs are working for Liv?"

"What the hell do you mean?"

"It's like this. She needs the vaccine that only I can get ready in time." She dropped back on her heels and looked at a suddenly stricken face.

Dave choked back a bubble of fear and rage that welled up inside him. He willed himself to stay calm, to think this through.

"No, Jennifer. I've fallen for your bullshit too many times. You're making it up. Liv never had the vaccine."

"Remember that big cut on her arm about four weeks ago. Remember her telling you how I medicated it for her? The first night you left me alone with her."

Dave remembered it clearly. It was the first night that he and Mel had left Liv alone with Jennifer. "How?" he asked. "I'm not buying it. She wouldn't let you just give her a shot."

"I gave her a gel to rub into the open wound. But it wasn't for cuts. It was the mutation."

Suddenly Dave realized she was telling the truth. "You bitch!" he said.

She stepped out of range as he lifted fists of rage.

"Why Liv?" he looked at her, fighting off both an overwhelming feeling of helplessness and a compulsion to beat Jennifer senseless.

She did not answer. She watched him as he tallied it himself. She watched his face contort from anger into guilt and grief.

"You risked her life to control me?"

"Could've avoided the whole thing. If you just weren't so damned principled. It takes a lot more leverage, a lot more temptation to own the soul of a good man. And, I'll give you this, Dave. You're a good man. The kind I wish I'd met a long time ago."

"This will catch up to you," he said, trying to restrain himself from hitting her. "I'll make sure of it."

"I don't think so."

"How can you be so sure?"

"I'm all you have, pal," she said before walking away.

Claire put down her mobile phone. She looked around the table at Pamela, Mossoumou, and Adrian. "That was Jennifer. Clement figured almost everything out somehow."

Mossoumou's eyes widened. "Then we have trouble," he said. "Should I arrange an accident."

Pamela placed a hand on his arm. "Relax, Joseph," she said. "We need Mr. Clement to carry out our programs at Prodeus. We knew this day would come and we have contingencies." Pamela turned back to Claire. "So did Jennifer advise him?"

"She did," Claire answered. "Sooner than we planned, but not too soon."

"And?"

"He's committed."

The Karanjas returned to the hotel by taxi at ten that night after a futile search for Jacob in the city. Dave waited, sitting on the floor outside their room.

"Thank God you're back," Dave said as he stood up. "We need to talk."

CHAPTER 49

Kono: Early morning
December 26, 6:53 a.m. GMT

The first gray light of dawn peered over the distant hills as Jacob and his band of small boy soldiers drove their Humvee near the town where Fr. Jim had been last seen. Roadblocks manned by MAD troops had been placed on the two roads into the village. The boys had avoided other roadblocks during the night by driving overland through jungle. That option did not present itself in Kono.

Hiding their weapons in the woods, the boy soldiers masqueraded as just boys, entering the village on foot playing hide and seek. They identified the location of the police headquarters where Fr. Jim and his brother had been taken. They asked curious boyish questions about the Vatican terrorists. The policeman at the front door freely told them what everyone in town already knew. The two perpetrators had tried to burn their way out of captivity. Mike Farley had been burned to death in the process. The priest, too, had been badly burned but still lived. He had been evacuated to a top burn center in Lagos where it was hoped he could be made well enough to lead authorities to the rest of the Catholic plotters.

"Where's Lagos?" one of the boys asked.

The policeman, thinking he was educating children, showed them a map on the wall in the stationhouse.

"That's a long way from here," said one of the boys.

"Over a thousand miles," the policeman said.

"Are there roads that could get you there if you had enough time?" Jacob asked.

"Sure," the policeman answered smiling. "Someday when you're old enough maybe you could drive there for an adventure."

Jacob studied the map for a moment, running a finger along the roads that led through the countries of West Africa to Lagos.

"Someday," Jacob said agreeably, but his grim look and the darkness in his eyes suddenly made the cop very uneasy.

CHAPTER 50

Tenerife, Canary Islands
December 27, 7:15 a.m. GMT

The call of gulls echoed across the beach to the veranda of the seaside condo reserved by Pamela Thatcher for her entourage in Tenerife. The long shadow of a single royal palm crossed the balustrade, carving its silhouette in the pink sunrise that skipped glistening along the peaks of the ocean's aqua swells. Sipping coffee, an exhausted Dave gazed out to sea, watching and listening to the waves, seeking to immerse himself in them, to find the peace the ocean normally brought him. He looked at his watch. Pamela expected him upstairs.

Conversation on the flight from Freetown to Tenerife centered on events in Kono. The consensus seemed to be that the implications for lifelong Catholics, for religion in general, could not be much worse. Mel, Liv and the cabin crew engaged in animated discussion about it. Pamela occasionally offered a declaration about Vatican corruption. Claire said nothing, choosing to wear headphones and listen to music. Jennifer immersed herself in her laptop studying 3D models of CEM15-D and analyzing DNA snipping tools.

Dave remained silent for most of the flight, clearly preoccupied, pondering the secrets he had learned, secrets he knew he could not share with Mel without putting her at risk. He had finally been able to access Sheila's cloud folder. The password **tedsplace** had been the key there as well. The folder contained the same information that had been on Evan Conger's phone, but with a personal note about Liv. That note confirmed what Jennifer had said about Liv's HIV. It contained a warning to get Liv into hiding immediately, that the Aldrich had given her the standard HIV clade, but would give her the accelerator to convert it to the aggressive mutation in order to gain full control of Dave. The note alluded to the password placed in the Clements' mailbox at home. Dated the day before Sheila died, it said: "By now, we'll know if Jennifer is working with us or against us. I'm meeting her at the Silver Grill right after I drop the envelope with the password in your mailbox. Since you're reading this, you obviously got it. Over the weekend, I'll upload a note on how it went with Jennifer. I'm hoping she'll listen to reason. Her heart was always in the right place, but she's a statistician, easily blinded by the logic of forecasts and numbers." Of course, Sheila never made it to Fort Collins.

It was almost two weeks after Sheila uploaded that note that Jennifer gave Liv the accelerator. Dave second-guessed himself for not more aggressively trying to figure out Sheila's password before then. If he had, he would have saved Liv from the mutated HIV. And he would be in a better position to stop the vaccine in Sierra Leone.

Now, sitting oceanside in luxury, thirty-six hours after learning from Jennifer what she had done to Liv, Dave still struggled with incredulity. How could she and Claire be so cruel? And how could he have exposed his daughter and wife to these horrors? He wanted to strike out at Jennifer and Claire – and Pamela – and squeeze the life out of them with his bare hands. But he wouldn't. That would be signing Liv's death warrant because it would cut off the path to her cure.

He prayed silently. Catholic prayers learned in a Church that he may have helped undermine in the worst way in modern history. He prayed that Jennifer would quickly resolve the AIDS vaccine, that Liv would survive this nightmare. He prayed for the Karanjas and all the people of Sierra Leone and the newly expanded MAD empire. He put his coffee down and headed for the elevator.

Claire's two-story suite sat atop the ten story resort. Catering had set a table on the veranda, adorning it with orchids, birds of paradise and colorful bowls of papaya, mango and oranges. Pamela and Claire enjoyed casual conversation with Dave, discussing the weather, the deep blue of the sea, the breeze, the "smashing" success of the press coverage of the malaria vaccine and the discovery of the HIV clade.

Dave found it awkward, to say the least, to interact with these people. He felt as though he were living in a horrifying, surreal nightmare. His work no longer proved a mere impediment to his relationship with Liv. It literally threatened to kill her. Tens of thousands of others would die in the next several months. Yet the administration of vaccine continued, more and more potential victims being created with each passing hour – and he intended to do nothing. Because he could do nothing else

After all finished omelettes filled with cream cheese, strawberries and confectioners' sugar, Claire excused the help.

"Ok. Time to lay it all out on the table," Claire said. "We're alone now, Dave. We had the room de-bugged last night. Speak your mind."

"Did you find any bugs?" he asked.

"No, but we always take precautions. Allows us to speak freely."

"I'm sure you have things to say," Pamela said.

"You're right. I'm angry as hell."

"Understandable," Pamela said.

Claire nodded her agreement.

"How can you be so smug? You're killing my daughter."

"No, Dave," Claire said. "We'll get her out of this."

"You can't know that. Not for certain."

"We took a calculated risk, one that's proven appropriate."

Dave did not have to ask how. The damage to Liv forced him to be compliant. He glowered at Claire. Her intensity had always come through in the past, but today she seemed different, drained. Her matter of fact demeanor came across in an odd way – for her -- almost as though her trademark willfulness had evaporated. Pamela kept grabbing her hand and squeezing it reassuringly.

"Have you told Mel?" Claire asked.

"Trust me. You don't have to worry about that. I'm struggling enough with my own rage. The burden of hers might just push us both over the edge, something I don't think you want any more than I do."

"Wise man," Pamela commented.

"So where do we go from here?" he asked. "I assume you're shutting down the program until there's a new vaccine without the HIV mutation."

They just looked at him, "no" written clearly in their glares.

"Does the malaria vaccine even work?" he asked.

"Absolutely," Claire answered. "And more effective than we hoped. The DNA profiles of the Leoneans are much more amenable to the chemistry than originally anticipated."

"The PDNA made that understanding possible," Pamela said. "You made that happen."

"And a lot of other people made that happen, too, including Brian Middleton and the two engineers you killed."

Pamela crinkled her face. "That was a traffic accident. In a blizzard."

Dave contained his rage. "Hepp sent them out," he said.

"Bad judgment," Pamela said.

"I don't believe you for - "

Pamela cut him off. "It doesn't matter, does it? You hold very few cards in this hand. So let's not waste time on what can't be changed."

He glared at her. When she did not react, he reached for his coffee, tempted to crush the cup in his hands. "Then, let's talk business," he said. "Side effects?"

Claire looked at him quizzically.

"Of the malaria vaccine."

"Mild," Claire replied. "With one completely unanticipated exception. One in ten thousand react in a way we never anticipated. A super-mutation of the malaria is generated in their bloodstream, one to which the individual with the mutation is immune. Unfortunately, no one else is, not even the other vaccinated."

"That should have been picked up in the trials, Claire."

"I agree, but it wasn't. This one's a complete surprise. Probably has to do with the genotype of the target population. It may not even be an issue with other populations."

Dave quickly thought through the epidemiology of a malaria mutation. "We'll just have to keep artequin and other options out there then," he said. "It can look like any other malaria, but with many fewer victims. That may still be a good thing."

"Except that it doesn't respond to artequin combination therapy or anything else we've used historically. It appears to be extremely deadly, much more so than the known strains."

Dave felt rage swirl like smoke inside him, rising to his face where he felt the heat from his rushing blood. "Then you have to pull the vaccine," he said. "If a single mosquito gets a taste of the super-mutation in someone's bloodstream, things could be worse than ever."

"We know," Pamela answered.

"So then you are pulling the vaccine, after all?"

Pamela placed her hand softly on his. "Dave, the good news is that we can readily identify the carriers of the super-mutation within a week of vaccination. The vaccination site becomes particularly inflamed when the mutation occurs. It forms a pustule that turns into a keloid that resembles the planet Saturn."

"Interesting. So you can try to hunt down people with Saturn-like scars and quarantine them. But you can't quarantine the mosquitoes."

"Essentially."

"Pamela, you will never - and I'm confident Claire will agree with me - completely constrain a mosquito-borne disease by isolating each of its human carriers. It's an impossible task."

Claire spoke. "We've really wrestled with this one. The damage is done. We can't pull it back. Whether there are ten human carriers or ten thousand, the mosquitoes carrying it will ultimately multiply exponentially."

"So what will you do?"

"Slow it down while we do more research," Claire continued. "Dramatically slow it down. Mossoumou's troops are tracking every vaccinated individual. Anyone discovered with the mutation - and it's easy to spot with a visual check - will be immediately taken off line - "

"Killed?"

"Removed from the population pool."

"But mosquitoes will get to some of these people before they're discovered. Some may never be discovered. You won't find every mark of Saturn."

"We created the mutation," Claire said. "So we can stop it. We just need time to study it and identify what common factor is unique in the individuals where it mutates."

"And what if you can't?"

"Dave, we've figured out how to stop AIDS. And that's nature's doing. Trust me. We have no doubt we can fix our own handiwork."

"Meanwhile, we just slaughter the carriers?

Pamela's disdainful look said enough. "President Mossoumou is a friend. Yours, too, by the way. He admires your work. His troops are continually rounding up anyone that manifests this mark of Saturn. They're killed quickly, in a very humane way. Then they're cremated and their ashes bulldozed into the ground."

"Why be humane now?"

"In the big picture, we are the most humane people on the planet," Pamela responded. "But in this case, we have to be efficient. Mosquitoes can swoop in quickly. Managed right, the whole malaria issue will be no more than a minor hiccup. The HIV mutation and cure are what matters here."

"More than a little Machiavellian, Pamela. Don't you need to keep a good sample of these mark of Saturn people around so you can study their chemistry."

"Claire's already working with Mossoumou on that."

Dave looked out to sea and pondered before speaking again. "So when do my daughter and I become as expendable as those people?"

"We're all expendable. You. Me. Claire. Any of us. But if everyone is on the same page, there's no reason to hurt anyone. If you aggressively support our program, keep the PDNAs rolling, keep the World Health Organization in our camp, work with us on future firmware adjustments — if you do all this, you're on the team. You've been on the team, anyway. You just didn't know the whole game plan. Remember, Dave, in the end, this is all about saving lives, tens of millions of them. Not taking them. Plus the quality of life for the survivors skyrockets when the twin burdens of malaria and HIV are eliminated. Can you imagine the lift in life expectancy, in per capita productivity?"

Dave looked again to the ocean, listened to the waves crashing. He shook his head slowly in dismayed amazement.

"What about Liv?" he asked.

"Or the tens of thousands of others who have the HIV mutation now?"

"Exactly."

"We'll save Liv. As long as you're on the team."

"Not the others?"

"We'll try. Depends on the work of Jennifer, Eldridge and the lab team. Jennifer's already back in Colorado working. Time is of the essence."

"Most of the vaccinated will die then from the accelerated AIDS," he said.

"There's no way we can deploy adequate vaccine in the timeframe required to save all of them, especially since we have to divert resources to deal with the malaria super-mutation."

"Then why are you not stopping the vaccinations? Tens of thousands more could be vaccinated before you get the cure out."

"It will be more than that. Much more. Millions of doses of the vaccine sit in a warehouse in Mossoumou's capital."

Dave's mind cleared. "He wants them dead?"

Neither Pamela nor Claire commented.

"Sure," Dave answered his own question. "He wipes out the weak in a year – and garners the sympathy and financial support of the world community. The world thinks it's a natural epidemic. Genocide without populist hate-mongering. No more Rwandas, right?"

"Right. Completely counter-productive."

"So Mossoumou stops disease from draining the MAD economy, and that drives productivity through the roof. But he can only do it with an iron-fist, one not possible before he deposed the democratic regimes in Sierra Leone and Nigeria. But with the new MAD empire… What's in it for you, Pamela? What's your cost-benefit equation?"

Pamela scrutinized him, poured just a little more cream in her coffee, stirred it. "The peace dividend," she said. "Everyone gets the peace dividend that only force or the threat of force can bring."

Dave knew that for many, a peace dividend as Pamela envisioned could bring oppression and misery. For others, it could mean new markets and increased income. In the world of investment banking, everything required cost-justification. Investment banking, by definition, maintained a firmly agnostic stance when it came to ideologies; only the financial bottom-line existed as a universally accepted valuation of action. Public companies as extensions of investment bankers and institutional investors demanded bottom-line thinking, absolutely convinced that a healthy bottom-line provided the best outcome for everyone. Increased value to shareholders equaled the best outcome for all. Flawed logic in Dave's mind, but the most important commandment in the religion of money. Dave knew it; he trained in it. He once believed in it.

"What's the bottom-line?" he asked. "What's in the peace dividend?"

Pamela smiled slightly, almost smirking. "Improved health care for all the citizens of the new MAD empire - "

"Skip the niceties, Pamela," he said. "You have me committed. I don't have any choice. You can be boldly honest with me. What's the real bottom-line? What are you taking back to your investment portfolio?"

She nodded, glanced at Claire who turned away. "Sweet, sweet crude," she said. "Light, cheap, easily refined West African oil. The end to Middle Eastern dominance of one of the most basic fundamentals of our economy. And leverage against the Russians and the Chinese."

"In exchange for West African dominance?"

Pamela reached across the table and latched on to Dave's hand. "My boy, don't think for one minute that Joseph Mossoumou is in control of anything. We can move him a helluva lot easier than we can the state of California. We have drones in Niger that can surgically take him out in a minute. And he knows it."

Dave pulled his hand back slowly. Slipping back into his seat, he digested the conversation. He pondered MAD as an American state without the bill of rights, without a lawyer on every corner, a state driven by markets and opportunity, not politics.

"Brilliant," he said.

"I knew you'd be on board. Claire assured me you would be reasonable if we got your attention."

"What about the priest? The whole anti-Vatican thing in Kono?"

Claire re-entered the conversation. "The Vatican's power elite is a collection of thugs," she said. "The good priest is an IRA killer for whom the Vatican provided sanctuary. No matter what he told you, he meant to kill Jennifer in your guest room. He and others like him are protected by men who rule with no accountability except to a God who changes to suit their political agenda."

"Then, do you think there is no God?"

"Oh no, Dave. I believe in God. We're doing her work."

"Does she condone what you've done to my daughter?"

"Condone?" Claire smiled. "Insisted on it. Life is an enormous jigsaw puzzle. Sometimes, we have to act on faith alone, knowing that we don't know what the finished puzzle looks like."

"What if Jennifer can't finish the AIDS cure in time?"

Claire leaned toward him and looked him straight in the eye. "She will."

Pamela canted her head toward Dave. "What if she doesn't?" she asked. "Would you have us throw away a healthy future for the world for the sake of one girl? The horse is already out of the paddock and you can't stop it."

Dave felt his head go numb, a wave of anger and hopelessness intruding.

"You're with us?" Pamela asked.

He choked back his fury. He knew resistance would doom Liv. He nodded affirmation.

"Good," Pamela said. "In the end, you will feel very good about your decision."

"One other very important thing," he said. "Mel and I need to get Liv home right away. She has no meds. She gave her Fuzeon to Chief Karanja's little girl."

Claire leaned forward and placed a hand on Dave's forearm. "We know. You have a special kid. A package with what you need is inbound from Spain and will be here this afternoon."

Pamela lifted a mimosa and smiled. "Now, let's enjoy the beach for a few more days. We're going to be very busy when we get home."

CHAPTER 51

Fort Collins, Colorado: Poudre Valley Hospital
February 14, 1:09 p.m. Mountain Standard Time

Liv pressed the touchpad on the side of the bed, raising her head to where she could more easily read the Valentine's Day cards. The IV tube poking into her left hand poured a steady drip of antibiotics into her system. Just in the last ten days, her face narrowed, becoming gaunt as the small fat pads on her cheeks wasted away.

More sudden than the Clements feared, the downturn threatened to kill her in weeks if the doctors could not get her CD4 count back up. For now, she had little immunity to anything, making her easy prey for opportunistic diseases. The sniffles and coughing spasms of the last several days had finally driven her into the hospital. The pneumonia diagnosis had driven them all to their knees.

"Thank you so much, Mommy and Daddy," she said as she closed their card. "I love you with all my heart, too."

Mel stroked her hair with a hand scrubbed in an antibacterial wash the doctors insisted on before letting anyone into Liv's room.

"Michael Winston sent me a card, too. He wants to know when he can see me."

"See," Mel said. "True love overcomes everything."

"True love would be nice, Mom, but we're a little young for that."

"So what is it with Michael?"

Liv blushed, a grin spreading across her pale face. "We're just really good friends."

Mel tilted her head skeptically.

"I just want to kiss him, Mom. And he says he wants the same. The doctors just need to find out that this form can't be spread by kissing."

Dave made a mental note to have Claire manufacture some finding that supported that position. The doctors would never know this form came from a lab. "The researchers are making fast progress on this one," Dave said. "I'll bet they'll have the answer you want on that by the time you lick this pneumonia."

Liv smiled, her eyes sparkling, their rich color back for a moment. Suddenly, she jerked forward, squeezing her eyes shut. She coughed a deep hacking cough. Dave placed a handful of tissues under her mouth. She spit green phlegm into them. Dave placed the tissues into a covered receptacle beside the bed.

Her head pressed back against the pillow, she struggled for air. "Sorry," she gasped.

"For what?" Mel said. "For being sick? You don't have anything to be sorry for."

"I did this to myself somehow, Mom. I'm sorry for that."

"No, sweetheart," Dave said. "You did not do this to yourself. You have the new mutation. It looks like it could be passed in different ways. You were exposed to this sometime last spring or summer. You don't have any responsibility for it."

"Did you bring it back from Sierra Leone, Daddy?"

Dave took both of her hands in his. "It's very possible, Liv. I'm so sorry."

"Don't be. No one could have known. And you'll get this fixed. I believe in you."

The knife of heartache plunged deep into his mid-section. Part of him wanted desperately to tell her the true source of her disease, to completely assure her that she was in no way responsible. Yet, even if Thatcher and Claire had not warned him to keep the secret from his family, he did not think he could bear Liv and Mel knowing that he had somehow allowed his ambition to hurt his little girl. If the unthinkable happened with Liv - not that it had not already happened - if the worst happened and Mel knew of his involvement, he would lose Mel as well. He needed her now more than ever. And she would need him.

So he lied, passing false data on to Mel and Liv with the help of Claire and Jennifer. He advanced the theory that the new HIV might be passed readily through food contamination, a rarity but possible. Since no previous testing had been done for the new HIV in the food supply, no data yet existed for its extent. Additionally, labs had not tested for this HIV clade in the United States, the general approach being to assume the standard clade. Additional testing had begun in the American HIV community with a few cases turning up in the homeless community, leading to further speculation about a dietary related cause of transmission.

For Liv Clement, the doctors theorized she simply had a very bad break in somehow getting exposed to this new pathogen, either when she went to Sierra Leone or perhaps earlier. Mel believed it happened earlier, that Dave brought it back from one of his African trips. The doctors thought that possibility held promise as the root cause for Liv. That alone had generated several angry, irrational outbursts by Mel, faulting Dave for their daughter's sickness.

"You!" she had shouted just a few nights earlier. "Damn you! You did this to her. You and your damned job."

He listened to her, agreed with her, said he understood. After a few minutes, she calmed down, hugging him.

"I'm sorry Dave. I'm wrong to blame you. I know it's not your fault. It's just so unbelievable. Makes me wonder where God is in all of this."

He held her, wanting to tell her the real truth, knowing that he never could, convinced that she could never forgive him, afraid that Claire would hurt her if she knew. He thought she would figure it out when she died, with the omnipotent perspective he expected of heaven. But he figured she would then see the whole picture, understand how this trap was set for all of them.

If there was a heaven. If there was a God.

Now, in the hospital room, he and Mel sat in chairs beside Liv's bed. On her nightstand sat the Bible and a Guideposts magazine. Liv still believed. So did Mel. He prayed for his own faith.

Peering at the snowflakes drifting down outside Liv's window, he remembered the bright heat of Sierra Leone. He remembered Hamara Karanja – thought of him every minute of every day – hoping the chief had set sail by now. He prayed that the ragtag fleet of Leoneans made landfall in the United States soon, that the weather in the Atlantic would be good, that the Coast Guard would not stop them.

And he prayed that his prayers ended up at someplace more significant than the vacuum of outer space.

CHAPTER 52

Cameron Pass, Colorado: Aldrich Lab
February 15, 10:46 a.m. Mountain Standard Time

The little orange illustration representing the HIV virus readily penetrated the T-cell wall in the animated presentation. Eradicated by Vif-D, the CEM15 protein no longer slowed down the penetration of HIV into T-cells. The Vif-D protein attached itself to free HIV virus in the bloodstream. When it reached the T-cell wall, Vif-D disintegrated the CEM15, depriving the cell of its key protection against HIV.

Once inside the cell, HIV virus re-produced itself repeatedly, drifting back to the cell wall to exit into the bloodstream, ultimately causing the patient's viral load to skyrocket. This led to symptomatic AIDS within a few months of Vif-D mutating the HIV.

Jennifer explained as Eldridge and Claire watched a green circle called CEM15-D, the mutated CEM15 designed by the Aldrich, attach to the exterior cell wall. CEM15-D, unencumbered by the presence of CEM15, locked the virus inside the T-cells, preventing the viral load from going up.

"Once this happens," Jennifer said, "the HIV is trapped inside the T-cell. Ultimately, the T-cell dies from malnutrition. The HIV inside the cell dies as well, systemically eradicating HIV – with one nasty side effect."

Eldridge nodded knowingly. Claire commented. "This is more of what we've seen before," she said. "The CEM15-D basically shuts down the entire immune mechanism, more aggressively than HIV ever did. And it does it quickly."

"Exactly," Jennifer said. "That's where Sheila and the team were when the project went on hiatus. But Sheila also figured out the science necessary to go the next step. Through DNA profiling, compatible RNA can be designed and introduced directly into the cells. These RNA are coded to co-exist with the CEM15-D. Once the RNA is inside the cell, it merges into the HIV virus. This creates a virus killer that's harmless to the T-cell, but exits the T-cell to scavenge and kill free HIV in the bloodstream."

Jennifer paused waiting for them to digest the animation. Both knew the subject well but neither had been updated on the chemistry since Jennifer took over the project.

"So this is where we are today with those HIV patients vaccinated. Any HIV negative person that receives the malaria vaccine will continue to have healthy CEM15 activity on the walls of their T-cells, leaving their immune systems intact."

"And anyone who contracts HIV after vaccination," Eldridge said, "will develop the mutation because their blood contains the Vif-D as a result of the vaccination."

"Ensuring that the victims will not linger and drain their society's resources," said Claire. "But that much we knew. The real magic is in step two. Introducing CEM15-D and locking down the viral load. This is one of the places where Sheila got hung up. She could introduce the CEM15-D, but without the RNA necessary to further mutate the HIV to an HIV killer."

"So it wasn't an issue of the CEM15-D not adhering to cells?" asked Eldridge.

"Only in an oversimplified kind of way," Jennifer said. She pressed the advance button on her presentation. A slide showing the RNA structure popped up on the screen.

"This is where the DNA profiles come in. Once we know the major DNA profiles, we can re-configure the RNA to be compatible, allowing free movement within the cells and ultimately through reverse transcriptase, we have an HIV killer virus that harms only HIV."

Claire squeezed her hands together. "And you think you've solved Sheila's last problem?"

"Yes," Jennifer said. "Her team couldn't get the CEM15-D to adhere to the cells after the initial tests. But it was a timing issue. The fundamental challenge is that Vif-D takes six or more weeks to bind with the HIV virus in the bloodstream and begin effectively penetrating the T-cell walls. Sheila's protocol introduced CEM15-D before the natural CEM15 was eradicated by Vif-D. In that case, the CEM15 blocked the CEM15-D, making it ineffective. It has to be a two-step. We didn't know it, but the CEM15 has to be gone before the CEM15-D can be introduced."

Claire sat back and put her hands behind her head. "So, at last we're headed for the finish line," she said. Claire's eyes softened, the ice gone from them.

"We are," Jennifer responded.

"What's the timeline?"

"Adrian Guerra's team worked with the W-H-O team in MAD to get a broad selection of DNA samples from the region. We now have sufficient sampling to complete the profiling. Within 30 days, maybe less, we should be able to conduct our first human trials with a high probability of success."

"What about Dave Clement's girl?"

Jennifer grew solemn. "Liv's in trouble. The mutation is wrecking her immune system. She's in the hospital with pneumonia and zero defenses of her own to stop it.

"Her only hope is to introduce the RNA-engineered vaccine as quickly as we can get it completed. We won't have time to wait for trials of any kind. Even once the RNA is introduced, it takes almost a week to begin its work. So we can't waste a moment if she's to have any kind of chance."

After the presentation, Claire walked back to her office with Eldridge.

"I like that she's personalized this so much," Eldridge said. "The Clement kid is keeping the urgency right in front of her."

"She is," Claire agreed.

"By the time another 30 days are up, Mossoumou will have vaccinated over 70% of the people in his new empire, and over 10% of them have HIV."

Claire folded her hands behind her back and turned toward Eldridge. "We have to assume that almost all of that 10% will die," she said.

"Frightening, but remarkable," Eldridge said. "He ends up with the healthiest nation in sub-Saharan Africa and the highest productivity levels, a burgeoning economic miracle that will overwhelm its neighbors."

"I'm still hopeful that Liv Clement comes out of this intact," Claire added. "Dave's proven to be a good soldier. And she's a sweet kid. Reminds me a little of myself at that age."

"Before the car bomb?"

"After actually. Seems to have the same grit as I did in the face of adversity. More really. That deal with giving her medicine to the little Karanja kid. Very impressive."

Eldridge placed a tentative hand on Claire's shoulder. She did not resist. "You've become much more…"

"Caring?" she asked. "Revenge was not as sweet as I'd hoped, Eldridge. I thought I could watch them burn, but I walked away."

He did not know about her videotape. Nor did he know that the torture and burning of the Farley brothers had been edited in. And he could not know that, after finishing the editing, Claire had never again viewed the footage.

"Don't get your hopes up too high for Liv, boss," Eldridge said.

"Why?"

"At least thirty days to the vaccine, Claire. From now. She has pneumonia and no CEM15. Her viral load is moving off the charts. She'll never last that long."

Claire sat down in front of her fireplace after Eldridge left. Snow fell heavily outside her window, hiding her view of Mt. Clark. Mossoumou could kill more than a million people with her creation, but one teenager in Fort Collins kept her up nights. For years, she had obsessed about her revenge, building in her mind the fantasy she finally lived. Then it was over in an evening. She felt no joy. Only horror at what her life had become. And a sense of completion. A chapter over. But no sense of celebration at all. Part of her even had a soft spot for the priest. He faced years of pain and recovery ahead.

Since that trip, Liv Clement had haunted her. Never one to second guess her decisions, she had repeatedly played out what other ways she may have found to leverage Dave without sacrificing his daughter. But she would not accept any as better options. She did not want to know they existed. Her plan worked. Brilliantly. And that's what mattered.

She poured herself a glass of red wine. She thought about the problem of getting vaccine to Liv in time. The vaccine designed using the antibodies of the West Africans might not help her since her genotype was very different. And there was no time to experiment and find out that it would not work.

She reached for her phone and pressed speed dial "3".

"Jennifer, I have an idea. A longshot but maybe it could work.

CHAPTER 53

Lagos, Nigeria
March 3, 4:17 p.m. West Africa Time

After eight long weeks, Jacob and his boys arrived in Lagos. The trip had been delayed repeatedly by fighting. In Liberia, Mossoumou's MAD forces invaded, shutting down all traffic in and out of the country, leaving the boys stranded and in hiding. In the Ivory Coast, a government crackdown led to the detention of the boys at a roadblock as well as the seizure of their weapons and ammunition. After a week, they were released, but they no longer had a Humvee or firepower. Trekking into the bush, they stole weapons and secured a jeep for transportation. That jeep took them into Nigeria.

Crowds no longer teemed in the streets of Lagos. Under the new MAD regime, a harsh order had been imposed. Before driving into the city, Jacob wisely had the boys hide the weapons underneath rocks near a stream.

Automatic weapons fire erupted to their right.

"Stop, boy!"

Several MAD soldiers rushed up to the jeep. Jacob braked the jeep before the firepower was turned on them.

"Where did you get a jeep, boy? You're way too small to drive."

"It's my father's, sir," Jacob lied. "He was killed in the north. All of us are orphans. We've come to Lagos to find work and new lives."

"The violence in the bush is regrettable," the soldier said. "We're here to stop it. For the first time in two years, there is order in Lagos. I'm sorry about your parents. I wish we had come sooner." The soldier smiled and slapped the hood of the jeep. "Now, go. And stay out of trouble."

Jacob ground the jeep into first gear. But as he started to press the gas, someone yelled "wait." A pair of hands roughly yanked him out of his seat and into the street. The other boys were ordered into the street and the jeep confiscated.

Over an hour later, soldiers tossed Jacob unceremoniously from the back of a truck. He landed in dust outside a walled courtyard. Two waiting soldiers dragged him through a heavy iron door into the courtyard. As he passed through the door, Jacob's head filled with the overwhelming odor of burnt human flesh. A small bulldozer pushed charred dirt into a pit.

The soldiers pushed him forward, causing him to stumble to the dusty ground. Jacob filled with rage. He wanted a weapon. These soldiers had no idea who he was, how dangerous he was. Angrily, he jumped up, grabbing the rifle of one of his captors. He had nearly wrestled it free when someone slipped a rope around his neck from behind. The rope tugged, yanking him to the ground, taking his breath away.

Jacob desperately wrapped his fingers around the rope, trying to free his windpipe as a burly soldier dragged him. Ahead of him, another group of soldiers pushed and dragged ten civilians toward a distant corner of the yard where the wall stood highest. Blood splattered the pockmarked wall. The civilians - men, women and a single young girl - cried and screamed at the soldiers. The soldiers responded roughly, hitting and kicking them, always driving them toward the bloody wall.

Having hauled Jacob through a tall iron gate into a smaller patio area crowded with people of all ages and genders, the big man kneed Jacob in the forehead, reclaiming his rope while the boy lay dazed in the dust. The soldier slammed the gate shut, securing it with a padlock.

"Sorry for you, boy," said a well-manicured woman in her mid-thirties. She examined him, helping him to sit up.

"Why are we here?" Jacob asked, knowing by the woman's skirt and torn blouse that she must be rich.

She caressed a kind hand along the edges of the knot forming on his forehead. "Make your peace, boy," she said. She nodded toward the courtyard.

Jacob watched as the soldiers shoved the civilians against the far wall, knocking them down with kicks, rifles and fists. A young girl, no more than ten, latched on to one soldier's leg, her mouth wide in hysterical screaming. Jacob waited for the man to bash her skull with his rifle butt. Instead, he slammed it against her back repeatedly until she slipped to the ground.

"They don't want our blood on them," the woman said to Jacob.

"Why?"

She shrugged her shoulders.

The soldiers had now corralled the panicked civilians into a knot in front of them. Popping sounds echoed through the courtyard. Blood exploded from heads and bodies as the screams stopped, the executed flopping to the dirt.

The soldiers stood back. They watched for movement. When they saw it, a fresh fusillade of fire followed. When satisfied their work was complete, they walked away. Two other soldiers poured gasoline on the dead and lit it.

Jacob glanced around the patio at the faces of the others. Some cried quietly. Others wailed. Still others chanted prayers aloud. Small groups comforted one another.

"When?" he asked.

"They collect a new group when they finish burning the last one."

Jacob saw that dusk approached. "Will they continue during the night?"

"No one knows."

A few steps away, a woman stopped wailing as she seemed to choke on something. Suddenly, she started vomiting. The people near her stepped back.

Jacob let his caretaker help him to his feet. "I need one of their weapons," he said.

She studied the skinny little boy who came only to her armpit. "The rifles are bigger than you," she said.

He glared confidently at her.

Her eyes widened. "Dear, Lord," she said. "I know what you are."

CHAPTER 54

Atlantic Ocean off the coast of South Carolina
March 3, 11:35 a.m. Atlantic Time

Hamara looked at the elaborate boats and helicopters hovering around his little fleet. The pursuers said they were beaming video images back to the United States, that the whole world now watched their exodus. Hamara explained into one camera that they sailed for America looking for good health care and a better way of life.

"But please go away now. If the American Coast Guard finds us, they will turn us back."

"Not as long as you're in international waters," the interviewer said.

"But we'll need to enter US coastal waters to come ashore," he said.

"Good luck with that one, Chief. The whole world is watching, waiting to see what the President of the United States wants to do with you."

That night, in the dark, after the cameras had left for the day, Hamara sat on the deck with his family. Mariama now looked sicker than Sara. Her HIV had advanced. Sara rebounded for a time with Liv Clement's medicine. But the medicine had run out quickly and Hamara could not find it, let alone buy it, in Freetown. Over the last two days at sea, Sara had taken a hard turn for the worse. Emma remained without symptoms, having been HIV negative, raising a question as to how Sara contracted it and when Mariama did. Ani, too, remained healthy. She had not been tested for HIV. Hamara held out hope that she was negative. He himself, though HIV positive, remained asymptomatic.

In the darkness, he found his way to the shrimper's galley. He opened the refrigerator and again confirmed the blood samples from his tribe were still there. Underneath a cabinet, he lifted the cover off the PDNA Dave had asked him to bring to America. He pondered the metal box that represented the best hope for the survival of his family and thousands of others. His ears could still hear the radio and TV ads calling upon all the citizens of the new Middle African Democracy to do their patriotic duty and vaccinate. He would pass the lines in the streets, knowing that many of the people celebrating the new hope of the MAD leadership would be dead in months from the genocidal Trojan horse hidden within the vaccine.

Musa set up an underground newsletter attempting to warn the population. MAD soldiers raided his small shop in an abandoned Freetown office building, murdering him and seven others. Immediately thereafter, the government provided guards as a "courtesy" to the refugee camp, a camp no longer under the aegis of the Catholic Church after its expulsion from the region.

Finally, the market day they awaited arrived. On that day, 487 refugees, among over ten thousand now in the camp, left for the Freetown market with no intention of returning. As they did every week, the 487 thronged with thousands of others, pulling carts and carrying sacks to fill with food.

As night approached, the 487 slipped away from the market, weapons appearing out of their sacks and carts. At nightfall, they seized pre-designated boats in the harbor. They risked no mercy on the crews of uncooperative vessels, hanging weights around their necks and dropping them into the deep harbor.

Since they could not risk the government discovering their whereabouts, a diversion of some of the camp's sickest people had been set up in the mountains southeast of the city to cause the troops to think they were returning to their village lands. Hamara and the others had no doubt that Mossoumou would order them massacred without discussion.

Now, they finally approached America. The cameras of the international press corps, with them since the Canary Islands, provided their best protection against any precipitous action. The public relations sensitive Mossoumou could not risk televised atrocities.

But Hamara knew the survival of the HIV-mutation victims relied upon getting the PDNA ashore in America quickly. If the American Coast Guard interdicted them, they could be put out to sea or the PDNA confiscated. Somehow he needed to get it to shore un-noticed. Dave told him to take it step by step, to trust that the right answers would come when needed.

Hamara heard the repeated clicking of a crutch followed by the thud of a foot landing on the deck outside the galley. Closing the cabinet, he stood up quickly.

"Hamara," Ani said, arriving in the doorway, the pain of her effort clear on her face.

"You should not try to move around on these decks with your leg."

"You mean without it," she said, a broad smile crinkling the weather-beaten sides of her young face.

"You amaze me," he said.

"I'm afraid I don't have good news," she said, her smile fading, her face darkening.

He waited for the rest, subduing his fear.

"We can't wake Mariama," she said.

CHAPTER 55

Liv's Journal
March 3, 9:15 p.m. Mountain Standard Time

I never thought I would actually sit down to write again. My energy has been sub-zero. Until tonight. It's weird, but I have this sudden feeling that I can do almost anything. Doc Resnick said my pneumonia's improving. Guess so. He says he's given me more antibiotics in a few weeks than he's given all his other patients in the last year. Dr. Ellis, the infectious disease specialist, visited me with him the last few times. She's really nice. I seem to matter to both of them.

It's been a while since I dropped to my knees and prayed. You can't believe how tiring getting in and out of bed is. Going to the bathroom has become a huge ordeal. So I try not to drink too much.

But I get to church more than ever. Or it comes to me, actually. A priest comes to the room and gives me communion every day. Priests are so cool. At least this one is. He's a good friend I can trust. He doesn't lie and tell me everything will be all right. It's not that I hold it against Mom and Dad. They think they're saying the right thing. I'm not stupid, though. I know I could die any day. If this pneumonia took a sudden turn in the wrong direction, I'm history.

Sometimes, I think that would be okay. It's pretty amazing how peaceful I get about it. God has me in his hands. He has a better place for me.

Not tonight, though. Tonight it scares me. I won't even lay down with my hands folded on my stomach. That's how dead people are set up in their coffins. I don't want to be like that. I keep my hands at my side or lay on my side. There was this dream where I looked up and saw the sky. Then I realized I was in my grave. They were shoveling dirt on me.

Oh, God. I just want to scream! Please God, no!

Oh, God. Just please be there. Make there really be a heaven.

Some of the writing's going to look a little sloppy now. It's just wet. Right. I'm crying again. I hate this.

CHAPTER 56

Hartsfield International Airport: Admirals Club
March 4, 4:10 p.m. Eastern Standard Time

Dave's eyes shifted back and forth between the departure monitors and the TV hanging over the bar in the Admirals Club. Karanja screwed up. As soon as Hamara's face appeared on the screen yesterday, Dave made reservations to get to the South Carolina coast in a hurry. Under the Secretary of Homeland Security's interpretation of the Patriot Act, ships could be interdicted in international waters if the intent of their passengers or cargo to violate US law could be demonstrated.

Hamara's statement on CNN that he planned to put ashore on the US mainland had stated what the world already took to be obvious, but it also gave the government firm enough standing to act without risking Federal Court or UN protest.

Now, the news channels showed maps of the little fleet's position. Still nearly 140 miles out to sea, they should have had plenty of time for Dave to get to them first. But news reports now headlined Coast Guard vessels steaming toward the fleet's location. Escort duty did not seem to be the objective, though some commentators held out hope that the US might show that kind of compassion. The savvier knew that the US would not let the vessels land because Mossoumou did not want to encourage a further exodus of MAD refugees to America.

Dave looked at his watch: 4:10. He picked up his briefcase, loaded with his laptop and a change of clothes, and headed for the concourse. His connection to Savannah left in 30 minutes.

He stopped at a payphone, making a collect call. He could not risk mobile calls being tracked. Nothing connected with his whereabouts could be logged into the nation's infrastructure. He did not use a credit card, even paying cash for his airfare. Unfortunately, there was no way to not use his name for the flight. ID was required. He was hopeful that the absence of leading credit and phone activity would keep his trackers from reviewing flight records.

Most painfully, he could not call Colorado to check on Liv's status. After a hopeful few days, her conditions had deteriorated during the night, but the last Dave knew, it had not become desperate. He still held out hope for the vaccine. He knew it to be Liv's only hope.

He also knew that his actions tonight could result in her being denied the vaccines. He knew, too, that if the Coast Guard confiscated the PDNA, the genocide in West Africa would continue unabated. No amount of praying had unburdened him of this choice. He prayed the vaccine would be ready and administered to Liv before Hamara arrived so that Claire would not withhold it from her in a fit of pique. His next best hope was to make sure no one knew of his involvement.

Throughout the flight, he prayed for Liv and for Mel. And for himself.

"I'm on schedule," he said into the pay phone. "We'll need to leave immediately upon my arrival." He listened to a protest on the other end. "Watch the news," he said. "You'll know exactly where."

CHAPTER 57

Fort Collins: Poudre Valley Hospital
March 4, 2:20 p.m. Mountain Time

Liv's relapse did not surprise Paul Resnick. Working closely with the infectious disease specialist, he now knew more about AIDS and opportunistic infections than he ever wanted to know. Without a functioning immune system of her own, Liv relied entirely on antibiotics to fight off the bacterial pneumonia. For the streptococcus pneumonia, it spelled enough time to learn to outsmart the latest antibiotic. Those lessons learned, the antibiotic now proved useless and another antibiotic had to be tried.

He raised the head of Liv's bed to better drain the fluids down her throat, to help keep her from choking. A whistled wheeze emanated from her mouth with every breath. At the head of the bed, he pulled Liv's medical record out of its pocket. The data disappointed him; it did not surprise him.

He mumbled a prayer over her before walking into the hall. He dialed his mobile.

"Mel... It's Paul Resnick. It might be time you camped out down here... We're still trying... Not for a minute... I agree. Odds are just numbers..."

CHAPTER 58

Route 14: Poudre Canyon
March 4, 3:50 p.m. Mountain Time

As she rounded the S-turn, Jennifer glanced at the small case on the passenger seat. She did not want it to fall. The update on Liv arrived on-line from the hospital 90 minutes earlier. Jennifer and Claire consulted immediately.

The vaccine had not been fully tested, but Liv had nothing to lose. Claire and Jennifer had arrived at a way to harvest Liv's own antibodies from blood drawn at the hospital and use that to build vaccine for her. It amounted to a real long shot, but, if it worked, it not only could fight off the HIV virus, but also jump start Liv's immune system within one week to help fight off the opportunistic diseases like pneumonia that were overwhelming her body. Still, Liv's antibodies had taken a beating and past research had identified a risk of rejection by the body of its own antibodies. But it provided a fighting chance.

For Jennifer and Claire, with all the hundreds of thousands affected, with the tens of thousands already dead or dying at the hands of the Aldrich, saving this one girl ranked above everything, providing a singular path to redemption for all the harm they were doing. Jennifer's resurrected hope for her own life lay struggling for air under an oxygen mask 43 miles away. She tried to self-justify her actions by telling herself that she was just following orders when she infected Liv, that she believed in the certainty of a cure. When she lay alone at night in bed remembering the reassuring touch of Mike Farley, she re-lived her role in fooling him into carrying tainted vaccine into Kono. While she did not know that he would die as a result, she certainly realized that her action placed him and his brother in danger. At the time, a part of her felt like he deserved retribution for what happened to Sheila so she told herself she didn't care. Now, neither Mike nor Sheila remained, her life a lonely round the clock marathon to complete the dream for which her friends had killed and died. Claire tried to contact Dave as soon as she and Jennifer reached agreement to bring the experimental vaccine to Liv. When Dave failed to answer after several attempts, Claire told Jennifer to head down to Ft. Collins anyway. With Liv's situation so precarious, neither woman could imagine either Dave or Mel rejecting the opportunity.

Both agreed that Dave had been an enthusiastic partner accepting the strategic direction as his own since Freetown. Claire did not want to lose his skills and relationships, especially with Ed Hepp's Parkinson's becoming far more acute.

But more importantly, Jennifer did not want to live with Liv's murder. She hoped it wasn't already out of her hands.

CHAPTER 59

Tidewater Estate, Virginia
March 4, 6:20 p.m. Eastern Time

Her finger pressed the automatic starter and the gas fireplace whooshed on, quickly filling the room with soft flickering light and heat. Pamela pulled the blanket up to her chin, curling into the oversized cushions of her couch. In the two months since Freetown, she had been home only twice, each time for a long weekend. She missed home, but often preferred travel. The big Tidewater Estate seemed too lonely at times, especially in the winter when night came early, especially when the temperatures chilled her, finding her with no one to cuddle.

Tonight, she had a work of fiction on the end table beside her, a Donna Leon mystery novel about an Italian detective. She looked forward to mentally going off on a fanciful tour of the canals of Venice, hot on the heels of some dastardly killer. She let one side of the blanket down, sliding a hand out to pick up the book. Beside the book sat her television remote. The idea of conversation filling the room, even if just a talking head, appealed to her. The news stressed her, but the remote still compelled her. She grabbed it instead of the book, aiming it at a panel in the corner of the room.

The panel dropped revealing a big screen. CNN blinked on, the news ticker below the picture scrolling from right to left with headlines and sports scores. In the upper left hand corner of the screen, a box showed a map of the Southeast coast and the western Atlantic. A voice talked over the sound of wind and rain as a sopping woman reporter, lit brightly in the darkness by camera lights, held a microphone in one hand and held on to a rail with the other.

"There's concern tonight that if the seas get any rougher, some of these small ships could sink. As we've seen over the last several days, many are not very seaworthy vessels. Perhaps, as importantly, their crews are not experienced sailors, but refugees desperate for freedom. Fortunately, the storms have stayed further out to sea thus far. Still, meteorologists forecast a very rough night ahead. We don't know what first light will bring for this gallant fleet."

The screen split into two large halves above the ticker. The reporter on the ship on one side, a well-coiffed anchor in a studio on the other.

"Will the Coast Guard help them if their ships get in trouble?" the anchor asked, the timbre of her voice carefully calibrated to express concern.

"I would certainly think so, but the Coast Guard is not expected to arrive for several hours. The bigger question is, if they have to rescue anyone, what would they do with rescued refugees? A source here has told us the Coast Guard's orders are to allow any refugees to ride out the storm on Coast

Guard vessels and then re-deposit them on the surviving boats – boats that are already overcrowded."

"What will they do with sick or injured refugees?" the anchor asked.

"What our source tells us is that all refugees will be deposited in the surviving boats, whatever their condition."

The screen now filled with the anchor who faced the camera somberly. "Thank you, Courtney Kiser. A very sad and dangerous situation off our Atlantic coast this evening. In other news…"

The anchor pressed a finger to her ear. "It looks like there's been a development. We're going right back to Courtney Kiser. Can you hear me Courtney?"

The screen again split.

"Yes, Grace, I can. A helicopter just arrived and is hovering over one of the fleet's boats. It may be a Coast Guard or even a Navy chopper. We are trying to get a good camera angle to see it through the drizzle. Because of the limited range of a helicopter, it would have to be from the American mainland. This may be an attempt on the part of the US government to negotiate with the refugees."

The split screen went away again, this time bringing in the view from the Atlantic. The view wobbled as the handheld camera turned aboard the rocking ship, trying to zoom in on the helicopter nearly a half mile away.

"We're going to turn our CNN ship and try to sail closer to the helicopter," Courtney spoke, but her face no longer was in the picture. "We may not get far. For everyone's safety, our ship's captain and those of the other media vessels out here have been very committed to maintaining a perimeter with a wide buffer zone."

The halo of lights in the distance came into sharper focus. Pamela watched with intense interest. What the hell is the President doing now? she wondered. They had committed to Mossoumou that the refugees would not be allowed to come ashore. She hoped the penchant of the White House occupant to "do the right thing" would not once again interfere with governing.

The camera shot grew clearer. More vivid shapes could now be seen. A cable dangled from the helicopter, a closed basket at the end of it. The basket swung dangerously over the deck of a Leonean shrimp boat. Over a period of five minutes, several of the Leoneans maneuvered around the basket, finally getting their hands on it to steady it. Water and wind whipped around them from the wash of the rotors.

As the CNN ship came closer to the refugee vessel, the picture came into sharper focus. Pamela could make out facial features now. A short Leonean man appeared on the boat's deck, carrying a metal box of some kind. Another joined him carrying a small ice chest. The others opened the basket and helped the men get the box and the ice chest into it. The box looked familiar to Pamela, maybe a personal computer like one she used. No. Not a computer.

Pamela sat upright on the couch, dropping the blanket to the floor.

"You sonuvabitch," she said. "You clever sonuvabitch."

CHAPTER 60

Atlantic Coast
March 4, 7:24 p.m. Atlantic Time

Dave peered out the chopper's door, watching the crew slowly wind the basket in from Hamara's shrimp boat.

"Keep the phone, Chief," Dave said into a headset. "It's a satellite phone. We should be able to stay in touch wherever you end up. Just keep it charged."

"Take Mariama with you," Hamara shouted into the phone. "She's breathing, but we can't wake her."

Dave turned to the pilot.

"Too risky," the pilot shouted into his headset over the cacophony of the rotors, wind and rain. "Too rough and windy. And it's getting much worse. We could drop her into the sea and then we'd never get her back. I'm barely holding the stick now as it is. Unless you're willing to risk certain death for your friend as well as the cargo we already have."

Dave looked through the wash of rain and wind to Hamara. Dave ached for his friend and his wife. "I can't," he finally said into the phone.

Hamara looked up to him, the anguish clear on his face. Dave knew that he and Mariama loved each other very much. Dave turned away. As the chopper began to rise, the basket with the cargo still not yet to the hatch, he heard Hamara on the phone.

"Okay, then," Hamara said. "Our prayers are with you. Please pray for us."

"I will," Dave answered. "Please be careful. Give me some time. Somehow we'll get all of you ashore."

As soon as the basket was aboard, the helicopter crew closed the hatch. They removed the PDNA from the basket and handed it to Dave who toweled it off. They put the ice chest down beside him.

The pilot turned toward Dave, tapping his headset to tell him to listen.

"The Coast Guard's going to be very curious now," the pilot said.

"Any radio chatter yet?" Dave asked.

"They haven't scrambled any air support yet if that's what you're asking."

"It's because they don't know what to do with the world watching. Is this weather going to keep me from flying out of Statesboro?"

"Not if we get this chopper back there intact. You sure the fate of the world is riding on this?" The pilot laughed as he finished speaking.

"Of his world," Dave answered, watching his friend below cling desperately to the grab rail on the shrimper's lurching deck.

The helicopter turned west for land.

CHAPTER 61

Aldrich Mountain Lab
March 4, 4:35 p.m. Mountain Time

Claire rubbed her ear as she hung up the phone. Rarely had she ever heard her aunt so angry. And scared. They both reached the same conclusion: the PDNA from the boat had to be one with the original firmware. Clement had played both of them. They could not find him earlier in the day because he had gone to the Southeast to get the box. Now, Pamela desperately wanted to know where he planned to take the PDNA. "And what the hell is in that ice chest?" she ranted. "He's just killed his little girl. Does he not understand that?"

They discussed the range of possible places to which he might go. Washington perhaps. Maybe he had been working behind the scenes with someone in the Congress. Tony Wayne was working to get Homeland Security on alert. He wanted to get someone watching for Clement at every DC area airport and at the train stations. Ideally, roadblocks could be set up at access points into the city.

Pamela told Claire that, thus far, bureaucracy had slowed the process down. They could only give Clement's name and picture to the media as a final option. The last thing they needed was for the news people to get to him first.

Claire suggested other research institutions or hospitals as possible target locations. Pamela asked her to put together a list of every institution that might have the expertise to decode the PDNA. Claire explained that if Dave somehow had the original object code from Brian Middleton's reverse engineering effort, much less expertise would be required, substantially expanding the range of possibilities where Clement could turn for help.

"We need to find him, Claire. Find him and arrange an accident. Damn fast. And do not give that kid the vaccine. She's dead. And he killed her."

When the call ended, Claire wandered to the window. No snow fell tonight. Instead, moonlight cast a sparkling glow over Mt. Clark and down the cascade of snowpack leading to her office window. It surprised her that she did not feel the same anger Pamela manifested. Since Kono, the fire had gone from her. She remained as focused as ever, but oddly calm, almost melancholy. She squeezed her eyes to blink away the images from the videotape she edited. The screaming. Howling. Flesh melting like wax, blood oozing everywhere.

Their faces. Mike. Angry to the end. Horrified. Disbelieving. It appalled her that she missed him tonight. Wanted to be able to talk to him about handling the situation with Clement.

"He killed my mother and sister," she whispered into the frosted window.

"I cannot want him back."

And Jim. Sean. On the video, the pain showed on his face, in its unavoidable contortions. But something else showed. In his eyes. Something that at first horrified her. Peace. The man had peace, a peace and acceptance she did not expect to see in him. She had not looked at the tape since that first review.

She opened her eyes again to the snowscape. In the shadows formed by the moonlight and the snowdrifts, she saw Jim's contorted face. She saw the peace again. Then saw a sea of black faces. And Liv Clement.

She walked back to her desk. Picking up the phone, she hit the speed dial for Jennifer's mobile. Pamela had ordered her to pull the vaccine from the kid. Dave had betrayed them from the outset. Jennifer's mobile trilled.

"Jennifer, it's Claire. Where are you?"

She listened as Jennifer described pulling into the Poudre Valley Hospital parking lot.

"Pamela called," Claire said. "She knows where Dave is."

On the other end, Jennifer asked if Dave had okayed the vaccination. Claire sat down, the perpetual tension in her shoulders suddenly melting away. "Yes, Jennifer. Yes. That's what Pamela wanted me to tell you. Dave's okayed vaccinating Liv."

She hung up the phone and turned her chair again toward the window and snow. She had avenged her family. She had set in motion a cure that would eradicate two of the planet's most deadly scourges. Her actions would provide hope for more people to rise out of poverty and the conditions that produced the kind of terrorism that killed her family.

But her actions killed innocents as collateral damage. She cried for innocents when she watched her video montage. Yet she stood to kill as many as almost any mass murdering dictator. So, instead of lasting peace through her work, she now felt only a hollow anxiety where once her soul had thrived on hope. For weeks, she had tried to speak beyond the grave to her father, but she heard no answer. All alone, she felt that not only God, but even the devil, if he existed, had abandoned her.

"Enough," she said, placing her palms on the cold glass of the giant window.

CHAPTER 62

New Jersey: Teterboro Airport
March 5, 3 a.m. Eastern Time

The twin engine Cessna landed in the fog at the Short Hills airfield at 3 a.m. The instrument-experienced pilot glided in on the field's radar vector, making a soft landing. As Dave descended the short staircase to the tarmac, the pilot wished him luck. A moment later, Dave entered a cab. He entertained powering on his cell phone, hoping that a trace would not be on it this quickly, but he knew better. He had no way of getting an update on Liv's status without the risk of giving away his location, risking the lives of everyone that could benefit from his work this night.

Instead, he prayed. He prayed that Liv beat the pneumonia, that the vaccine would be in time for her, that what he set in motion tonight would not prevent her access to it. He prayed for Hamara and the fleet off the Southeast coast. The news reported them caught in severe storms for the last several hours, invisible to the ships tracking their progress. Coast Guard cutters stood by within a few miles.

Aboard the plane, Dave had opened the ice chest, finding a note from Hamara. Jacob had not made the trip. Hamara did not even know where he was, only that he promised to follow the family as soon as he completed his work. Mariama had grown very ill. Hamara's note asked Dave to tell Liv that her sacrifice had brought nearly two months of improved health to Sara, giving her a much fuller life for a time, briefly bringing back his little girl, long enough for him to appreciate her more than ever, to show her his deep love as a father. Sara's reversal three days earlier disappointed all of them, but it had been expected knowing what Dave had told him of the mutation. Now, the band of refugee sailors prayed and were determined to do everything they could to get to medical help in the United States. Dave wondered if Hamara still did not realize that the traditional HIV therapies worked for only a very short time to mitigate symptoms, that Sara and the others needed the new Aldrich vaccine in order to survive. Unless they came ashore, they had no hope of even receiving that.

Fifty-five minutes later, still more than two hours before sunrise, Dave's cab drove into New York City's East Side. There in the cold and the dark, members of the UN Secretary-General's staff awaited him and his cargo.

CHAPTER 63

United Nations, New York City
March 5, 4:05 a.m.

The Secretary General greeted Dave enthusiastically. They had known each other for years, having been introduced by Evan Conger when Dave consulted for WHO. Six weeks earlier, they met again secretly very early one morning at a deli several blocks from the UN. There, Dave told Secretary Khalfani of the un-sanitized PDNA and depicted Mossoumou's vaccination campaign as genocide. At first, Youssef Khalfani, an Egyptian hero of the Arab spring, seemed to discount Dave's story as a paranoid fantasy from someone who either did not understand or did not have all the facts. At one point, the man, noted for circumspection, grew extremely uneasy, glancing several times at his security escort watching attentively from a nearby table. If not for their history together, Khalfani would have cut the meeting short or avoided it altogether,

Instead, he probed Dave over several cups of strong black tea, using two fresh tea bags for each cup. He asked Dave about his business, about the extent of his relationship with Pamela Thatcher. He asked about his family. And Dave gambled. He told the Secretary General about Liv's AIDS, that she had the Leonean clade allegedly discovered by the Aldrich in December. This struck a chord with Khalfani, a father of six.

"How did she contract it? It's only been a few weeks since you were there. Surely, even this new form does not become this severe so quickly."

"It doesn't. One of their people, a woman they had me employ, confided to me that she infected my daughter with the mutation."

"Why?"

"To be certain I had no choice but to support their ongoing work. If I turned them in, progress on a cure would stop. Liv would die."

"So why are you willing to talk to me now. "

"By the time we get what we need to prove what's happened, they will either have the cure ready or it will be too late. Every day we delay, more are getting the malaria vaccine and its Trojan horse. I'm cutting this as close as I dare."

Khalfani leaned forward and scrutinized Dave's face. "I believe you," he said. "It's too insane to be fiction. I also know that Pamela Thatcher is both arrogant and half insane."

"Do you think the President knows?"

"The US President? Not a chance. Pamela and her crew went entirely off reservation. They have, however, handed your President quite a problem. He just doesn't know the extent of it."

"How can that happen? Here you have the most powerful office in the world and – "

"Dave, even a President has to trust people. You can't be everywhere in a bureaucracy with millions of employees. And no person can know all the answers."

"Will you talk to the White House?"

"Not yet. Without hard evidence, the President and his staff will want to believe a long-time supporter and icon like Thatcher. Word could leak to Pamela. In that case, she would definitely come after you. You can't risk that with Liv's situation."

"I'll get the evidence."

"Good. I also have other ideas. I can confide in a good friend at the Clinton Global Initiative."

"Who?"

Khalfani narrowed his eyes. "A friend who could invite members of his very small club into the discussion. We'll figure out a game plan to press the right buttons once you get the data to me."

Dave did the political math. "Is that secure?"

"That's a club with some hard lessons under its belt. I trust them implicitly."

He gave Dave a private number for communication, asked him to use it only from pay phones or mobile burner phones. Any contact between the two men needed to remain secret until the PDNA arrived in the hands of the United Nations.

This morning, as Dave entered the Secretary-General's offices after his nighttime journey from the Southeast coast, Khalfani greeted him with a bear hug.

"You certainly like the early hour," Khalfani said, noting the 4:05 a.m. time on a wall clock.

He asked after Liv, genuinely disturbed to hear that her health had declined even further. He explained that he had people ready to move forward for a rapid analysis of the situation using the Lokoma's PDNA, the preserved blood samples from the tribe, and a copy of the CD Middleton had provided Dave.

"Once we have the preliminary work done, my associates and I are ready to press the necessary buttons," Khalfani said.

He had a breakfast of cold cuts, fruit and breads brought into his office. "This morning, you will enjoy good tea the way I like it," the Secretary General said. He poured a cup from a silver service and handed it to Dave who sipped it tentatively.

Dave did not know if he lit up because his body instantly absorbed the much needed caffeine – or if it was the combination of very strong tea with honey and cinnamon. He thought the drink must have been one-third honey. He liked it.

"You know, Youssef, this is probably exactly what I needed. Something very sweet and tasty to dilute the bitter taste of the last several months."

"We'll try to complete that job for you with what you've brought us today," Khalfani responded. His phone trilled. "Yes," he said into the phone. His face grew stern. "Thank you. I'll handle it." Pressing the end button on the phone, he looked grimly at Dave.

"I'm afraid you may have been found out. American Homeland Security has issued an alert to find you."

"Me? What the…"

Khalfani grabbed Dave's wrist. "What did you think, friend? You've just fired a dart in the Eagle's eye."

"How did they find out so fast?"

"Does it matter?"

"Will the President help?"

"Only after we get the evidence to him. Without it, he's not going to interfere with law enforcement. I think the best thing is to get you out of the country until we fix that."

Dave did not hesitate. "No. No, thank you. I need to get home and be with my family. My daughter needs me. You need to keep your promise."

"There is no need for worry there. I will make every effort to insure the American government pushes the vaccine effort forward. Your daughter will be one of the very first to get it."

"What if the administration stonewalls it?"

"We went through all this six weeks ago. Nothing's changed. If this evidence is everything you say it is, this administration will not want the world to know. They'll work with us."

Dave chewed the inside of his bottom lip. "Can you help me get home?" he asked. "Public transportation, the rental car agencies – all their computers will generate an alert the minute my name shows up."

Khalfani smiled. "I just so happen to have a private plane going to Colorado for a ski trip. There is surely a seat available."

Three hours later, Dave found himself the only passenger aboard a Gulfstream G450. As the twin-engine jet reached cruising altitude after a steep and rapid ascent, he pressed a button and raised the telescoping footrest. He tilted his seat back and turned his face toward the panorama outside the wide oval window. Beneath him, amidst a vivid blue sky, puffy clouds drifted over a wintry landscape of snow, barren trees, and sparse patches of straw-colored grass. Creation in all its glory, he thought. He attempted to mumble the Our Father.

"Our Father, who art in heaven, hallowed be thy name. Thy kingdom come…" He stopped. He could not bring himself to say the next line.

"No, Lord," he mumbled. "Not 'thy will be done.' Not if it harms Liv. You have to intervene. You need to show your compassion. I need you now. Not just after we die. You can't keep letting everyone suffer like this. It's dead wrong."

He felt a tear slip over his eyelid. "Dammit," he said, wiping the embarrassing drop away.

The decision to bring Hamara Karanja ashore had generated violent discussion at the White House. Then, Joseph Mossoumou called. The MAD president did a 180, suddenly wanting the Americans to provide sanctuary to refugees he had called terrorists as recently as 12 hours earlier. The Americans could use freedom as a trading card for their silence. Otherwise, the press would inevitably report everything on the mind of the sea-bound band of renegades.

Mossoumou insisted on one odd condition for his concurrence, however. In the face of considerable opposition, Tony Wayne called the condition reasonable. The President agreed, nodding at Wayne when the group finally reached consensus to accept the condition: Pamela Thatcher would be present for the interrogation of Karanja.

CHAPTER 64

Mayport Naval Air Station near Jacksonville, Florida
March 5, 10 a.m. Eastern Time

Hamara looked at Pamela Thatcher and his other interrogators. They made it conversational and pleasant, but Hamara knew it for an interrogation. Velvet glove, but an interrogation nonetheless.

They sat in a conference room with coffee, tea, sodas and food. Hamara felt guilty about eating the food, the best he had enjoyed since Dave Clement hosted him at the Kimtumani Hotel in December.

The refugee fleet had survived the storm intact, but seasickness from hours of violent pitching had made the vessels nearly unbearable, the stench of illness permeating the holds. Once the weather cleared just before dawn, nearly everyone huddled topside on the boats, hungrily gulping in the sea air.

They were still outside US territorial waters, but Hamara agreed to let the Coast Guard board to provide medical aid and food to the refugees. He agreed to go ashore himself in exchange for hospital care for Mariama and others who would benefit from it.

Subsequently, the Coast Guard airlifted Hamara and fourteen others. The fourteen went directly to the hospital on the base while Hamara was flown to another area. Pamela Thatcher greeted him as he stepped off the chopper, treating him like a dignitary.

They took him to a conference room where Homeland Security personnel rained a checklist of questions on him about the health of the boat people, his intentions, anything on board that might be construed as a threat to the security of the United States, whether any of the boat people had visited the states before or if any, in fact, already had US citizenship.

Of most significance, Hamara acknowledged that fully 75% of the Leoneans had HIV. Of those, only a handful had not received the malaria vaccine. The Homeland Security personnel did not understand the significance of that link.

It surprised Hamara that they asked no questions about the Mossoumou regime. He surmised they knew more than he did.

Pamela slowly picked apart a bagel as the bureaucrats performed their jobs. She ended up eating less than half of it, downing it with unsatisfying, lukewarm coffee. When it was her turn, she asked to be left in the room alone with Hamara. She asked, too, that the video camera and recording devices be turned off. The team leader said that could not be done. Pamela called the President. The team leader agreed to the condition.

She did not bother with further niceties with Karanja. "What do you know?" she asked.

Hamara blanched. "About what?"

"The portable DNA analyzer. The PDNA."

"That it analyzes DNA to optimize drug treatment."

"You know that's not what I'm asking."

"What else is there to know?"

"Enough that you made sure you brought a PDNA along on your little adventure. Enough that you passed it on to Dave Clement at sea last night."

She bluffed. She did not know with any certainty if Clement had been in the helicopter. She did feel confident that he was deeply involved.

"Have you talked to Clement?" Hamara asked.

"No, but you could help with that. Where is he?"

Hamara sighed. She made it easy. He needed only be honest. "Not a clue."

Pamela sat back, taking the measure of the man. "Chief Karanja, your people will get temporary asylum here. You and I both know that many of them won't live more than a few months without a vaccine. I control the vaccine. Cooperate with me and you save lives. Don't and they're as good as dead."

He glared at her, wanting to slam a fist into her face. She continued to look him square in the eye.

"Including your wife and Sara," she added.

"What about the rest of the people back in Mossoumou's new empire?"

"So you do know?"

Hamara thought quickly. "I know that this new HIV seems to be spreading very rapidly."

"Chief, you think you know that the malaria vaccine causes the mutation. I've seen the misguided little newsletter your friends tried to send out."

"So why are you bothering to ask?"

"I want to know where Dave Clement is and I want to know what state that PDNA is in."

"What state?"

"When did you take it offline, Chief?"

He studied the smooth laminate surface of the conference table. He ran his fingers over the top of it. He did not recall ever sitting at so fine a table before. His people would have many finer things if they came ashore. "In time," he answered.

"That PDNA is not Clement's property and it's not yours," she said, her face reddening.

"We have blood samples, too," he added. "Samples that demonstrate the vaccine is the likely source of the HIV mutation."

"How can you... Who else knows?"

"I've told everyone I could, but no one believes it. They think it's the rantings of a paranoid savage. I've been compared to the imams in Nigeria who said HIV and infertility were delivered with the polio vaccine. Nonsense, of course. And my claims are viewed as equally without merit."

"As they will continue to be."

"Guarantee the vaccinations will be stopped and I'll tell you what I can about Dave Clement, but not until everyone on the boats is ashore in the United States with a written guarantee of permanent asylum."

"The vaccinations are not negotiable, but asylum is. Your people badly need medical care."

"The vaccine is killing people."

"The vaccine saves people," Pamela countered. "Too bad I can't say the same for you. You seem ready to sacrifice your refugee fleet in exchange for some conspiracy theory."

"You know it's real."

"Real or not, Chief, the only thing you can do is help your own people. It's that or let them die while you tilt at windmills."

Hamara weighed his options. He realized he had none. He knew Pamela was right. All he could do was help his own people and tell her what little he knew. The rest had to rely on Dave Clement. If Pamela did not find a way to stop him first.

"Permanent asylum then," he said.

"Temporary. Homeland Security and State will never go for permanent asylum. That would set a precedent that would be unacceptable. A year guaranteed."

"Five."

"I'll make the phone call. Now tell me about Dave Clement."

"The call first."

CHAPTER 65

Fort Collins, Colorado: Poudre Valley Hospital
March 5, 10:15 a.m. Mountain Time

The smell of antiseptic and the fresh, frequently recycled air of the hospital filled Dave's head. The limo hired by Khalfani's people took him straight to here from the Fort Collins airport. On the plane, he learned that while he made the watch list, Homeland Security had been careful not to publish the search. They had no interest in involving the media.

The elevator dinged as it arrived on Liv's floor. Dave stepped out double-time, marching through the corridors until he arrived at her room. He opened the door and saw Liv asleep, an IV running into her wrist, an oxygen tube in her nose. He stepped to the side of the bed. She looked peaceful, her breathing even. The blood pressure and pulse monitor showed her pressure to be very low, her pulse at 78.

"I told her to go ahead," Mel said from behind him.

He turned to find her rising out of a chair. They hugged. "Go ahead with what?"

"The vaccine," she said. "I had to make a decision."

Jennifer stepped into his view. "Claire authorized it last night," Jennifer said. "Against Pamela's instructions as it turns out. Claire confided the details to me this morning on the phone. Pamela's not very happy with you."

"Where have you been?" Mel asked. "Why haven't you called?"

"It's a long story," he said. "Tell me about Liv first. The vaccine? Her pneumonia?"

"No, Dave. You just disappeared. You're not part of our lives."

Jennifer placed a hand on Mel's shoulder. She shook it off. "Mel, listen to him. He had to do what he did. To protect you and Liv for as long as he could."

Mel turned toward the younger woman. "How do you know?" she said, her eyes drilling in on Jennifer.

"Homeland Security. Dave made the watch list last night."

"My God, Dave…"

"Please trust me. I'll try to tell you everything. But I just flew over 2,000 miles on a private jet just to find out how my daughter's doing. I couldn't call. Not until now."

Mel's face grew completely rigid. She pulled him out of the room. In the hall, she stuck her face in his. "She's dying," she whispered. "Dying. She got this damned mutation and you brought it to her."

"Mel, it's not what you think…"

"I'll tell you exactly what I think. You're killing her. That's what I think. You and you're damned dreams."

"Did she get the vaccine?" he asked.

"What do you care? You haven't been here."

"Did she get the vaccine?"

She stood before him, trembling. "Now I'm doing it, too. I'm killing her. To save her. It's the only hope."

"Mel. Please answer me. Did she get the vaccine?"

"Yes, dammit. That's what I'm talking about."

"I don't understand."

"Jennifer explained that the vaccine effectively shuts down all remaining immune function for seven days until it becomes effective. If she makes it through the seven days, she lives. But she's very vulnerable. Right now. Since ten o'clock last night. And I had to make that decision. Without you. It's all on me. I hope you're happy."

He placed his hands on her shoulders, looked at her, watched her melt into tears and pulled her close, if only so that she could not see his tears. She wrapped her arms around him and squeezed, pressing her face as far as she could into his chest. He slowly stroked her back.

"You made the only decision you could," he said. "It's the right decision. I know its risks, but, for God's sake, she has no immune system anyway. The only thing fighting off infection is antibiotics."

"Thank you," she mumbled.

"I love you, Mel. With all my heart."

She re-fortified her hug.

"Let's go back inside," he said after a moment.

"No, not yet." She pulled away. "Why is the government after you?"

"You know the boat people from Sierra Leone."

"Right."

"Hamara Karanja and his family are among them."

"Including Sara? Is she all right?"

"Liv's gesture bought her quality time, but she's turned for the worse again."

"She needs the vaccine."

"A lot of them do, but there isn't enough made yet. It will take months to deploy enough doses to cover every one concerned. By then, thousands and thousands will be dead."

"We should save who we can save."

"It's not up to us, Mel."

"Who then?"

"President Mossoumou in MAD. Pamela Thatcher. Claire McQuaid."

"They'll help those people. What's this have to do with you?"

"Mel, the cause of this mutation is the malaria vaccine."

"It... I'm confused."

"Our PDNAs are covering up a plot to spread the mutated vaccine to every HIV victim in the new MAD and throughout all of sub-Saharan Africa - if someone doesn't stop it."

She stepped back further. "What are you saying, Dave? It sounds like the mutation was by design."

"Exactly."

"The mutation our daughter has?"

"Yes."

"And you knew about this?"

"Not until the end of our trip to Sierra Leone. Pamela and Claire confirmed it in Tenerife."

Mel held her hands to the side of her head, trying to absorb this information, to contextualize it. "But... but, Liv didn't get the malaria vaccine," she said.

"Mel, Liv did not catch HIV from anyone. Jennifer injected her with it and with the mutator."

"She what?"

"Injected her with it."

"Why the hell..."

"To control me. At Claire's direction."

She looked down at the floor, looked at Dave. Her eyes reddened. "You let that bitch into our lives," she said just before slamming the door open to Liv's room.

Mel grabbed Jennifer by the hair, yanking her out of her chair and slamming her to the ground.

"No, Mel. Stop," she pleaded.

"Why, Jennifer? Why did you do it?"

"I didn't know this would happen. I swear."

Mel latched a hand under Jennifer's jaw and lifted her with super-human strength. She threw the redhead against the door. Jennifer scrambled on her knees into the hallway, but Mel came up and kicked her in the backside, sending her sprawling on to the hall tile. Dave followed them out, closing Liv's door behind him.

Four large men in dark suits entered the corridor. They rushed up and grabbed the women, holding them apart until they stopped fighting. Soon Mel and Jennifer stopped struggling and stood glaring at each other in the grip of the peacemakers.

One of the men approached Dave. "Dave Clement?" he asked.

"Yes."

The man held out a badge. "Homeland Security. You're under arrest."

CHAPTER 66

Lagos, Nigeria; Old Mission Grounds
March 6, 2:35 p.m. West Africa Time

The smallest of the condemned, Jacob identified an escape route within the first hours of his confinement. The space in the thick, shrapnel-freckled wall looked little more than a crack, but a boy used to surviving alone in the jungle, a boy trained in the fantasy of Rambo movies, found opportunity wherever a glimmer of hope appeared. And Jacob had a friend to be rescued. If not that, then a tyrant to be stopped.

The others, seeing Jacob crawl up to the crack, anticipated his move. They also knew they could not fit in the tiny cavity. His woman friend encouraged a group to huddle in front of the spot, hiding Jacob from the prying eyes of any guards that might pass the gate. Jacob nodded to the others and slipped into the crack. Inside, he chipped away a concrete obstruction with a small rock, all the while hoping the clacking of rock against concrete would not be heard by the guards.

Finally, he popped out on the other side, finding himself in an abandoned chapel. He walked behind the altar into the sacristy. He peered through a crack in a stained glass window. Seeing no one, he opened the outside door to the sacristy. Around the corner, he could see uniformed soldiers talking, smoking and waiting for new orders.

He walked in the opposite direction, hoping to quickly blend into the city's crowds. A few blocks away, he found a dead body lying on a side street. The man, dressed well, had been shot twice in the head. His long-sleeved shirt had no blood on it, no holes in it. Jacob pulled the fabric of his tank top to his nose. He did not need to sniff it to know it smelled like a sewer. If they did not identify him by sight, they would smell him. He bent down and undid the buttons of the dead man's shirt. He carefully slipped it off without staining it in the blood puddle by the man's head. He put it on, rolling the extra-long sleeves up and accepting a tail that nearly touched his knees. With the body lying sprawled on the ground, Jacob had not realized that the man had been nearly two feet taller than him.

Jacob sucked in a deep breath. He mumbled a prayer. "Jesus, help me find Father Jim. Help me and I promise I'll stop killing after I finish here. But I have to finish. Your father understands that. He let that happen in the Old Testament before you came. There's a place for it."

The image of Christ crucified flashed through his mind, the Christ that forgave his enemies on the cross. He thought of the crucifix Father Jim would set up before Church. Jacob touched the nun's small wooden cross that still hung around his neck. Christ forgave. Then his memory thrust vivid images at him, plunging him into a replay of his friends being tortured and killed ruthlessly in the jungle, their screams again piercing his ears as he watched helplessly from his hiding place. He re-lived the breathless horror of discovering his grandparents hacked and sprawled across each other in senseless death on the floor of their home. He flinched at the unwelcome memory of the screams and wailing of the nuns that night outside the refugee camp. A seemingly endless onslaught of images and sounds popped like fireworks in his mind and squeezed his heart in a suffocating vice.

He lifted the cross from around his neck and jammed it in his pants pocket.

Trying to appear natural, he stepped out of the side street onto one of Lagos main thoroughfares. He did not know where to go. He only knew he needed to find a hospital with a burn unit and figure out how to get inside. Jim would still be there – if he ever arrived there in the first place. It had only been two months.

As Jacob's stride grew more confident, the boy worried about the people he left behind in the makeshift prison and execution chamber. He wondered how he could get them out. He could think of no alternatives without a weapon.

CHAPTER 67

The United Nations, New York City
March 6, 9:15 a.m. Eastern Time

It surprised Under-Secretary Wayne to find Secretary General Khalfani so cordial. Normally, the man treated Wayne as a great nuisance, disagreeing with him on important policy matters as a matter of principle.

Now, Khalfani had requested an urgent visit. The US Ambassador to the UN had deliberately not been invited. Khalfani needed to be one-on-one with Tony Wayne. Alone with Wayne, he confronted him immediately.

"I figured it out, Tony," Khalfani said, sitting on the front edge of his desk. "Alas, the United States has learned a little about subtlety."

Still standing without an invitation to sit down, Wayne looked puzzled. "What is it you figured out, Youssef?"

"With oil at $150 a barrel, it was only a matter of time, wasn't it? I'm rather glad you spared the Middle East this time."

"Not a lot of oil in Egypt."

"No, just a lot of unhappy Muslims because of the greed of the leadership in Arab oil-producing countries."

Wayne placed a hand on the back of a wing chair and impatiently tapped his fingers. "Why am I here, Youssef?"

"To deal. You have things I want. I know things you want kept very quiet."

"We all have secrets. Which ones did you have in mind?"

"The President doesn't know, does he, Tony? It amounts to treason. You know that, right?"

"I'm a patriot. The President knows that."

"Not for long. The administration's going to need some help with the mess you've made. After we've finished here, friends of mine will be calling the White House to offer help."

"I don't know where you're going with this, but you're way out of line."

The Secretary General pulled a photo of the Karanja's PDNA out of his desk drawer. He placed it on the desk in front of Wayne.

Tony looked it over, his composure instantly taking a hit.

"You know what that is?" Khalfani asked.

"No, do you?" Wayne responded.

"I know exactly what it is and how your friends have used it. So do you."

"This picture doesn't tell me anything."

Khalfani produced a report. Wayne skimmed it quickly. A team spent the last thirty-two hours working non-stop to assess the firmware of Karanja's PDNA. Confirming Dave's claims, the device had the earlier firmware version that insured the data falsely reported that all HIV-positive individuals showed the biomarker that made them candidates for the malaria vaccine. The firmware also falsely identified everyone with HIV as having the new mutation before they ever received the vaccine and its Trojan horse.

"So you have a statistical anomaly," Wayne said. "Maybe there's something to be learned about the vulnerability of HIV to the Aldrich malaria vaccine."

"What's to be learned is that this PDNA doesn't have the firmware update that hides your fraud in West Africa," Khalfani said, handing Wayne two more reports. "Unfortunately, there's more to this."

The first report was the PDNA report on the HIV of Hamara Karanja and twenty-four other people in the refugee camp. The other report was a brand new analysis of the blood samples brought to the States by Hamara.

"You'll see that the reports are in conflict," Khalfani said. "Chief Karanja instructed his elders and the men of his village to be among the last to get the malaria vaccine, making certain the women and children received it first."

He leaned forward and pointed to a column on one of the reports Wayne held. "These six men listed here never received the malaria vaccine. The PDNA shows them to have the mutation along with the other 19 tested on these reports. You and I both know that's impossible without the vaccine. Recent blood tests prove those men don't have the mutation. They have HIV-1 clade G, the clade found throughout much of West Africa until the so-called Aldrich discovery. A little strange, isn't it?"

Wayne threw the reports down, indignant. "Some kind of statistical anomaly. There's not enough data to be meaningful."

"Tony, that response doesn't even make sense. The evidence proves that the 19 others tested got the mutation from the malaria vaccine. We can make this a public discussion, fighting it out in the face of world opinion or we can fix things quietly. Reach a few understandings that might be in the interest of good people everywhere. "

Wayne dropped back in his seat. He picked the reports up, making a show of looking at them. "I'll need time to analyze this data. If what you say is true, it's appalling."

Khalfani frowned. "Tony. I'm not stupid."

"All right, Youssef. We're grown-ups. Tell me what you want."

CHAPTER 68

Fort Collins, Colorado
March 7, 7:10 a.m. Mountain Time

Homeland Security released Dave from a guarded room at the Fort Collins Courtyard after less than 48 hours. They never questioned him or explained why he had been placed on the watch list. Dave did not need explanations. He knew more than his captors. He knew his information had been parsed into carefully compartmentalized units in the Federal bureaucracy to keep anyone from sorting out the whole story.

When, on the morning of his release, he saw the small article on the inside pages of USA Today, he knew that his effort had been meaningful.

"MAD cancels malaria vaccine program," said the small headline over the short article.

The article explained that the Aldrich Institute, manufacturers of the vaccine, had discovered a bad batch had been released. While both the Aldrich and MAD's President Mossoumou expressed confidence that none of the bad vaccine had been administered, caution dictated that all vaccine be recalled and analyzed until the breakdown in the manufacturing process could be identified and rectified. The article quoted Claire McQuaid as saying the bad batch would do no harm, that it simply did not work because of sedimentation in the vials.

Rather than go home or to the office, Dave had the agents drop him at the hospital after his release. He had not even been allowed to contact anyone while in custody. He had barely slept, praying and worrying about Liv. When his mobile phone was returned upon his release, he immediately called Mel.

"It's not promising," she told him.

Arriving at Liv's room, he felt a rush of relief when he saw her eyes open, a weak smile for him on her face. She flipped the hand without the IV palm up so that he might take it. He sat on the edge of the bed and took her hand in both of his.

"I've missed you, Liv," he said.

"You, too, Daddy. I missed you, too." She croaked, her voice dry and weak. He bent down and hugged her gently.

"I'm getting out of here," she said. "Soon."

"You bet you are," he said optimistically.

"No, Daddy," she corrected. "Not that way."

He inhaled a long breath.

"It's time," she said. "If God wants me this bad, I think I should go."

"Honey, don't talk that way. We -"

"Shhh. I love you, Daddy. I know how hard you tried for me. How hard you've worked. Mom told me. I know you've done everything to get the vaccine out to save not only me, but millions of people. You could not have made me more proud."

Tears drifted from her red, tired eyes. He wiped them gently with the tips of his fingers.

"I'm the one who should be proud," he said. "You gave us all a reason to live. You're what keeps me going every day."

"Then I'm sorry I'm going to let you down."

"You could never let me down. I saw Chief Karanja. Sara's alive because of you."

Liv's face lit up. "She is? Is she getting better?"

He lied. "She's strong enough that we think the vaccine will save her."

"See, Daddy. You have a lot of other reasons to keep going." Her face pinched back tears.

He swallowed hard, letting his tears flow freely down his cheeks. Mel came over and intertwined her hand with theirs.

Liv smiled. "This is how I want it," she said quietly. "Exactly like this."

She closed her eyes, falling asleep, her fingers tightening their grip on her parents' hands as she did so.

When Liv coded that night, Mel had fallen asleep sitting up, her head on Dave's shoulder. Dave's eyes remained open the entire afternoon and evening, watching Liv sleep, listening to her breathe, studying her innocence. On the handful of occasions when she had briefly awakened, he had been there to listen to her and finally to pray with her as darkness settled in outside.

"The night scares me," she said. "I'm worried that's all there's going to be on the other side."

"No, Liv. There's light on the other side. The brightest light ever."

"I know," she said. "I've seen it in my dreams. But then at nighttime, when I'm alone, I get scared."

He squeezed her close to him.

"Don't let go, Daddy."

When the medical staff ended its efforts to bring back Liv's heartbeat, Mel crumpled into the bed, sobbing quietly, whispering "I love you, Liv" over and over.

Dave stood behind her, a hand on her back, his other hand squeezing hers. He closed his eyes, trying to feel Liv's spirit in the room. He heard her, clear as a bell. Not in his head, but in the room.

"Daddy, it's so bright. So beautiful."

He looked toward Liv's body. It was perfectly still. No movement. The monitors showed no activity. He bowed his head and prayed.

Thirty seconds later, he heard a beep. And then another. And another.

CHAPTER 69

Lagos State University Teaching Hospital: Burn Unit
March 8, 5:14 a.m. West Africa Time

In the darkness, Jacob entered the hospital through a side entrance. He told hospital personnel that he had come to visit his uncle in the burn unit. They took pity on the little boy. No one from the countryside seemed to have ID, many of their houses and possessions completely wiped out in the fighting. They gave him directions to his uncle's room.

Jacob approached the burn ward cautiously. He expected guards. There were none. From across the ward, he thought he recognized Fr. Jim. His face had thinned considerably, but his eyes, the eyes that drew Jacob in, that allowed him to believe – those were Jim's eyes. While his eye sockets had hollowed through his ordeal, the priest could not hide the life inside them.

Jim turned his head, recognizing Jacob immediately. He smiled, reaching a hand out. Jacob took the hand and then threw his arms around his friend. The priest flinched but held on.

"Thank God you're all right, Jacob."

"What about you, Father? We heard you were almost burned alive."

"Almost, but it appears the good Lord's not through with me down here."

"Where are the guards?" Jacob asked. "Surely, the government has you watched."

"No guards. The imams, even those that disagree on other issues, have issued fatwas that no one is to harm me. They want people to see what they've done to me. You're looking at living proof that Islam is superior to the Catholic church."

Jacob tilted his head, pondering his spiritual leader with eyes too tired for a young boy. "But it's not true. Is it?"

"No. It's not."

Jacob thought for a moment. "Well, I guess you don't need rescued," he said.

Jim laughed a little bit. "It depends on how you define the word. I'm still depending on our Father in heaven to rescue me from the world."

"How can you? After he let this happen to you."

"He didn't let this happen. I invited it."

The boy's eyes narrowed. "The people in Kono did this to you. I don't believe you were trying to hurt them."

"I wasn't. Neither I nor the Church would commit such horrors."

"So then where's Jesus in this?"

"Probably looking at me wondering if I learned my lesson."

"I don't understand."

"I did something a very long time ago. Something horrible. And God forgave me. But I couldn't forgive myself. My soul never rested. Until now."

"Because you've been punished."

"Ha-ha. Not sure I understand it myself, lad. I know this. I've suffered not for the crime for which God forgave me, but for my pride, for my arrogant attitude that God's forgiveness was not enough. I needed to be able to forgive myself and I refused. That's the lesson here."

Jacob fingered the bedrail, studying it for a moment before lifting his eyes back to the priest. "So you were punished so that you could know that you didn't need punished?"

Jim smiled. "Maybe. I know God did not want me to go through this ordeal. That was all me. But I'm more peaceful now. Much more."

"How? After what they did to you and Mike."

The priest looked closely at Jacob as his thoughts formed. "I'm very sad for my brother. I hope he made peace with God before his last breath, but I fear he may have been overcome by his anger. That part bothers me. Very much. I worry that I failed him, that I could have done more."

"But don't you want to get back at them? Aren't you mad?"

"No anger. Just sadness. And peace. Acceptance. At last."

"I don't understand you, Father."

"Starts with a kingdom not of this world. Seems simple but it's not. Took me a few decades to figure it out myself. Don't be too hard on yourself."

Jacob squeezed Jim's hand and pressed his face against the back of it. Jim felt the boy's tears on his skin.

"So tell me about your father and the rest of your family," Jim said.

Jacob sat up and inhaled deeply. He proceeded to bring Jim up to date on Hamara's journey to America. He told him how a vaccine in the United States represented the only hope to save the lives of Sara and Mariama.

"So what will you do?" Jim asked.

Jacob grew grim. "I have work to finish here. Adrian Guerra betrayed us. And Mossoumou needs to go."

Jim pondered the boy. "No, son. That's not your work. You need to be with your family. Go to America. Get an education. Then come back to Sierra Leone and do some good."

"I can't, Father."

"If you finish this work, what do you think will come of you?"

Jacob thought of all the friends he had lost in war, of the civilians executed by Mossoumou's soldiers. "I don't know," he lied.

"You do know. They'll hunt you down and kill you. And do you think anything will change here because of it? Things will only get worse because the government will be more fearful of the people."

Jacob turned away from the priest.

"I despise Mossoumou as much as you, Jacob, but to replace him through violence will just lead to more killing. Someone worse is likely to replace him. That is, if you can even get near him and survive to do what you're thinking."

"What about Adrian Guerra?"

"Adrian? He just carries water for people back in America. He's not worth your blood."

Jacob turned back. "Who in America?" he asked.

After Jacob left, a nurse helped Jim to the bathroom. He needed to become more mobile. In a few weeks, he would be leaving for the Vatican to help attempt to rebuild what he had inadvertently helped tear down.

He leaned on the sink to catch his breath. Straightening up, he laid out the special washcloth and lotion the burn unit provided. He removed his clothes. The bandages had all been removed, the oozing almost completely stopped now. With his hands, he traced his wounds. Grafting had moderated much of the damage, but in his disfigurement, he saw the outline of Claire's scars, the sin carved by fire into his flesh.

The next morning, Jim listened to a radio report. It said that just before dawn, grenades and automatic weapons fire massacred MAD soldiers at the old mission grounds. The government reported that dangerous criminals had been released by the young attackers. Mossoumou's minister of the interior promised to hunt them down.

CHAPTER 70

Barrier Island, South Carolina Coast
September 25, 11:20 a.m. Eastern Time

SIX MONTHS LATER…

She came because she still loved him. She simply could not bear living with him, faced constantly with the reminder of what had happened. Maybe someday, but not yet. Intellectually, she knew Dave had made reasonable choices, but emotionally she remained convinced those choices turned Liv into a vegetable.

It angered her that Pamela remained untouched and that Claire and Jennifer remained protected inside the Aldrich. The Federal government had quickly buried all evidence of what transpired. It had no choice. Mel knew that a prosecution would have been likely to disrupt refinement and availability of the vaccine. Too many West Africans would pay the ultimate price if that happened. She tried to accept that outcome and to find peace with it. Some days she could. Other days, she fought constantly to repress her rage.

Both she and Dave had, however, accepted the rewards associated with the initial public offering of Prodeus. Since Dave no longer worked there, he was able to sell much of his stock at a higher price early and without restriction. Blood money, he called it. Mel agreed. So they allocated enough to pay off their mortgage and their cars. They placed a large sum into a medical trust to provide care for a comatose Liv for decades if needed. Another chunk went to research to find a way to wake her up. And they set aside enough to provide an allowance for a modest lifestyle for the next five years. They purchased no new cars or furniture. They took no trips to Tahiti or Europe. Instead, they put the substantial remaining balance into the Olivia Clement Charitable Trust.

From that fund, they each would take a small ongoing salary for finding ways to allocate the proceeds from the fund to help the children of West Africa, just as Liv had helped Sara.

Dave liked to say that Liv gave him the most precious gift. He told Mel about hearing Liv describe the light after she flatlined. Initially, Mel wrote it off to him hearing what he wanted to hear, but the depth of his conviction chipped away her cynicism to the point where only a thin veneer remained.

Walking on the beach with him this afternoon, she heard him repeat his mantra. "She went to the light," he said. "She went there because she always kept hope alive. Sharing it when she could, even when it cost her. We owe it to her to build on her hope here."

Mel squeezed his hand. "She may have gone to the light, Dave, but she came back. She's in that body, waiting for it to get well enough to wake up. The vaccine worked. There's no HIV left in her system. She will wake up one day and then she can visit a healthy Sara Karanja and others for whom she made a difference."

He stopped and turned to look out to sea, watching the waves crash and then rush to where they stood. "Selfishly, I hope you're right," he said. "But I know she touched the other side."

"I want to believe that, Dave. I want to believe there is someplace beyond this, someplace better. But I pray every day that she gets a full lifetime first. She deserves that."

He changed the subject after that. They finished the administrative business of the trust, outlining the plan for Mel's trip to Freetown in the late summer.

They said their good-byes. As she walked back over the sand dune to the little shack and her rental car, she thought about Liv. She saw her smile again, laughing on the beach in Tenerife, expounding on the physical and personality virtues of Michael Winston. She remembered her tears as the heartache of her illness wore her down, heard her weeping secretly in the night. She felt the hot tears on the soft skin of her face as she hugged her and told her she loved her.

And she remembered the peace, the acceptance that Liv portrayed in her last weeks of consciousness. In that memory, Mel touched the unreconciled anguish of her own soul. She recoiled.

At the car, she paused, put on sunglasses and faced into the stiff wind and the blowing sand. She looked back at the refugee camp where her husband worked. Through the fog of sand and sea spray, through the film of her tears, Dave's image shimmered like a holograph. Completely still, he appeared covered with fine grains of pure white sand. Then, a gust blew up and she could not see him at all.

Entering the quiet of the car, she placed the key in the ignition and wondered if he had gone over the edge, losing his bearings altogether.

Or if he had only now found them.

CHAPTER 71

Western Atlantic Ocean
October 4, 1:25 p.m. Eastern Time

Pulling himself up to the rail, Jacob gazed upon the other small boats in this new fleet. Humble boats, many built for rivers and not the open sea, lurched violently on ocean waves, causing their occupants to latch on to anything that could steady them. Seasickness had been epidemic on the passage.

Jacob's parents went to America just this way only nine months earlier. He had discovered that Mariama had died but everyone else, including Ani and Sara, survived in a new land, some in treatment, some mending and some whole again.

These boats had sailed from Monrovia, a fleet of troublesome Liberians and Leoneans that Mossoumou happily let sail to America. He did not care if they made it or not. His new empire could not afford unproductive people. With the UN's new interest in MAD's internal activities, Mossoumou had to minimize executions as a means of managing dissent.

Much to Mossoumou's satisfaction, the malaria vaccinations had been 75% complete before he was forced to abort them. AIDS victims had begun dying at an accelerated pace. Not nearly enough AIDS vaccine would be available in time to save most of them. So through attrition, MAD promised to be a highly productive, nearly AIDS-free nation within a few years.

Jacob wanted to help his people, but, for all he learned through his ordeals, he did not yet understand the science of what had been done, nor did he think in anything more than simplistic terms. He knew he wanted to go to America to be with his family. He also planned to track down Adrian Guerra's bosses.

As the eastern tip of Long Island appeared on the horizon, Jacob sucked in the air of what he hoped would be an all new and better life. He felt for the wooden cross that once again dangled around his neck, thankful for a new beginning and a chance to return to his family.

He swatted at a mosquito that threatened to land on his arm. It surprised him that the pests could be found so far from land. Until he received the vaccine, he normally worried about malaria from a mosquito bite. Not anymore. He no longer had anything to fear from malaria. He reached under the sleeve of his shirt and rubbed his vaccination mark for reassurance.

He ran his fingers around the scar. He still did not know why the MAD troops selected him and the others for execution at the mission church in Lagos. He remembered he had something in common with most of them, though. Their vaccination marks resembled the planet Saturn.

Two more mosquitoes hovered near his bare arms. He slapped at them, taking out one, but the other managed to land in the crook of his elbow. He swatted at it, just missing as it flew away from the ship with a fresh snootful of his blood. The boy wondered if the journey across the water would kill the little nuisance or if it would reach Long Island even before he did. Inexplicably, he found himself rooting for the tiny mosquito's survival.

CHAPTER 72

Fort Collins, Colorado
December 24, 11:49 p.m. Mountain Time

Only two nurses and a single aid worked the floor this night. At the nurses' station trimmed in garland with red and green lights, they treated themselves to egg nog with just a touch of rum. The slightly giddy aid smelled like a musty cross between skunk spray and crayons, apparently having celebrated Christmas with a little weed on her break. The supervising nurse let it go tonight. They all deserved a little leeway for working Christmas Eve.

Three doors down the hall from where they sat, the only light in the closed room came from blue diodes and a single monitoring screen. Fluorescent green EKG waves tracked Liv's heartbeat against the monitor's black background. The EKG showed a healthy heart, but a PET scan two days earlier showed Liv's brain metabolism remained very low with no reason for optimism. A feeding tube led from her stomach to the bedrail where the nurse had clamped it after the last meal. The nurse had also moved her on to her right side, part of a ritual done every two hours to change Liv's position to avoid lung congestion and minimize the risk of pneumonia. The staff carried out their functions in soldier-like fashion, but nothing about Liv's responsiveness and brain activity offered hope.

Until now.

"Daddy?" a small voice whispered from the bed.

# # #

The Characters in Public Offerings return in...

Courtship of Innocence

...The dominos continue to tumble on top of humanity in the plot set in motion by Claire McQuaid. Dave, Mel and Jacob all have unfinished business to tackle.

Look for it in your favorite bookstore in 2018.

Learn more at www.PublicOfferings.net

Follow at www.Facebook.com/PublicOfferings

APPENDIX

PUBLIC OFFERINGS

ABOUT THE AUTHOR

With the *Public Offerings* series, Bob LiVolsi won the Writers League of Texas prestigious manuscript contest for best thriller. In the same competition, Bob was also a finalist for best narrative non-fiction. He started his career as a journalist and was managing editor of the Daily Kent Stater at Kent State University in the aftermath of 1970 shootings. There, he won the national Sears Congressional Internship for his investigative coverage of racial tension on campus.

A high tech executive on teams that took two companies public, Bob applied his experiences in the mercenary world of high-stakes investment to *Public Offerings*. As a vice president with Hewlett Packard and in his roles in building new companies, he traveled the world partnering with large corporations, governments and other international organizations. Bob is currently CEO of VRI, a humanitarian vaccine systems company. He has a certificate in vaccinology from the Pasteur Institute in Paris, and he has been a mentor for a vaccine formulation company in the National Science Foundation's regional Innovation Corps program. His and his wife's private support of missions in the Middle East, Sub-Saharan Africa and Central America brought him closer to the day-to-day challenges presented by disease, poverty, war and tyranny. In the mid-1990s, he began online communication with a missionary priest in Sierra Leone where he learned about the horrors there not yet reported in the western press. The priest disappeared and was assumed killed. He became the inspiration for Fr. Jim Reilly in *Public Offerings*.

Bob lives with his wife of 35 years in Austin, Texas. He is writing *Courtship of Innocence*, the sequel to the *Public Offerings* series.

CHARACTER SUMMARIES

Clement Family, Fort Collins, Colorado

Dave Clement

> Dave is the father of Liv Clement and husband of Mel Clement. As VP of Operations and Business Development at Prodeus, he is the main driver of partnerships to deploy the Portable DNA Analyzer (PDNA) with malaria vaccine pilot in West Africa. Dave is the likely successor to Ed Hepp as CEO of Prodeus. Claire McQuaid, Executive Director of Aldrich, relies on Dave's partnership and his relationships in the pharmaceutical industry and with international aid organizations

Liv Clement

> Fifteen year old daughter of Dave and Mel Clement. Liv is a good student and volleyball player at Ft. Collins High School where she is a sophomore. She is on anti-retrovirals to manage HIV. She insists to her parents and doctors that she has participated in no risky behaviors that would lead to HIV. She has not had a blood transfusion, another possible source of HIV. She keeps her HIV very secret; her friends, teachers, and coaches do not know she has it. She frequently writes in a diary to help her cope

Mel Clement

> Liv's mother and wife of Dave Clement. Mel works as a mortgage broker, but now seldom goes into the office, working from home to be present for Liv. Mel is frustrated with Dave for constantly prioritizing work over family and feels he is not doing enough to help find answers for Liv's HIV.

Aldrich Institute, Colorado

Claire McQuaid

> Executive Director of the Boulder, Colorado-based Aldrich Institute. She has spearheaded the development of the malaria vaccine to be tested in Sierra Leone with the Lokoma tribe and others. Claire's body is disfigured from wounds incurred when she was young. She is passionate about her work and feels a duty to change the world on a grand scale. She helped put Ed Hepp and Prodeus in business where she sits on the board. She plans to have Dave Clement replace Ed as CEO when Ed's Parkinson's disease advances to the point where he cannot carry the CEO workload. Importantly, Claire relies on Dave to smooth the way for cooperation with locals in Sierra Leone and with significant allies such as Evan Conger at the World Health Organization (WHO).

Sheila Stratemeier

> Lead developer for the malaria vaccine at the Aldrich Institute. Sheila works out of the Aldrich's secretive mountain lab in northern Colorado's Rawah Wilderness, high up in the mountains near the Medicine Bow Range. Sheila is troubled by the alternatives that Claire and the Aldrich are considering for deployment of the malaria vaccine; Sheila and Jennifer Winter, who works for Dave Clement at Prodeus, are close friends going back to the days when they were protégés at the Aldrich Institute fresh out of grad school.

Eldridge Perry

> Director of Drug Discovery for the Aldrich Institute. Eldridge works out of the firm's mountain lab in Colorado's Rawah Wilderness. Sheila Stratemeier and Jennifer Winter both reported directly to Eldridge when they worked there together; he is still Sheila's manager today. A very secretive and mysterious man, Eldridge compartmentalizes work assignments among his researchers and developers so that no single one of them has a complete picture of the company's plans and strategy.

Lokoma Village, Sierra Leone

Fr. Jim Reilly

Irish missionary priest who serves the people of Sierra Leone. Fr. Jim feels a special fealty to Chief Hamara Karanja and the Lokoma tribe. He baptized Chief Karanja and the tribe members when they converted from a local tribal religion three years ago. He is itinerant, traveling from village to village and often saying Mass outdoors. Dave Clement and Fr. Jim have been friends since Fr. Jim gave a fundraising sermon at Dave's church in Colorado eight years ago. Since then, Dave and Mel have contributed funds and time to help the Lokoma through hard economic times during the civil war in Sierra Leone.

Hamara Karanja

Paramount chief of the Lokoma nation in the northwest mountains of Sierra Leone. Hamara considers Dave Clement a friend through Dave's efforts to bring medical missions to the Lokoma, bringing items such as eyeglasses and prescription medicines. Hamara is married to Mariama Karanja who has given birth to two daughters: Ketta and Sara. Ketta died recently at age seven from malaria. Sara is five and her family dotes on her, particularly since the loss of Ketta. Hamara's oldest child Jacob, age 10, is his son by his first wife, Ani. Hamara was married to both Ani and Mariama simultaneously, but had to choose one when he converted to Catholicism, as polygamy is outlawed by Church law. He chose Mariama. Jacob holds this against his father.

Jacob Karanja

Hamara's oldest child, Jacob was born to Hamara's estranged wife Ani. Age 10, he lives with Ani, his birth mother, in the chief's compound along with Ani's parents, Mariama and his sister Sara. Jacob aspires to be a chief like his father and seeks ways to demonstrate his manhood.

International Aid Organizations (NGOs)

Adrian Guerra

The West African Country Director for the World Bank, Adrian is based in Freetown, Sierra Leone, the capital city. Adrian visits Lagos, Nigeria, to persuade Dave Clement to place the malaria vaccine pilot in Sierra Leone, not strife-torn Nigeria. Adrian wants Chief Karanja to move the Lokoma people to sell their ancestral land to another tribe ostensibly to get the Lokoma to more reliable medical care and safer environs away from the criminal bands that still wander the bush, years after the official end of the civil war. Chief Karanja is against such a move, believing he owes it to his tribe and to their ancestors to keep the Lokoma where they are. Adrian has to sign off on the World Bank funds needed to subsidize the malaria vaccine project in Sierra Leone. Dave's long-term relationship with him helps make that happen.

Evan Conger

Director of sub-Saharan tropical diseases for the World Health Organization (WHO), Evan is a reliable and experienced hand in health care administration and drug discovery. He served as Executive Director of the Aldrich Institute until the President of the United States tapped him to be Surgeon General. After serving in the administration, he could not go back to the Aldrich where Claire McQuaid was doing an effective job as his replacement. Instead, he took the job at WHO, hoping to make a difference there, particularly with regard to malaria. He started the malaria vaccine research at the Aldrich and is working with Dave Clement to bring the pilot project for the vaccine to Sierra Leone. WHO's endorsement of the effort will be critical to its deployment and its financial success. Evan and Dave have known each other for years and have a close, trusting relationship. Evan is the kind of man everyone looks up to as a mentor.

Author's Note July 2014

On the next page is a short bibliography where more information can be found about what the situation on the ground is really like in West Africa. Much of the developing world remains in turmoil, facing daily trials that those in the developed countries may rarely, if ever, encounter. Thanks to the Gates Foundation, The World Health Organization, Doctors Without Borders, pharmaceutical firms (big and small) and others, including many small faith-based NGOs, help is reaching many of the people. But not nearly enough. And stability is extremely difficult to maintain.

Some true-to-life facts mentioned in the Public Offerings series:
- Many in the region really believe that vaccines are a western plot delivering HIV and infertility.
- One in five children in Sierra Leone dies before age five.
- So-called rebel bands still roam the bush even where civil war has ended, and civil wars are still ongoing or brewing. Maiming, murder and rape are common in these situations.
- The Boko Haram in Nigeria and extreme elements of both Christian and Islamic groups in the Central African Republic keep life dangerous and short in their respective countries.
- A form of AIDS that kills at an accelerated rate has been discovered in West Africa.
- There is, in fact, evidence that a malaria vaccine may cause more virulent strains of malaria: Mackinnon MJ, Read AF (2004) Immunity Promotes Virulence Evolution in a Malaria Model. PLoS Biol 2(9): e230. doi:10.1371/journal.pbio.0020230; http://www.plosbiology.org/article/info%3Adoi%2F10.1371%2Fjournal.pbio.0020230
- Sierra Leone, according to many studies, remains the poorest nation on the planet.

Some Selected Readings:

Nigeria Polio Vaccine Workers Killed, Boko Haram Suspected
http://www.huffingtonpost.com/2013/02/08/nigeria-polio-vaccine-workers-killed_n_2647539.html

MalariaVaccine.Org: The website for the Path Malaria Vaccine Initiative

Newly Discovered HIV Strain, A3/02, Linked With Faster Development of AIDS
http://www.huffingtonpost.com/2013/12/02/new-hiv-strain-a3-02-development-aids_n_4372428.html

A Long Way Gone: Memoirs of a Boy Soldier by Ishmael Beah – Autobiography of a former child soldier in Sierra Leone, Farrar Strauss & Giroux 2008; also Ishmael's website:
http://www.alongwaygone.com/index.html

Sierra Leone: Treating Malaria in Children
http://www.doctorswithoutborders.org/article/sierra-leone-treating-malaria-children

World Health Organization Website on Sierra Leone:
http://www.who.int/countries/sle/en/

Rigzone for news about Oil in West Africa:
http://www.rigzone.com/news/oil_gas/r/3/West_Africa

IRIN Humanitarian News and Analysis Sierra Leone:
http://www.irinnews.org/country/sl/sierra-leone

International AIDS Vaccine initiative:
http://www.iavi.org/Pages/default.aspx

The River: A Journey to the Source of HIV and AIDS by Edward Cooper, Little, Brown & Co 1999

Polio Eradication Initiative: Challenges in polio and politics of Nigeria:
http://www.polioeradication.org/Infectedcountries/Nigeria.aspx

Sierra Leone Demographic and Health Survey Key Findings 2008:
http://www.measuredhs.com/pubs/pdf/sr171/sr171.pdf

Sierra Leone Still Suffers Legacy of Child Soldiers:
http://www.ipsnews.net/2012/04/sierra-leone-still-suffers-legacy-of-child-soldiers/

Oil Pirates and the Mystery Ship:
http://www.foreignpolicy.com/articles/2014/01/28/oil_pirates_and_the_mystery_ship

The West African Oil and Gas Market 2013-2023:
http://www.marketwatch.com/story/the-west-african-oil-gas-market-2013-2023-2013-09-18

The Characters in Public Offerings return in…

Courtship of Innocence

…The dominos continue to tumble on top of humanity in the plot set in motion by Claire McQuaid. Dave, Mel and Jacob all have unfinished business to tackle.

Look for it in your favorite bookstore in 2018

Learn more at www.PublicOfferings.net

Follow at www.Facebook.com/PublicOfferings